RECKLESS

Viper Force, Book 3

MARLIE MAY

 Created with Vellum

Acknowledgments

For my critique partners:
Lee, Jes, Stephanie, Lana, Katrina
Linda, Laura, Renée, Alex, & Becky
I'm grateful to have all of you in my life.

For Mom. Miss you.

For my children who give me endless support.

And, last, but not least, for my own personal hero,
my retired Seabee Chief husband.
I couldn't do this without you.

RECKLESS

**Trapped together on an uninhabited Caribbean
island and hunted by killers,
can Haylee & Jax survive long enough to find
their happily ever after?**

While on assignment for Viper Force, Haylee, a former
Navy Seabee gunner's mate, barely lived through an
"accident" in Mexico. When someone tries to finish her
off while she's recovering in rehab, she begs her secret
crush and fellow Seabee Chief, Jax, to hide her before
the next attempt is permanent.

Jax fell for Haylee months ago and while he knows she
can't stand him, he'll do whatever it takes to keep her
safe. A cat and mouse chase sends them to a cruise ship,
then fleeing in a helo over the ocean. They crash-land
and swim to an uninhabited island. The killer follows,
determined to exterminate both of them forever.

It'll take their combined military experience and some tricks from Viper Force to survive, all while fighting the attraction they're helpless to resist. The Maestro plans to eliminate Haylee and Jax, and only the victors will escape the island.

Jax

Some dude I'd never seen before, a guy who was *not* Haylee's nurse, stood beside her bed, injecting something into her I.V.

A week ago, they turned off Haylee's sedation, saying they wanted to see how she responded. Short of a wince when they rubbed her chest—hard—we had nothin'.

Five days ago, they pulled the tube from her lungs, saying she could breathe on her own.

They moved her out of ICU and then to rehab, saying it was time for her to progress after the "accident".

They'd increased her physical therapy. Even played her favorite music and TV shows 'round the clock.

But she hadn't moved. Hadn't opened her eyes.

Not even when Clyde, the guard someone high up in the government had sent, turned on the TV and watched some stupid game show, blaring the volume throughout the room.

Or when her dad, her only surviving parent, squeezed her hand and pleaded for her to come back. If nothing else, that should've done it.

And now someone was trying to kill her.

Again.

I hadn't been there for her when someone forced her car into that ravine. Or when her dad arranged for her to be shipped by helo from Cancun to Miami.

But I sure as hell was here for her now.

Rushing across the room, I flung my scalding-hot coffee into the startled face of a guy fifteen or so years older than me. Black hair with graying temples. Brown eyes. Slight build. A meaty fist that connected with my jaw. He'd been aiming for my throat, hoping to crush my larynx.

Dude. I'd learned how to deflect worse blows than that by the time I turned sixteen. Living on the streets will do that for a kid.

I growled, and *my* punch didn't miss.

Gagging and clutching his throat, the man stumbled backward before he pivoted and bailed across Haylee's bed. He crashed against her side table then onto the tile floor on the other side of the bed.

Haylee winced and groaned. Her eyes opened, and her gaze met mine.

"Jax?" Though scratchy and weak and lacking her hallmark spunk, just hearing her say my name was enough to make me tremble. But the asshole who'd tried to end her life permanently had sprung to his feet and was raging for the door.

"Be right back." Breaking eye contact with Haylee, I gave chase, hitting the solid panel with my fist as it swung back in my face. With a grunt, I blasted the door open. It ricocheted off the cinder block wall with a bang as I bolted from the room and into the hallway. I only paused long enough to seek someone fleeing. A hunter, I'd catch the perp then show him a few moves I'd learned on the streets.

Down the hall, the elevator dinged and the doors whooshed open. The guy leaped inside as I charged that way. As the panels pinched closed, I shoved my fingers in the narrowing slot and pried the doors open.

Not getting away. Not until I'd pummeled him.

With his legs spread in a shooter's stance, the guy stood inside the empty elevator with two hands supporting a 9 mil at chest height. Safety off. The barrel drilled my way.

While my lungs heaved, I lifted my hands, palms exposed, and stepped toward him.

He nudged the gun in the air. "Don't even try me, man."

"Who sent you?"

His dry laugh burst out. "Maybe instead of asking me questions, you should look in on your girlfriend."

She wasn't my girlfriend. She'd never be.

The doors started closing, and a smirk rose on his face. "Just injected her with a boatload of potassium."

At the nurse's station, a heart monitor alarmed shrilly.

Fuck. Haylee.

Wrenching backward, I spun and bolted for her

room, my pulse aflame. My breathing raged as I hit the door at a dead run and slammed inside.

Blood.

On the bed. The floor. Spattered on the walls.

My horrified gaze followed the splotchy trail to where Haylee slouched in the very corner I'd held up for too many sleepless nights. She stood on her good leg with the injured one bent, dressed only in her flimsy cotton hospital gown. Shivers wracked her frame, and tears of pain and fury streamed from her blazing eyes. Blood dripped down her arm from where she'd yanked out her I.V. She'd hefted a hunk of her dismantled I.V. pole overhead, ready to smack whoever came inside the room.

"Jax," she whispered. The pole dropped. It clanged on the tile floor as she slumped forward.

I caught her. I'd always catch her.

Until she sent me away.

"Got you," I growled.

"Jax."

"Here, sweetheart."

"Sweetheart?" Her eyelids fluttered and an unexpected half-smile rose on her face, but she lifted and shook her finger near my face. "Sounds like flirting."

As I shifted her in my arms, aiming for a comfortable position, she groaned.

"Sorry," I hissed out.

"Hurts."

Her leg or her ribs? Or, hell, the entire right side of her chest that had taken a direct hit in the car crash? For all I knew, she was talking about her concussed head.

I turned, holding her as gently as possible, but she gasped—a shallow puff from her lungs the only movement her tortured ribcage would allow.

"You killed him," she spit out.

"Nope." I carried her around to the side of the bed. The side rails were still up. She must've dragged herself off the end. "I wish I had."

"Too bad."

Damn right.

"Guess I'll have to do it for you," she whispered.

My chuckle rushed out of me as I carefully lowered her onto the bed. Easing her feet to the side, I tugged up the sheet and blanket to cover her goosebump-riddled body.

"Take my clothes off," she said.

My hands stalled. They shook so badly I nearly dropped the blanket.

Get control of yourself, Chief.

She was joking.

"On a first date?" I croaked. Not sure where my daring came from. Usually around Haylee, my words stalled on my tongue, unable to slide free. But there was something vulnerable, sweet, and approachable about a wounded Haylee. I wasn't freezing or stuttering like I always did whenever she was around.

"I didn't mean anything like that," she said.

Nope. She never would.

I lifted the blanket up to her shoulders and tucked it down snug.

"I know you hate me," she said, tears leaking from

her tightly closed eyes. Creases of pain lined her beautiful face.

"Not too much." Not at all. How could I? I'd liked this woman from the moment I met her, when I joined Flint's newly formed business, Viper Force. The business was made up of a group of ex-Navy Seabees brought together to test new weapons and handle "special" projects for the military.

"Can you do something for me?" she bit through her clenched jaw.

"Anything, sweetheart." This endearment, I forced out. Joking between us was one thing, but I more than half meant it.

One hundred percent meant it.

Reaching up, her hand clamped around my wrist. "Get me the hell out of here," she said with terror lifting her voice. "Before they kill me."

2

Haylee

J ax roared across the parking lot, and the tires of his SUV squealed as he drove the vehicle out onto the main road.

While he watched the side and rearview mirrors, plus the road, I braced myself in the passenger seat, trying to keep my ribs from puncturing my right lung. Puncturing it again, I supposed, since the stabs ripping through the sensitive tissue each time we hit a bump suggested my lungs had taken a hit or two already.

Damn, I ached. From my head to my right leg to my left pinky toe, plus everything in between. White lights flashed around me brighter than those on the main strip at Vegas. I took in a bunch of shallow breaths and prayed I wouldn't pass out.

The backward hospital gown Jax had carefully fed my arms through to use like a robe over the other one had ridden up. Nothing beat bare thighs plastering themselves to leather.

Hell. At least I wore undies.

The stunned looks on the nurse's faces…and the strangers'…as Jax carried me from the room, down the hall, and out the front door, would remain in my mind for days.

"How long was I there?" I barked, not because I was angry but because I could barely hold myself together. My scream kept rushing up my throat, desperate to break free. I wanted to gnash my teeth. Clamp my hands into fists until the nails bit through my palms. Cry.

"Rehab?" he said, sparing me a quick glance. "Three days. Four hours. Twenty minutes. We're in Miami, by the way."

"We're in Florida?"

"Your dad had you life-flighted from Cancun."

Cancun. Yeah, that was right. I remembered now. Gabe, a fellow Viper Force employee, and I had flown to Cancun on assignment. Ex-Seabees, we both worked for the owner, Flint, who'd also been in the Navy with us. Viper Force specialized in testing top-secret weapons for the military and performing special ops assignments handed to us by my dad, a retired Admiral who did government consulting to keep his mind active—his words, not mine.

Our assignment had been to seek out intel that could be used to take down a small branch of a big drug cartel tree. We needed to gain evidence implicating cartel sympathizers high in the Mexican government. This information would then be used to discover who the organization was affiliated with in the U.S. One man—

or woman—who controlled the entire northeast operation.

The Maestro.

Gabe and me, we'd… I shook my head. Everything that happened after we flew into Cancun felt cloudy, as if I stood on a pier in Portland, Maine, trying to see through heavy fog banks rolling in from the Atlantic.

Arms flexing, Jax wove the vehicle through a bunch of side streets until even my brain was scrambled, and pulled into a big box store parking lot. He wheeled around to the far side of the building to take a spot, and then sat with his foot on the brake. Drumming his fingers on the steering wheel, he studied the surroundings via the mirrors before his back loosened. He shut off the engine and popped free his seatbelt. "I'm going in. Need to pick up a few things."

"You got the munchies?" I spit out, still bracing myself in the seat. We were no longer moving. Why did my head keep spinning?

"Assume you want to wait here?" he asked, pulling the key from the ignition.

"If my outfit doesn't draw attention, you carrying me around the store might." I'd yet to determine if I could walk more than a few jagged steps, but the long scar on my right thigh plus the burning ache in my chest suggested I'd be better off not pushing for distance.

There was no need to face plant in the chip aisle.

When we'd gotten into the vehicle, he'd pulled a 9 mil from behind his waist and dropped it on his lap. He lifted and offered it to me.

"Thanks." Exhausted from the escape and what had

almost happened back in the room, I appreciated the extra insurance. I'd never shot a weapon while drunk, but I imagined doing so while trying not to pass out would feel about the same. I might not hit dead center, but I'd be able to graze the outer circle.

"Won't be long," he said, handing over the keys as well, giving me an out if I needed one. Worse case, I could bolt for the store. In a hospital johnny, but people wore weird clothing in department stores all the time. I wouldn't stand out too much.

His hand pinched the door handle but he paused, awaiting my confirmation.

I gave him a sharp nod and watched as he got out of the SUV and, using the vehicle as cover, scanned the area again.

With a click, I engaged the vehicle locks as he strode toward the store.

While I had a feeling I'd already slept three lifetimes, it seemed my body disagreed. Blackness dragged my mind to the edge of a cliff and I teetered. I didn't mean to nod off, only lay my head back against the seat and rest my eyes...

Startled awake by a tap on the window, I bolted forward, groaning when agony shot up my spine. Spasms took over my body, and my teeth clattered together. I really needed to lie down, but I doubted a restful sleep was in my foreseeable future.

Jax stood patiently beside the SUV, a bunch of shopping bags bunched in one hand and his other bracing a pack draped over his shoulder. A tag on the strap spun in the breeze. His face, like always, was solidified in a mask of indifference.

Heat flooded from my chest to my cheeks, and I scrambled to pick up the gun that had slipped from my hand and onto the floor. It was a damn good thing the safety was on.

Jerking my hand out, I unlocked the doors.

Beyond Jax, a few rows away from where he'd parked, a man I'd never seen before leaned against a light blue vehicle. About thirty years old. Average height and build. Dirty blond hair. And an intent gaze that watched our every movement.

While Jax walked around behind the vehicle, I watched the man.

He tossed a cigarette onto the ground and snuffed it into the pavement before getting into the vehicle and pulling out of his spot. He didn't look this way as he turned toward the exit.

Probably nothing.

After tossing everything into the back, Jax climbed into the driver's seat and took the keys from my limp hand.

"You okay?" he asked, staring forward. He avoided my gaze either because he didn't want me to see the disgust filling his features or he didn't care. Both notions stung equally.

"Yeah," I said. "I'm perfect. I was just catching up on my beauty sleep."

He started the car and, bracing his arm on my seat, backed up and then drove through the lot. As we pulled out onto the main road, I swore I heard him say, "Can't improve perfection."

I had to be mistaken.

After weaving through enough back streets to confuse whoever might've picked up our trail, he drove the vehicle onto NW 7th. About half of his attention remained focused on the road, forty percent on the mirrors, and the last bit on me.

"Where are we going?" I asked, hoping he had a plan, because mine had consisted of *get me out of here before someone kills me.*

"Since you're a princess, thought we'd go to the ball."

"Sure." I was anything other than royal. Being the sole child of a Navy admiral had brought me a considerable amount of grief during my time in the Seabees. Princess was one of the nicer names I'd been called. "But really. Any ideas?" I assumed a hiding spot, perhaps where he'd drop me off then speed away.

He glanced at me before returning his attention to the road. "You trust me?"

"You can talk." I flapped my hand toward the thin hospital gown scrunched up to my mid-thighs. "I doubt I'm bugged."

His snort of laughter rang between us, and he darted me a shy smile. "Always did enjoy your sense of humor."

Interesting comment, considering he'd cringed whenever I tried to make him laugh in the past. And, attracted to him as I was, I'd tried a lot. "I guess you don't have to tell me where we're going. I'll find out eventually." Maybe he was winging it. "Somehow, I don't believe shopping at a box store and driving around Miami was on your agenda today, however."

"Nope." But his lips curled down as he stared into the mirrors.

My heart thudded once. Twice. Then picked up to race double time.

Carefully easing forward, I scooted around to peer out the back window. If I braced myself right, I could almost breathe. Pant. Whatever.

Traffic surrounded us but that was to be expected in a city. "Do you think someone's following us?"

"Maybe. Not quite sure yet."

"You'll ditch them."

"Yep."

"I might not be bugged, but what about you?" Inching around to face forward again, I took in the immaculate, dust-free dash and the floor mat beneath my feet that was clean enough I could eat off it. Messy might be my middle name but it sure wasn't his. "This isn't a rental. It's your SUV, isn't it?" He must've driven it from Maine or had it shipped.

It didn't mean anything. He'd needed a vehicle, and I'd been sick for a while.

"I'm clean," he said.

There were so many ways I could take that, but I was one hundred percent certain he wasn't implying anything sexual. Unfortunately.

"They must've followed us, then," I said.

"Likely."

"I saw someone watching us in the parking lot." I described the man and his actions.

"Light blue car, you said?"

"Yes." To think I'd dozed off when I was alone in the parking lot. My hands stilled on my lap and horror rose inside me like a gnashing beast. Someone could've crept up on me while I'd slept, maybe even the blond guy. Stupid moves like that would get me killed.

"Don't be too tough on yourself," he said, as if he'd read my mind. "You've been through hell."

"And come back alive." I wasn't sure about coming back whole, however. That had yet to be decided. "I'll be more careful." My voice shook more than I liked. "I won't let us down."

"Never dreamed you would."

"Are you taking me to a safe location?"

"You asked for help, and I'm giving it."

"Back at the hospital—"

"Rehab."

"Okay, at the rehab place, someone tried to kill me." Terror edged into my words. I'd woken to find Jax standing over me while someone I didn't know thumped across my body and onto the floor. The guy bolted, and it didn't take my former career in the military to tell me something horrible had nearly happened. "I think they'll keep trying."

"Trying's not doing, and I'm here to make sure it doesn't happen."

Tension eased from my body, and I slumped in my seat. "Thank you. I appreciate it."

"Welcome. I'm just grateful you're awake. That you're still you."

What wasn't he saying? "You had doubts?"

"We all did." His sigh whistled from between his teeth. "You were out of it for a long time."

I was still half out of it. The realization that I was weaker than a kitten hit me like a ton of cinder blocks. I couldn't breathe. Though it would make me shiver, I directed the vents to blast myself with frigid air. I gulped it in and tried to regain control, but telling myself to get over it wasn't working. My shakes wouldn't stop.

A few stray strands of my hair fluttered in the breeze. The rest of it hung in knots around my shoulders. My mouth tasted like I'd been sucking on a plastic tube for a month. Who knew when my teeth had last been brushed? Hopefully Jax had thought of floss and toothpaste while he was in the store.

Pulling his gaze from the mirrors, his hands that had been white knuckling the steering wheel loosened, telling me he believed he'd been mistaken about the tail. So far. "After the accident, Flint asked me to keep an eye on you."

Ah. So I was a job. I wasn't sure why I'd thought— started to believe—there was something more to all this than work. "How long did you say it's been?"

"Didn't. I assume you mean since the accident. Four weeks. Three days."

"And twenty minutes?"

He blinked, and his hands tightened again on the wheel. "Huh?"

"Nothing." Had the job watching over me been that awful? Why else count the time?

I slowly eased around to face him and propped my back into a stable position with the seat and the door. "How could I be out that long?" I could swear only hours had passed since... Gray mist filled my mind when I tried to remember.

"It was touch and go there for a while. Thought your dad would lose it." He peered at me briefly before his gaze returned to the road. "Why not ask him to help you now instead of me?"

"You mean other than the fact that you were in the room when the guy tried to kill me and Dad wasn't?"

"Sid could raise an army to protect you in about ten minutes."

Five minutes, if I knew my dad. "I don't want to endanger him."

"It's okay endangering me, though, right?"

My sigh chugged out. "You know what I mean. Dad's..." I shook my head.

"Retired doesn't mean he's ready for the nursing home yet."

"I guess that would be me." I rubbed the back of my neck. "Rehab you said?"

"Yep, they called it skilled rehab, though they admitted there wasn't much skilled stuff they could do beyond range of motion until you woke up."

"I've been in a coma?"

"Pretty much. EEG said you still had full brain activity, though."

"That's reassuring."

"You had a bad concussion, which meant you weren't doing anything for yourself for too long. Though lately, there were signs you were coming around. Purposeful movement, they called it. Your dad was thrilled."

What about my stepmom? She hadn't been thrilled about anything I'd done in years, if ever. It would be best not to ask, however, since Jax hadn't mentioned anything about her hovering at my bedside. If I knew her, she'd made a brief appearance then flown home.

"Lay it out for me, Jax," I said. "What am I dealing with here?"

"You broke seven ribs on your right side, multiple fractures to each rib. Flail chest, they called it. They put you on a breathing machine."

No wonder my chest felt like it had been hit by a boulder. I'd fractured ribs in the past and knew it took about three weeks before I could take a deep breath without believing I'd die. "Seven ribs."

"Then you got pneumonia. They said it's real common, but it set you back. Took a bunch of antibiotics to clear it up."

Huh.

"Then there was your right femur. Open compound fracture. You lost a lot of blood. They took you to the OR and plated your leg."

I traced my finger along the sharp, pink incision line on my thigh.

"But the worst was your head. At first, they thought you were out of it due to pain because, hell, it had to hurt like a bitch, but when they lightened the drugs, you didn't wake up."

He laid it all out in a dispassionate tone, but an edge of something I couldn't define came through in his voice. Not anger, but…

Had he been worried about me?

I studied him like I had so many other times when I was confident he wasn't watching. Solid, sure hands gripping the steering wheel. Shoulders wide enough to support the world. Sharp eyes intent on everything around us. So tall, his tight haircut almost brushed the ceiling when he moved. He'd been out of the military almost as long as I had, yet he still kept it high and tight. A good look on him, but I imagined he knew that.

Hot. That was clear the second I met him.

While I felt like I'd been run over by a train, my body still stirred, responding to his appealing presence beside me.

Muscular, hot men had been common in the military. We all worked out to stay in shape and to remain combat-ready. And there was something about being in danger that heightened attraction. I'd dated enough of those guys, too. But none had screwed with my insides like Jax did just by existing.

He was too hot. I needed to remember he wasn't interested in me.

"CTs, EEGs, and MRIs of your brain," he said. "All your tests came back normal. No head bleeds. Neurologist settled on a concussion for your diagnosis. Bad one, Haylee."

"I don't remember much of anything after Gabe

and I flew from Maine to Cancun except…" Gabe. "He was in the car with me!" My words echoed like a horn inside the tight space. "Is he… Did he…" Tears smarted behind my eyes. "Is he okay?" Please, tell me he was okay.

"His family shipped him to D.C. They…did all they could."

Fuck, fuck, fuck.

"Gabe—is dead?" I bleated. As if someone had reached inside my chest and clamped their fingers around my heart, it spasmed. I curled forward in protection, but it was too late. Slumping fully against the seat, I pinched my eyes closed, willing myself not to break down. Once I started, I'd never stop. "It's my fault."

"How can it be? You weren't driving. Someone shoved your vehicle off the road."

"I'd…" I shook my head and my lanky hair flopped past my shoulders.

"You'd what?"

"Nothing."

His sharp gaze pinned me in place. "What aren't you saying?"

I growled. Should I tell him? Withholding the information could endanger us both.

"I… It's worse than me not saying something, because I *can't*. I don't remember." I sorted through my mind, but my brain felt like it had been replaced with cotton. Each synapse refused to connect with another.

"What *do* you remember?"

"Flying to Cancun. Checking into the resort. Playing around in the pool for a day before slinking out of the hotel after midnight and out into the city. A long, dark gap after that." A black hole where memories should be. "Then the car roaring through the streets. Gabe yelling something about…"

A blank wall rose in front of me.

This was horrible. My brains had been scrambled. What if I never remembered?

I gulped and shook my head. "After that, the only thing clear is the crash and then nothing."

"Your contact?"

"Did we connect with one?" Even that detail wasn't clear in my mind.

A swear ripped out of him. "Haylee, I'm sorry. The docs said, if—when—you woke up, we weren't to push it. Don't worry about all that right now."

"Except someone tried to kill me. They killed Gabe! The missing details…" I swallowed past the solid mass in my throat. "Someone must be worried I'll talk. And the worst part about it is that I don't remember." My laughter snorted out but this was anything but funny. "They want to permanently keep me from talking when I have absolutely nothing I can say."

"Can't exactly put the word out on the radio that you don't remember."

"We'll hide, then?"

"For now. I'll get in touch with Flint once we're safe. Fill him in on the situation."

"The thing that surprises me most is that no one tried to kill me before today."

"Your dad and I didn't leave your bedside until they moved you to rehab. And the government sent someone

—Clyde—who stayed in the room whenever we couldn't be there…" He frowned.

"What?"

"Where was Clyde? When I came back with to your room, he wasn't there."

"The bathroom?"

"Not without telling us first."

"I hope he's okay." Had the guy who tried to kill me incapacitated Clyde?

"I'll fill Flint in on that, too." He swore. "That guy in your room must've been waiting for us to lower our guard. Your dad and I had stepped away this morning, gone for coffee. He stayed in the cafeteria to take a call while I returned to the room."

"We should let Dad know I'm okay, too."

"While I'm confident I'm clean, I'm less certain about my phone. Once we're secure, I'll use a phone in a hotel or wherever we end up to notify everyone."

Dad would be freaking out, but there wasn't anything we could do about it until we hit a secure location.

"I appreciate it." The words trembled out of me and reaction set in. Mourning Gabe and struggling to hold back my tears, I slumped against the glass and stared out the window as the world blurred by.

Jax pulled up to a light and turned onto NW 20th Street.

"By the way, I don't hate you," he finally said. His fingers tapped a rapid rhythm on the wheel.

"Okay." What was I supposed to say to that? I'd just been thinking he was hot. This comment wasn't a hand reaching toward me, urging me to take it. He was just clarifying a simple point, contradicting what I'd said back at the rehab place. "For what it's worth, I don't hate you, either."

"Okay."

A long silence followed as we continued east.

Jax had said more to me today than he had during all the months we'd worked together combined. Why go silent now?

He'd called me sweetheart but he couldn't mean it. He'd used the endearment with both Mia and Ginny on multiple occasions. It was a form of teasing, like something that would go on between a brother and a sister. But they were all friends. Me and Jax? Coworkers was as far as I could stretch it.

A shadow of a memory skated through my mind, but I couldn't see through to grab it. Something about the vehicle chasing us… The driver…

I scowled, frustrated it wasn't clear.

My eyes stung as I remembered Gabe joking around with me, teasing me, just having fun. Kind of like Jax with Ginny and Mia.

Gabe. I'd flirted with him more times than not, but we'd only been friends. He'd known I had a thing for Jax. Had Gabe had a thing for someone, too? If he'd liked someone and hadn't told them, it was too late now.

Pinching the bridge of my nose, I struggled not to break down. Do. Not. Cry.

"I'm sure your memory will come back," Jax finally said.

"What if it doesn't?" My voice came out shrill, filled

with pain for my loss. Gabe had been dead for over a month, and I hadn't known. I hadn't been there with him when he'd passed away. I hadn't been able to tell his family and friends I was sorry.

So, so sorry. I—

"Hey." Lifting my hand from where it lay beside my thigh, Jax squeezed it. "Trust me?"

When he'd asked me earlier, I'd hesitated. This time, I squeezed back.

Jax's gaze darted to the mirrors again, and he swore. Dropping my hand, he slammed his palm on the steering wheel. His foot compressed the gas pedal, making the SUV leap forward.

My left side was shoved against my seat.

"Hold on!" Jax belted out.

3

Jax

I lied when I told Haylee we weren't being followed.

Thought I'd ditched the black Mercury sedan while weaving through town, though. So much for that idea.

My foot compressed the gas pedal, and the four hundred horses under the hood roared, blowing us back against our seats. I dodged through traffic, ignoring middle fingers and blasted horns. The vehicle behind us kept with me, riding so close to my back bumper, I braced myself for the hit.

Dude wasn't shoving *me* into a ditch.

Haylee's breath came in sharp spurts. She clutched her thigh, her other hand splinting her ribs. It killed me to see her hurting but it sure beat the alternative.

I dashed around and between vehicles while the Mercury hugged my spine.

We had to get away, but where? While in the store, I'd used a payphone at the courtesy desk to call a friend. I asked him to put an escape plan into action and gave him a list of what I'd need. First on the list was to ditch my vehicle. Second, take us far from here, to a place where no one would ever find us.

An old Navy buddy, Dwayne would do all he could to make it happen.

This entire situation was too organized, too planned out. First Clyde disappearing at the rehab place, then the guy being in the room one of the few times both of us had left the room.

While I could activate government contacts, the idea made my spine itch—a sure sign something was going on I hadn't yet figured out. And I sure as hell couldn't sit around and wait for the feds to handle things, let alone Haylee's father, whose connections were good but not that good.

Haylee could barely hobble. I'd happily carry her from here to Alaska but, while doing that, we'd stand out in a crowd.

She needed time to heal and time to get strong enough to protect herself. For that, we needed to disappear.

I flew through a red light and slammed on my brakes before I hit the white Toyota in front of me. Jerking the vehicle to the right and then forward, I ignored the other drivers, some shaking their fists out their windows, others jabbering on their phones. Calling the cops.

Really needed to blow this place.

I barreled out onto NW 3rd, heading south, and back onto 17th, then 4th, snaking around a park, trying not to turn anyone into a statistic. Rows of palm trees dwarfed by high-rise buildings blurred on my right.

Fuck. I wasn't losing the Mercury behind me.

My heart slammed against my ribs and, though I hadn't run one single damn step, my lungs were on fire. Fury and desperation made my hands sweaty. Moisture trickled down my spine, making me itch.

Haylee swayed in her seat, her eyes wide with panic and her mouth ajar. Was she reliving what happened that morning when Gabe was mortally injured?

"Sorry," I huffed out, not daring take my eyes off the road or my hands off the wheel for more than a sec.

"It's not your fault."

I compressed the brake pedal to keep from hitting a bicyclist then roared around another vehicle. Tires squealed and horns wailed, and I did my best to ignore them. I didn't like endangering others. I had to end this. Right away. "I'll lose him."

"For now." Her voice came out bleak. Defeated.

I growled my frustration. "Forever."

"He'll keep coming." Her wry laughter must've made her chest hurt because she gently rubbed her right side. "This job has been a shit show from the moment we took it on."

"We'll find a way through this. Someone's taken the lead and they're after us, but we'll bring them down along with the entire cartel."

"If you say so." Her fingers traced along her scar. "So, this leg of mine."

"Yep?" Sunlight slaked through the side windows, and a quick glance at the clock told me time was ticking down. For my plan to work, we had to get to our destination soon. But I couldn't bring our tail with us.

Haylee set the gun in the drink holder and unbuckled. "Am I going to rip anything apart inside my leg or chest if I do some acrobatics?"

"You planning on climbing up onto the roof?" I wasn't joking. I knew Haylee. There wasn't much this woman wouldn't try.

Well, except me.

"Not yet," she said.

"Your leg's plated. Ribs are secure. Docs said, if you'd been awake, you would've been shuffling around a week or so ago with a walker."

Her lips twisted, and her eyebrows rose. "I'm part of the geriatric crowd, am I?"

"You would've been a hit with the old guys."

The snort she released made my pulse surge.

I really needed to focus on my driving.

While I rushed through traffic, Haylee turned and rose onto her knees, hissing at the discomfort. She held onto the oh-shit bar and there was no hiding her shakes.

"I forgot my walker back at the rehab place," she said.

"No problem." Seeing a gap between the lanes, I goosed it and the car surged forward. "You've got me."

"You can't carry me everywhere."

"Watch me."

Compressing the button, she dropped the passenger window and ducked her head out. Wind worthy of a category three hurricane whipped through the car.

She groaned as she stared behind us. "Talk about black car cliché!"

We wove and swayed, dashing around cars with them in hot pursuit, Haylee hanging on and hissing through the pain.

I half-watched in the rearview mirror, and my gut sank when the matching passenger window in the Mercury dropped and someone shoved their head and a weapon out the opening.

An Uzi. Great. A blur of clicks peppered the air. And my SUV. Sounded like a pencil poking through foil.

"Nice paint job you've got here," Haylee said. "I hate seeing it get dinged up."

"Bullet-proof." Mostly. It wouldn't survive a lengthy barrage.

More bullets encroached on the passenger side of my vehicle, rushing toward Haylee.

"Get back in the car!" I roared. With her head leaning out, she presented the perfect target.

"One second, hero," she belted out through gritted teeth. "I've got a plan."

I grumbled while squeezing between two cars. Up ahead, the light turned green, and I shot through the intersection.

"Can you get us somewhere quieter?" she yelled. "Not interested in friendly fire."

"On it."

Where? We were talking Miami. I wheeled around a corner, another, and the Mercury kept pace.

No clue why we didn't have an entourage of cops on our tails, too.

A siren rang out, and I slammed my palm on the steering wheel. Jinxed us.

We flew down a narrow street, and I was pleased to find it less crowded than the others. "This is it," I called out. "The best I'll find. Make your move."

"Hey!" Haylee yelled at the other vehicle. "Your big boy's all muscle but this little lady in my hand has got brains." She took quick aim with the 9 mil, while I held the wheel steady. A sharp crack and the car behind us swayed.

They kept coming.

"Losin' my touch," Haylee said limply.

Her spunk had fizzled quicker than a popped soap bubble.

More sirens burned through the air. In seconds, they'd be all over us. We didn't have time for lengthy explanations. We needed to leave town fast.

"Do you have a clean-up crew on hold?" Her hand smacked on the roof, and she groaned as she tried to maintain her balance.

"Yep. Just do it, sharpshooter."

Her lethal reputation preceded her. Flint wouldn't hire just any old Seabee. He wanted the best. Which was Haylee. She'd been a weapons specialist and gunner's mate in the military.

I swerved to avoid a bicyclist, and she started tumbling through the window.

I slapped my hand on her ass. Not on purpose. Just to help keep her from sliding out onto the pavement.

But damn. Her ass. So…firm. Rounded.

Hot.

Shouldn't even be having the dirty thoughts running through my mind.

Securing a hold on her hospital gown, I kept her from falling out.

"Getting kind of frisky…aren't you, Jax?" she said dryly.

Like every other time she teased, my breathing stopped. My tongue froze. I wanted to give it back to her as fast as she delivered it, but I didn't know how. What if I said something stupid?

Wincing, she lifted the gun again and, bracing herself against the door, sighted down the barrel. "Hold it steady. On one…two…three."

A crack was followed by tires squealing and a grinding shriek. Tire blown, the Mercury bailed to the side, dragging its side along a row of parked cars before coming to an abrupt stop when it slammed into a sign.

As I reached a second intersection and turned right, the guy who'd injected something into Haylee's IV leaped out of the car and, weapon wavering, sighted down it as I careened out of view.

Haylee gingerly climbed back inside, emitting tiny pants, her face florid with pain. She carefully lowered herself into the seat, leaned forward, and cupped her face. "Crap. I'm going to pass out. If I do, could you make sure my hospital johnny's hiked down? Don't want to show off my ass." Easing to the right, her face fissured as agony shot through her. She put up the window. The gun dropped from her unresisting hand and onto the floor. "Safety's on," she gasped out. As she dragged her hand up to her shoulder and wrenched the seatbelt forward to snap it into place, she hissed. "Don't let me do that again, okay?"

"Sure thing." Ah, and that was a smooth response on my part. Not. I scurried to find something worthy to tell her instead, because this woman literally blew me away. "Love how you work, sweetheart," was all I could drum up.

Haylee

The world slammed into focus when the driver's door clicked shut beside me.

Arms splaying wide, I pinched back a groan and stared around with blurry eyes.

Jax's SUV sat in a parking garage surrounded by other unmoving vehicles. The silence inside the cabin was broken only by the chilled whir of the AC and the soft hum of the motor Jax had left running.

Ahead, beyond rows of parked cars, a grate-covered slice of sky peeked into the building.

Were we still in Miami?

Jax crossed the open area between this row and the next and met up with a guy in his late twenties—about our age—whose tee and jeans hung off his tall, lanky frame. The men bro-hugged then pulled apart. Jax's grin came out loose and infinitely easier than I'd seen it before other than with Ginny and Mia.

The other guy's dark hair clouded around his face,

and his longish beard brushed his chest as he gestured and spoke. He reached toward his spine…

Gulping back fear, I scrambled for the gun I'd left on my lap, but it was gone.

My worry dropped three notches when the guy pulled a small leather portfolio from underneath his shirt and held it toward Jax. I'd thought he was going for a weapon. They'd hugged but it wouldn't be the first time someone had come across friendly only to shoot a moment later.

A second man joined them and slapped Jax's shoulder. Older, like mid-forties, the second man had red hair and was clean shaven. About the same build as the first.

Jax unzipped the portfolio and pulled out a couple of U.S. passports. When he opened them, his hands stilled. The first voice lifted, but I couldn't make out what he said.

After closing the passports and zipping up the portfolio, Jax released a jerky nod and tapped the guy's arm.

The three men turned and strode toward the SUV but the second guy stopped at the hood. A half-grin rose on his face when he caught me watching, and he lifted a limp arm to wave. His narrowed gaze followed Jax as he went around the driver's side to the trunk and opened it. After rifling around, he shut the back and came up beside me with a large pack strapped to his back.

Opening the door, he nodded when my eyes met his. "Good, you're awake. Was worried about you for a second."

"Only a second?"

"At least ten minutes."

I blinked, unsure if I should laugh or take him seriously. His neutral face and stormy blue gaze gave nothing away.

The black guy opened the driver's side door and dropped into the seat while the other waited in front of the vehicle. He dipped his chin my way. "Fine day." His voice came out like honey drizzling down a spoon. Slow and southern, his mouth cupped the words before releasing them. "Hope you two have an awesome trip." His deep brown eyes softened and, when his teeth flashed white in his face, I swore he held back a laugh. "Fixed things up nice for you."

"We've gotta go, Haylee," Jax said. "Dwayne, here, has come up with our out. We're ditching the SUV. Dwayne and Eben will take care of it now."

"Thanks, Dwayne," I said. I nodded to Eben, who just stared.

"Anytime. Anytime," Dwayne said. He leaned out the car. "Eben. Dude. Stop gawking and get into the back seat."

Eben stomped around the driver's side and opened the door. When he dropped inside, the weight of his gaze fell on me, though he said nothing.

I couldn't say why, but while I felt comfortable with Dwayne, I didn't with Eben. I shoved the thought aside. Eben was Jax's friend. I could trust him.

It hardly mattered. We were leaving, and I'd never see him again.

As Jax stepped back a pace, I swung my legs over toward the opening, holding my breath when my body protested the movement with spasms.

Seeing my hesitation, Jax reached inside and slid his arms around me. He scooped me up into his arms. "I've got 'ya."

Now Dwayne did laugh. "Almost want to go with you, dude. Watch the fireworks."

"Only rest and recovery where we're going," Jax said dryly. "You know I stay away from open flames."

"If I know you, that won't last but a minute," Dwayne said. "You always did jump into the fire before thinking things through."

Was Jax's friend also former military? And what about Eben?

Dwayne patted the dash. "I'll take care of your baby. You said bright yellow, now, right?"

Jax growled, his chest rumbling beneath my cheek. "Green. We agreed you'd paint it dark green."

"You sure?" Dwayne said with a laugh. "'Cuz I kinda like yellow."

"Ass," Jax said, and to me, "A new paint job and plates," he added to Dwayne. "That's it."

"Disguised?" I asked, shifting to get more comfortable. It felt odd snuggling against him like a child. Or, shit, a girlfriend.

Do not go there.

Yes, I should be protesting, insisting I could walk wherever we were going, but it felt too good to be held by him. He smelled like laundry detergent, cotton, and the deep woods on a hot summer's day. I wanted to close my eyes and nuzzle my nose into him, but I was confident he'd take me back to the hospital and demand the neurologist run more tests.

I was tempted to give into my weakness when I needed to be strong.

"Take care," Dwayne said, shifting the SUV into gear.

Eben said nothing, just stared. Creepy dude.

"Thanks." Jax bumped the passenger door shut with his butt and carried me over to a silver Hyundai sedan. He carefully lowered me to my feet on the driver's side as Dwayne drove the SUV out of the spot and toward the exit.

"You okay standing?" Jax asked, tugging my attention back to him.

"Yes."

"Hold on to me if you want."

"I will."

He opened the back door. "Would you mind lying across the back seat?"

"I just took a nap."

"You passed out."

"Some date I am, right?"

Jax's face shut down, telling me I needed to keep this serious and avoid jokes.

As if I'd commented on the weather, he continued in a practical tone. "Anyone who saw us enter the garage will be looking for a man and a woman at the exits."

Good point.

"I can lie down," I said. Turning carefully, I presented my rear to the seat and dropped onto the cloth cushion. Inching, I eased my way inside and bent my knees up, moving my legs until my feet wouldn't catch in the door, then lowered myself onto my back. Agony roared through me.

"Hurts," I choked out. Chuffing, I rolled onto my side, facing the front. While some might think lying on broken ribs would hurt more, it was actually more comfortable. The solid seat braced the fractures and allowed my good lung to expand to make up for the loss of the other.

Jax put the pack inside the trunk then came around and settled in the driver's seat.

"Go easy on the bumps, okay?" I gritted through clenched teeth.

"Yep." He started the car and eased it out of the spot.

We snaked through the parking garage to the exit.

Though it was a challenge to see his face, whenever he turned, Jax's lips remained in a thin line. His posture gave nothing away.

"You're Coral Jacobs," he finally said, braking to slow the vehicle. After lowering the window, he paid for the parking. When the gate lifted, he stiffened and eased the vehicle forward, joining traffic. Sunlight burst through the windows, blinding me.

"Coral? Cute name," I said, blinking fast. "What's yours?"

"Clark Jacobs."

"Are we passing ourselves off as brother and sister?"

Jax peered into all the mirrors at least three times before sighing. "You can sit up now."

I did, buckling in behind the front passenger seat.

Driving up to a light, Jax tapped his fingers on the

steering wheel. While he kept his gaze trained between the mirrors and the road, tension had eased from his shoulders.

No one was following us, then. And the sirens had moved on. Would we get away this easily?

"Here's the thing," he said. "For now, we're husband and wife."

"Did we get married while I was asleep?"

"Passed out."

Whatever.

"For now," he added. "Married for now."

"Divorcing me so soon?" We hadn't even consummated the marriage. Yeah. Definitely shouldn't be thinking of something like that with Jax, or my heart would burst from my chest.

When he said nothing, I lifted my left hand. "No ring."

He reached over his shoulder, dangling a gold band. Taking it, I slid it on my left finger.

And just like that, we were married. A disguise shouldn't make me feel squirrelly inside.

"What if I prefer silver?" I said, just to be ornery.

The way his snort popped out past his tight lips made me think he didn't like giving anything away. "We can change the bands later."

"I take it we're leaving the country, then?"

"Flint thought it'd be best. We're hiding you until he and the crew can figure this out. Clyde…"

"Who is that?"

"Bodyguard the government sent."

"Oh, yeah. He was supposed to be in my room."

"He's missing."

Not good. My gut sank. Another person endangered because of me.

"Your dad's on it. They'll find him," Jax said, injecting confidence into his voice that couldn't be real.

My shoulders curled forward. "I hope so."

"Flint approved of the plan Dwayne came up with."

"Which is…?"

Silence followed.

"I imagine it's a solid plan," I said to fill the growing gap between us.

Injured as I was, I was useless, unable to defend myself. Hell, I couldn't even run—walk—if I had to. "Are we going to the airport?"

"Not quite."

"You're keeping awfully quiet about our destination."

"As I said, Dwayne hooked us up."

Hooked up, huh? My chuckle came out jagged, and I gulped back my pain.

While Jax was driving as carefully as possible, each bump and clunk sent more agony shooting through me. "Is your friend a justice of the peace?"

More silence.

Well, that had gone over well. "I was joking." I couldn't figure out why I kept poking him, gouging away at the hard shell he surrounded himself with. Maybe I kept hoping he'd crack and let a different part of Jax shine through. A side of him that might…I don't know.

Flirt back?

I should give up. I'd been trying to find my way

inside his hardened exterior for months, without success. What made me think us being alone together would make a difference?

Mia said he was shy, that I needed to give him time, but I wasn't convinced. To me, he came across disinterested.

Damn my eyes. They kept watering.

I didn't need him. Not *that* way. It was the sunlight making me weepy. I'd been cooped up inside for over a month. I was in agony.

It was only natural for my eyes to be wet.

Maintaining the quiet, Jax drove down a narrow street, then another, and I was eternally grateful my tears shut down on their own.

"Think we lost them?" I asked. Maybe he'd believe the shake in my voice came from pain.

It did. Except it wasn't just my leg and ribs that hurt.

"They won't be working alone," he said, putting on the blinker and slowing the car.

"You're right. Men who shoot an Uzi in downtown Miami will have backup."

"No one on us so far."

But they would be. Their determination so far made that a given.

We drove through a long tunnel, following signs toward the terminal. Maybe we *were* flying somewhere and he'd wanted to keep it a secret for some reason.

No, wait. *Cruise* tunnel.

Cruise?

We emerged into daylight and streamed behind other cars, eventually pulling into a parking garage, where Jax spiraled us up to a top floor and pulled into an empty space way in the back.

"Dwayne'll come for the car," he said, tapping his hand on the stick shift. A tic in his temple was his only reveal. While he seemed to want me to feel confident we were safe, he didn't come across as convinced himself.

"We're leaving the car," I said. "Going…somewhere."

Jax checked the mirrors before turning off the engine and unbuckling. He reached to open the door but paused. "You'll need to change so I'll step outside."

"I assume there's clothing in the plastic bag you threw on the floor?"

"Yep. If you need help…"

And that statement sent a variety of wild ideas rushing through me, but I knew Jax meant nothing sexy by the statement.

"I can do it." I could only hope he'd bought simple-to-don clothing because my body wasn't up for wiggling into tight jeans.

"I'll wait in the lot. When you're ready…"

"I'll let you know."

He got out and shut the door, then leaned against it, presenting his back to me.

I shuffled sideways, snagged the bag off the floor, and tossed it onto my lap.

"Holy shit," I hissed as I pulled out a hibiscus-print sundress. Dark blue with bold pink and white flowers, plus a profusion of green leaves. I was a jeans and t-shirt kind of gal. This… I shook my head as I yanked off the tag, stuffing that back into the bag.

I held up the dress, scrutinizing the elastic waistline and spaghetti shoulder straps. It had a straight skirt with no flare that would hit just above my knees if I guessed right.

"How am I supposed to fight in a get-up like this?" Big assumption on my part that, if confronted, I'd be able to do more than throw a weak punch or generate a simple push kick no matter what I was wearing.

The hospital gown unsnapped at the shoulders and drooped around my waist.

Jax had included cotton granny undies but no bra, which might be problematic with my Cs. Okay, Bs, but still. I'd jiggle. Well, when I moved on my own. Not much jiggling going on if Jax carried me.

After shimmying into the undies, my jerky breathing echoed in the still vehicle as pain bit into my spine. I tugged the dress over my head and carefully shifted sideways to hitch the stretchy fabric down over my hips. With trembling fingers, I combed my hair and pulled it back with the cloth tie I ripped off the hospital gown. After, I slipped my feet into the yellow rubber flip-flops Jax had provided. After shuffling across the seat, I popped open the door.

Jax stared.

"What?" I said.

"What, what?" He said, color rising into his face.

"I've worn a dress before."

He blinked as if he needed to digest my words. "Have you?"

"Jax."

"Yeah?"

"Why are your eyes focused on my legs. They hairy? 'Cuz it's not like I've had a razor to shave them."

"Not worried about any hair on your legs."

"Then what are you worried about?"

"Not worried at all."

I sighed, realizing this conversation was going nowhere fast. "Where to next?" I asked. Trying to figure out why Jax couldn't take his eyes off me would take me about a thousand years, and it was clear he wasn't going to contribute enough information to make a solution possible.

As if relieved I'd changed the subject, Jax shifted the bag he must've retrieved from the trunk and strapped onto his back while I was changing. "Elevator. Terminal."

I'd assumed that already.

After a quick glance around that must've assured him we were alone, he lifted me out of the car and settled me in his arms. "I'll carry you to the elevators but once we're inside, you'll have to stand. Sorry."

"No drawing attention."

"Yep."

"I can do it."

He only nodded.

We boarded the elevator and Jax lowered me to my feet.

"Hold on to me, if you want," he said.

I did latch onto his arm. No one would think twice about me clinging to my "husband" and I wasn't sure how long I could even stand on my own. Others joined us as we traveled downward, and we all left the elevator together and streamed out into the sunshine.

Cop cars on the road made my already-slow footsteps stall. Fortunately, no one except a gray-haired guy in a tropical print shirt seemed to pay us any attention as we took the crosswalk.

The gray-haired guy watched as we climbed into a van to ride to the Terminal, but he didn't get inside with us. He looked vaguely familiar but I could swear I'd never seen him before.

Call me paranoid, but I'd be grateful when guys stopped staring at me.

We rode to the Terminal and after that, Jax didn't need to fill me in on what was coming next.

"Time to get on board," he said, flicking his free hand toward a big sign that said, *Bon Voyage*. "You do any sea duty?"

"Yeah. Served on the Enterprise as a gunner's mate. When I re-upped, I switched over to the Seabees." Stopping, I stared, and my jaw unhinged.

Beyond the terminal, looking shorter and wider than an aircraft carrier, a portly cruise ship rose above the water.

Royal Caribbean, huh?

Jax had been right.

I *was* about to become a princess.

Jax

"Everyone's going to think you're taking a cruise with your mother," Haylee said wryly.

She took a few more slow steps forward, wincing whenever she put weight on her right leg. A quick glance over my shoulder told me we'd gone about a hundred feet from where the shuttle had dropped us off. About five minutes ago.

Her breathing hitched, and it socked me in the gut to see her in this much pain, because I couldn't do a damn thing about it.

"Let me carry you," I hissed for what had to be the tenth time, as we crossed the sidewalk and started up the steps leading to Terminal A.

"We can't risk drawing attention," she bit out, focusing on placing one foot in front of the other. Take a step. Drag up her injured leg to join the other. Pause. Grunt. Another step. Etcetera.

At this rate, we'd reach the top in about twenty minutes and draw attention because of her slow pace.

"Until we're locked in a room." Her wheeze made me worry about her rib injury, but maybe she was getting short of breath from the increased activity. She hadn't done anything on her own for a long time. "We need to blend in with everyone else."

"A wheelchair, then."

I could almost hear her teeth grinding. "I can do it." Another step up. She stopped and braced her hip against the railing. Clung to the metal, actually, her fingers blanching from the effort.

I scowled. "You're stubborn." Too damn stubborn.

"You know it." Her pleading eyes turned my way, and her voice dropped to next to nothing. "I need to do it, okay?"

My grumble rose from deep in my chest. "For now."

Her lips twisted. "Don't go all alpha on me, Jax. Because then I'll have to knock you down a notch or two." The lift of her chin shouted determination, but it was negated by her quivering lips. "I could take you if I had to."

I couldn't help rollin' my eyes. "Back in Maine, before the accident? You'd make decent competition. But now?" I skimmed my gaze down her trembling body —damn woman should let me help her. "You're no challenge, sweetheart."

"Don't call me that," she snapped. "If you meant it…" Her teeth caught the words as if she worried she'd revealed something by saying them. Crazy notion on my part. "Forget that." She waved her hand between us as a frown took over her features. "You're using the endearment to mock me, and I don't like it."

What if I really did mean it? Because, when I said it, it sure didn't feel like mocking.

Fuck. I was teasing myself with what would never be mine.

"Okay," I said. "You're right. Sorry."

"Apology accepted." She swallowed, but her voice croaked when she spoke. "And I'm sorry I'm cranky. It's just…" Blinking fast, she stared past my shoulder. "It hurts like hell."

My irritation dropped to nil in a flash. I wasn't feeling impatient with her pace. Fear for her was gnawing at my bones. I needed to get her someplace safe and away from prying eyes, where I could let her rest. Drop her guard. Then she could sleep for as long as she needed, knowing I'd watch out for her. Protect her.

We reached the top and crept forward. People hustled around us, pulling roller suitcases, hefting carry-ons, and holding the hands of little kids who strained to break free. Stepping inside the terminal, we were greeted by a blast of A.C. and perky, tropical music.

Security loomed ahead, and my only concern would be our fake IDs. No weapon to worry about, however. I'd hated leaving my gun with Dwayne, but I had no choice. While Jackson Ramsey could carry, Clark Jacobs could not.

"You look too young to be my mother," I said, shifting my bag on my back. Not wanting to leave Haylee in the car for long, I'd grabbed the minimal amount of clothing at the store. We'd need to pick up more gear either on the ship or at our next destination. Both, probably.

Tipping her face back to look up to me, she grimaced. "I sure don't feel young. I feel at least a thousand years old."

"Don't look a day over nine hundred to me."

She looked startled for a moment before she socked my arm. "Are you joking with me?"

I shrugged as heat traveled up into my face.

"Whoa." Her pretty green eyes widened. "Watch out, Jax, or I might start thinking you like me."

I did like her. In a different way than what she was suggesting, however.

"You got a problem with that?" I asked, feeling bold enough to keep the subtle tease going.

"No." Her cheery mood fled. "Since we're in this together—for now—I would like it if we could be friends."

"Friends works."

"Yeah." She yanked her gaze from mine, dropping it to the gleaming floor. "Friends it is."

Would it be that horrible for us to be friends? It was a start, a direction we hadn't gone in yet. I wouldn't read anything more into it than that.

"We should go," I said, jerking my head toward the baggage area, and she nodded.

I checked my pack, and we took the escalators to the second floor.

"Did you check in online with the app?" a woman working for the cruise ship asked when we reached the top.

"Nope," I said. No phone, no data.

"Okay, then. It's not a problem." She smiled and

waved toward a desk. "Right this way, and someone will be happy to help get things settled. Then you can board and let the party begin!"

"You want to sit over there?" I asked Haylee, nudging my head toward a long row of connected chairs. "No need for you to wait in line. I can call you up when it's our turn."

"Sure." Leaving me, she hobbled over and sank down with obvious relief. While stretching her leg out implied utter relaxation, it was negated by the sharp way she scanned the vicinity. She'd have to be unconscious to let down her guard.

I joined the back of the line. When I reached the desk, Haylee limped over and stood beside me.

A woman with the nametag *Sandie* scanned our passports. Dropping them on the counter, she pulled up our information on a computer screen. "Oh."

My spine jolted, but I kept my face neutral. Was something wrong with our IDs?

"So exciting!" she gushed.

Maybe not our IDs.

Sandie's attention darted in my direction. "It says here you're on your honeymoon. How lovely! And you've booked a gorgeous suite. What a wise choice." She dimpled a grin at me as if I was responsible for all this.

Honeymoon, huh? I could almost hear Dwayne's snicker from here. I was gonna kill him.

After her smile encompassed Haylee, Sandie held up her index finger. "Because this is a special occasion, let me see if I can make it even better." A few taps on her computer followed. "Ah-ha. Oh. Yes!"

Haylee's eyebrow-raised gaze fell on me. The pinched skin around her eyes told me five minutes spent sitting had not been enough. She was flagging already.

What did she think about all this honeymoon stuff? Her lips twitched, which could mean she was pissed. Hell, for all I knew, she was holding back laughter. Might be pain, though. Her leg had to be killing her.

"Perfect," Sandie said, nodding at me. "I've arranged for a few complimentary items to celebrate your newly-wedded status, including an upgrade to a junior suite with a decent sized balcony. Since you're in a suite, your WOWbands will be in your room. They'll help you navigate the ship, and you can use them to charge your onboard purchases at any of the stores. You can even use them to make restaurant reservations." She tucked a strand of black hair behind her ear. "They work like keycards with a few extra options. And they're water-resistant!"

"Awesome," Haylee said. "This is really nice of you. Thanks."

"The concierge for your room is Maxym. Make sure you look him up after you're settled in your room. He'll be happy to help you with anything you might need. Perhaps you'd like to have a bottle of champagne delivered for this evening? Let him help with booking your excursions, which I recommend you do sooner rather than later, because some of the activities fill up fast."

"Like what?" Haylee asked, propping herself against the desk. To anyone else, the gesture would look casual and showed interest in the conversation, but it was clear to me she worried her knees would give way. "Where are we going?"

"Is the cruise a surprise?" Sandie asked, her voice bubbling as she crinkled her eyes at me. "Want me to keep the fun going a little longer?"

"Key West," I blurted out.

Sandie's shoulders drooped as if I'd ruined her own, personal surprise. "Yes, Key West is the first port we'll put into tomorrow. The day after that, we're in Cozumel. Wonderful snorkeling there."

"I'm not sure I'm up for swimming," Haylee said.

"There are lots of other options," Sandie said. "A full list of them. Such as a catamaran cruise or a botanical garden tour. You could go swimming with dolphins or rays… Oh, right. You said no swimming. How about shopping? Everyone loves finding a bargain. Don't forget to pick up vanilla and maybe a bottle of tequila while you're in Cozumel. Mexico's also known for Kahlua. And if you take the ferry to the mainland, it's a quick ride south to Coba, which features the tallest pyramid on the Yucatan. Even farther down the coast, you'll find Tulum, a crumbling fortress overlooking the sea. And then there's an ecopark, Xcaret. I know—"

"We're going to the Yucatan?" Haylee asked me quickly. Her face had lost all color. Not that she'd had much to begin with, having been lying in a hospital bed so long. "I'm not sure I'm up for Mexico."

I'd been concerned about how she'd take returning to where she'd been injured, where Gabe had been murdered, but this was the easiest way to disappear. I expected whoever was after Haylee to watch for her name on all outgoing flights. A cruise seemed like the simplest way to get out of the country.

"Are you worried about the sargassum seaweed issue?" Sandie asked. She leaned across the desk as if to share a secret. "I can assure you the towns of Playa del Carmen and Cozumel are doing everything they can to keep the beaches clean. Worst case, if you do choose to take the ferry to Playacar and you find the seaweed is a problem, you can stick to 5th Avenue. Shopping cures all ailments, am I right?"

"Sure," Haylee said weakly. "Shopping is what I need to make me feel better."

"We all set?" I asked, eager to grab our fake passports before Sandie scrutinized them further. We needed to get on the ship. Haylee needed to rest more than anything. I'd get her to our room, tuck her into bed, then get her something to eat. I was starved. I imagined she was, too.

"We are," Sandie said. "I bet you'd like to get started on your honeymoon." As if realizing how suggestive that had come out, her eyes widened and she coughed. "Yes. Right." Color filled her face, and her attention fell on me again before she sent a wink toward Haylee.

What did the wink mean?

Haylee turned to me. "Time to get on the ship." From the way her body drooped, she was past ready.

"Right this way." Sandie pointed to her left. "Be aware, however, that the ship doesn't depart for a few hours yet. If you'd like, you can relax in the lounge that's exclusive for those who've booked suites."

"We need to board," I said firmly. Before Haylee collapsed.

"Okay, then. Take a right partway down the hall and you can cross over to the boat. From there, you'll find an elevator that will take you to your floor. Your room awaits!"

"Thanks." Leaving the desk, Haylee took one step forward. Another. Her breathing came fast already.

This wasn't going to work.

Sandie's smile fell as she watched Haylee struggle.

I knew Haylee didn't want to draw attention to herself but how was this any different?

"Do you need help?" Sandie mouthed to me, her penciled eyebrows brushing the hair sweeping across her forehead.

I shook my head and caught up to Haylee. Sliding my arm around the back of her waist, I essentially held her up.

"Not liking this independence of yours," I said, knowing the comment would piss her off, but it hurt to watch her move with such pain.

"Jax." Warning rang out in her tone.

Got it. Didn't have to like it, however.

We made our way slowly down the hall and across a clear gangway connecting the terminal to the ship. Ahead, yellow lifeboats dotted the sides of the vessel, with rows of balconies above. Portholes peppered the lower portions of the ship.

I had to wrap my brain around the idea that some people saw this as a fun way to spend a vacation. Like Haylee, I'd done regular Navy before joining the Seabees, and I'd had my fill of a deck's slow rock beneath my feet during tours on more than one aircraft carrier. Last time I'd been on a ship, I'd served as an IC sailor on the USS Abraham Lincoln, working in tech and fiber optics. Essentially a communications electrician. Long shifts, almost no days off, and crappy food had been the norm.

Things might be different on the Royal Caribbean. If nothing else, I wouldn't have to go through shellback initiation if we crossed the equator.

"Doing fantastic," I told Haylee. She'd eased away from me and limped near the side of the gangway, leaning heavily on the railing.

"Is it my perky stride that makes you think that or the fact that you can barely keep up with my pace?" she asked, injecting a hint of her former spunk into her words. She swiped tendrils of her silky black hair off her face with a hand that shook.

I'd always been fascinated by her hair; she usually wore it in a long braid. When it spun across her waist, it became a mix of raven's wing and the deepest, darkest sea.

"Both," I said.

"Is she sick?" an older woman asked as she paused beside us. She made a tsk-tsk sound in Haylee's direction. "Poor dear. Queasy?"

Haylee nodded. Probably easier than mentioning the recent fractures of her femur and ribs.

"And you're not even on the boat yet," the woman said. "Cruise tip number one. If you ask the ship's doctor, they'll give you seabands—" She held up her arm to show the pink terry strap around her wrist. "—or a scopolamine patch you can put behind your ear. Personally, I use them both. Seasickness is my curse, but I still love to cruise."

"Thanks," I said. "We'll get in touch with the doctor."

Haylee lifted her lips and kept plodding forward at her turtle pace.

The woman made a sad face at me before moving around us and continuing toward the ship.

I followed Haylee, playing point, and we were soon swallowed by the enormous white beast.

A man standing beside a small podium inside the hatch smiled when we appeared. "Can I see your Set Sail Passes?" he asked.

After he'd checked them and wished us a happy cruise, we moved into the ship.

"We're on the port side," I said to Haylee.

"Lovely," she said in a monotone. "Why give us a room on this side, where it would be closer?"

"A few floors up, too," I added.

"Please tell me we don't have to take the stairs." Coming to a halt, she leaned against the wall and her eyelids slid closed.

I growled. "Alphahole or not, I can't stand this. I'm gonna help you."

A weak scowl rising on her face, she pivoted toward me so fast, she tilted sideways.

Not falling on my watch.

"Hang on, sweetheart," I said, sweeping her off her

feet. "Sorry about the nickname. Not sorry about taking charge."

I do like a man who takes charge, I could swear she whispered.

I must've misheard her.

As she gazed up at me, her eyes darkened. Anger? Her lungs released short pants, telling me she must be irritated with me already. While I'd hear about it soon, I wasn't putting her feet on the floor only to watch her stagger or fall.

"You just going to stand here?" she asked, her breathy tone making me immediately think of anything other than anger.

Mia always joked I was slow, but I was as savvy as the next guy. I could read social cues.

Haylee wasn't angry. She was…

Nah. No one would think of sex at a time like this.

"Jax?" Her hand waved in front of my face.

I grunted. Wasn't capable of much more at the moment.

I blinked slowly, trying to fathom this moment. She wasn't interested in me. Was she?

"Can we go to our room?" she asked while my brain spun in too many directions for me to handle. "Since you're now my ride, I might as well make the most of it. Perhaps we can take a tour of the ship while we're at it?"

"Wait." Somewhere, I found my tongue. "What did you just say?"

She lifted one eyebrow. "Our room?"

"No, I meant before that."

Her brow furrowed. "I don't know what you're talking about."

"Okay. Sure. Yep. We can go to our room."

This was about keeping her safe. Not about romance. Needed to remember that.

I could sort this out later, when I was alone.

"This really okay?" I asked gruffly, lifting her a bit higher to show her I meant me carrying her. If she insisted I put her down, I was all over that. Maybe. But damn, I wanted to help her.

Hold her.

Felt good to carry her in my arms. Too good.

"I… Yes," Haylee said. "I know I'm stubborn."

I huffed. More than stubborn.

Her lower lip trembled, and she directed her gaze downward. "I hate being a burden. I want—no need—to do things for myself. But I can't." The crack in her voice wrenched my heart sideways. "I'm broken. I just hope I can get my strength back soon, because being weak is killing me."

"I'm here to help you. I listened when the PT people were explaining what you'd need to do to get stronger. I even took notes." Which I'd left in my hotel room, but I'd pretty much memorized them already. "We can get you there together."

"Together." She rubbed her palms up and down her face. "I'm not used to leaning on anyone. Ever since my mom died and Dad remarried, I've taken care of myself."

"Your stepmom wasn't there for you?"

"She was there for him." A rueful laugh slipped past her lips. "But that's okay. It's what he wanted."

"How old were you when your mom died?"

"Eight."

"Too young to lose both parents at once."

"It wasn't quite like that. I know my dad loves me."

Love and caring for someone didn't always meet in the middle.

"It's okay to lean on someone every now and then," I said as I walked carefully down the hall. "You can lean on me."

"Thank you. I know I fuss and…"

I cleared my throat and was rewarded with her smile.

"Fuss. Yeah," she said. "But I don't think I could've made myself take another step farther." Her glance darted away from mine and took in the vicinity. "By the way, this place is… Wow."

Talk about opulent. It ranked up there with the time I'd been assigned duty at the embassy in the UK. Only that had been fancier. Lots of gilt and weird artwork.

I was a plain guy, happy with simple things. Running away from home when I was a teenager and then living on the street for a time until I straightened my life out and joined the military had done that for me. All this frilly stuff put me on edge.

Might as well face it. I was a loner. Didn't need anyone outside myself.

People kept bumping into me, crowding my space. Made me want to slink off and find somewhere quiet where I could let down my guard.

"What will everyone think of you carrying me?" she asked, shifting in my arms to get more comfortable. For a second, her head rested against my chest.

I liked it. Made my lungs puff even if this didn't mean anything.

"Can't say that I care one way or the other what other people think," I said as I strode toward the elevator. "Coming through, folks." My urge to escape the crowd was suppressed by my greater need to keep Haylee from being jarred. Banging her foot would mean pain in her leg, and I wasn't having any of that. "Comin' through."

More people crowded around us. Jostled us, making me growl.

As we moved through a big room with a vaulted ceiling, a server with a tray filled with foo-foo drinks dipped toward us. "Welcome onboard. Complimentary glass of passionfruit juice?" he said.

Haylee snatched a flute off the tray. "Need one," she gritted out. She'd lost what little color she'd possessed. My arm supporting her beneath her injured leg must aggravate her injury.

"These have alcohol?" she asked the server.

"No. I'm sorry. But we can certainly offer you something more substantial." He waved his arm toward another server and asked our room number, which I gave.

The second server dipped her tray toward us, and Haylee grabbed one of the new foo-foo drinks with fruit chunks linked together with a tiny spear and a paper umbrella on top.

She drained it in a few deep gulps then sighed. "Rum. Yay." She grabbed a second for the "ride". "Thanks," she told the woman server. "I needed this." Turning to me, she added, "It's been so long since I had a drink I can't remember when. At least four weeks and four days."

"Cruising can be stressful," the woman said diplomatically, only her bugged eyes giving away her confusion about Haylee's comment. "Fortunately, you have a …ride."

Haylee snickered and patted my shoulder. "I sure do. Hired him for the cruise."

The woman's eyebrows lifted and she gave me a second, lingering look. "Hired?"

Great. Now the woman thought I was being paid to have sex.

"Sure did," Haylee said, making me squirm. "Let me tell you. He doesn't come cheap, either."

"Gotta go," I said, plowing my way through the crowd.

We paused by the bank of elevators and waited for one to arrive. Other guests pressed from behind us, making my spine itch. I wasn't claustrophobic. Just didn't like being around lots of people. Made my heart race and my hands sweaty.

A quick scan suggested none of the other guests posed a threat. I wouldn't let down my guard for a second, though. If need be, I could lower Haylee to the floor and put her behind me. Defend her.

"Aw," a woman said from beside us, and I half-turned. About seventy. Gray-haired. Wearing a mint green capri pantsuit with white embroidery across the top of the shirt. Matching wedge heeled sandals were strapped to her feet. She twitched the sleeve of the Hawaiian print, button-up shirt worn by the guy standing next to her. Also about seventy. Average build. Brown eyes full of pleading when he turned them my way.

"Wish I had a sexy, muscular man to carry me around," the woman said. She elbowed the guy in the ribs, and his breath woofed out. "When was the last time you carried me like this, Francis?"

"Can't say I ever remember carrying you, Middie," Francis said. He put steps between them quickly as if he expected Middie to leap into his arms and ask for a ride around the deck.

Faking a scowl, she followed him and tapped his arm. "It was too long ago." Her beaming gaze fell on me again. "You two are newlyweds, aren't you? You're carrying your new bride over the threshold."

Pretty big threshold since we had to travel up a few floors still, but sure.

"Yes," Haylee said, linking her arms around my neck. "He seems to think I can't walk on my own."

"Let him do it," Middie said. "The honeymoon thrill doesn't last long enough, if you ask me." She elbowed poor Francis again. "Maybe you could—"

"No!" Frances said. Rushing forward, he jabbed at the button to call the elevator to this floor even though it was already lit.

A few women watched everything with grins on their

faces. One snickered though she covered it up quickly with a hand pressed to her lips.

"We got married last night," Haylee said, obviously feeding the story Dwayne had started.

She was good at this. Recently married made a great cover. No one would expect us to be social. We could hide in our room until things were in place for the next phase of my escape plan.

"And now you're taking a cruise to celebrate," Middie said. "How sweet. You make a handsome couple." Her eyes lit up. "Hey. I think you should kiss your bride. There's nothing like the thrill of young love. It's a feeling that should be shared with the world."

Kiss Haylee?

Middie flapped her hands our way. "Go on!"

"Do it," someone else said.

"Do it!" Another person clinked her fingernail on her fruit juice glass, like people did at wedding receptions.

Haylee's eyebrows lifted and her lips twitched.

This was a joke, right? Please tell me this was one big joke, because…

Her fingers trailed across the back of my neck. Just playing along. It didn't mean anything, but it sure felt good.

"Kiss?" Middie said with a big smile, her gaze flicking back and forth between us.

"I'm game if you are," Haylee said.

Must be the alcohol talking. No way did she really want to kiss me.

I one hundred percent wanted to kiss her, however. Lowering my face, I stopped before our mouths touched. My knees went weak. Other parts of me perked up and shouted hooyah. That part of me needed to chill.

Our mouths connected and heat seared through me. I gathered her closer while her arm tightened around my neck.

As quick as it started, we burst apart.

She stared at my mouth. I stared at anything but her.

Middie bounced on her toes and everyone cheered.

My cheeks went hot.

"So sweet!" Middie said. "I wish both of you all the best in your future. Maybe you'll make it to fifty years like me and Francis." She winked at me.

What was up with the winks? I mean, I got it. People thought we were going to our room to have sex, especially after that kiss. But did they really think I was viable marriage material for Haylee? She was gorgeous while I was just…average.

Haylee was fun and cute and spunky. She made everyone around her happy.

Sure she'd kissed me. But she'd never look seriously at a guy like me.

Where was the elevator? I chomped back my growl. Should've been here by now.

Haylee snickered and drank the rest of her second cocktail while I wedged us into the elevator the second the doors opened. "What's the hurry, hot stuff? Eager to drag me off to the bedroom to finish this off?"

An old dude standing in front of us turned, his bushy eyebrows flicking up.

"You didn't tell me you couldn't hold your alcohol," I said. No judgement. Just making a statement. If it wasn't patronizing, and I had the nerve, I'd tell her she was cute when she was tipsy.

"Hold your alcohol," she mimicked in a deep voice, doing a damn good job of sounding like me. "I'll have you know I'm barely feeling it. Those drinks were weak. Probably only half a shot each. If you plan to get me drunk and take advantage of me, you'll have to liquor me up with more rum than that."

I sighed. Heavily.

Sometimes—no, all the time—I didn't know how to take Haylee.

Haylee

S o maybe I *was* a bit tipsy. Not drunk because I never did drunk.

And maybe I was teasing Jax more than I should.

But that kiss…

My God, I wanted more. If only he'd meant it. If only it hadn't been faked for Middie. And if only I could forget about it because, to Jax, it had been nothing. He'd probably forgotten all about it already.

I couldn't help myself as far as the teasing went, however. He brought out my good and my bad and everything in between, solely by existing. I'd never been able to keep from poking him, hoping for a reaction.

My nerves went haywire whenever he was near. I lived in a perpetual state of flail. I couldn't stop myself from acting giddy, jittery, and squiggly. My impulses took over when they should keep their mouths shut.

I forgot how to think.

"I *can* handle alcohol," I said primly. My words lost some of their school teacher effect when I burped.

"If you say so."

"I do say so."

He grunted.

The elevator doors opened on our floor, and Jax turned sideways and swept me out into the hallway. He paused to study the signs directing guests, before turning left and striding down the hall.

We passed a man dressed in a cruise ship staff uniform.

"Welcome," he said in a perky voice. His gaze skimmed over me lying in Jax's arms and his face revealed nothing, as if men carrying women around on the boat was the norm. As we passed him, his smile fell quickly, taking on an odd expression I couldn't define. I watched over Jax's shoulder as the man went to the elevator bank and pressed the down button.

A hint of unease prickled down my spine, though I couldn't name why I felt squirrelly. Well, other than the fact I was being held by Jax. Never thought I'd find myself in this situation. Too bad I was too injured to enjoy it.

The cruise ship employee stepped into the elevator without looking our way, and I pushed him from my mind. We'd ditched our shadow hours ago, before we met up with Dwayne and Eben at the parking garage. We'd wound all through town, traveling at least twenty miles to get to the cruise port. Then we'd boarded the ship with fake IDs. I'd be amazed if whoever was after me had traced me to this location. Yet.

I wasn't exactly sure why someone kept trying to eliminate me. It had to be related to my last Viper Force assignment. Gabe and I had been close to revealing the Maestro, the leader of the American side of the drug trafficking organization.

We'd found a new contact who'd told us…

As quickly as the thought tripped into my mind, it slid back into the darkness. I couldn't grab hold of it long enough to bring it back into the light.

I'd heard enough about head injuries to know I needed to give this time. The details would either come to me on their own, or they'd remain hidden forever. But I was looking at this glass as half full, not half empty.

If this wasn't a life or death situation, I'd let it go. But I needed to remember every detail before whoever was after me ended things permanently.

By the time the slight buzz from the tropical drinks had faded, we'd arrived at our door.

Note to self: It was never wise to count on alcohol for pain relief.

"Have you ever cruised on a ship like this before?" I asked Jax, my momentary high replaced by a jittery feeling.

My belly rumbled. When had I last eaten real food?

"Nope," he said as he worked on the lock. "You?"

I shook my head. "I guess we're both cruise virgins." My voice deepened. "Be gentle with me, will you?"

When he stood there saying nothing, my face overheated.

Foot, meet mouth.

Would I ever be able to carry on a normal conversation with him, one that didn't beg for attention?

I'd crushed on Jax almost from the moment I'd met

him. We'd tested devices at the shop together and hung out with the guys after the day ended for a beer or two. We'd worked out in the Viper Force gym on multiple occasions, trading off equipment as we alternated reps. He'd never given any indication he saw me in the same way I saw him. Not even the slightest. I was a buddy like Cooper and Eli.

Now I was a burden. Weaker than a newborn puppy. I hated being dependent on someone, especially a man I liked.

Inside the room, he kicked the door shut and, walking into the main room, lowered me onto the king-sized bed.

It wasn't easy pretending everything was normal with him leaning over me, his big warm hands sliding across my back as he released me.

My inhibitions were eager to leap off the fifty-foot-high diving platform. They urged me to say something I'd regret. Or beg him for a kiss.

Yeah, his lips. Thin with just enough puff to make me wonder how they'd feel pressed against mine. How they'd taste.

How I'd respond if he feathered them down my neck to my chest…

He cleared his throat. His eyes…They'd locked onto my mouth as if he had similar thoughts of his own. But he wouldn't.

Straightening abruptly, he reeled backward and bumped into the wall.

It was a small room; that was why he'd stumbled. Or I made him uncomfortable. Had to be the first time for that. My endless hints were sinking through his hard-ened exterior. If so, hint, meet rejection. Welcome to the he's-not-interested club for the thousandth time.

"I think you should take a nap," he said, his gaze directed toward the balcony.

"Yes, Dad," I said with a pretend frown. "Will you read me a story? Tuck me in. Give me a goodnight kiss?"

His sharp inhalation rang out in the room, followed by what I took as a glare.

Definitely needed to zip my mouth shut.

"Never mind," I shot out before he could reply. Grumbling about how stupid I must sound, I rolled onto my side, away from him.

"I'll..." He cleared his throat. "I'll go sit down." His footsteps padded around the bottom of the bed and, as I peeked at him through my lashes, he dropped down onto the squishy chair parked in the corner next to the balcony. "You sleep. You'll feel better once you've rested."

Did he mean I'd feel better or I'd have better control of my tongue once I'd rested? Maybe both.

I closed my eyes but couldn't get comfy. I couldn't put Jax from my mind long enough to let my brain drop off.

He shifted in the chair.

Like I could sleep with him sitting there, staring at me? What if I snored? I hadn't before the accident but maybe I did now. Crap, I might drool all over the pillow. That would go over well.

"Could you sit on the balcony?" I asked, because my

fidgety-Jax feelings were rising up inside me again, eager to say something that would get me into more trouble. Slitting my eyelids, I watched him.

His hands that had been lying against his thighs twitched. He blinked. "I guess so. Sure."

While he got up, I rolled over, onto my other side, facing the wall. The balcony door slid open and a warm, balmy breeze buffeted the room. When the door shut, I was left alone in silence. A scraping sound told me Jax had moved a deck chair, maybe closer to the railing.

I thought I'd lie on the bed, unable to sleep, but I was out within seconds.

I dreamed...

The smell of coconut sunscreen hung in the air, choking my lungs.

My breathing ragged, I ran down the street, my sneakers slapping the pavement. I passed one well-lit resort after another, each filled with laughing tourists and gleaming lights. While I was tempted to dart into one of the resorts and find a safe place to hide, I didn't dare endanger others.

I had to reach our hotel and tell Gabe what I'd discovered.

The Maestro was...

My spine jarring, I woke. I lay still a long while, staring at the ceiling, wondering what sound had pulled me from the dream.

The Maestro was...

I ground my fists into the blankets. Why couldn't I remember?

Rolling onto my side, I faced the balcony. Sunlight slanted from the west, slicing beams across the open deck and highlighting the empty deck chairs and table.

Jax sat in the chair in the corner of the room again. Studying me.

Should I tell him what I'd remembered? The fragment—more a wispy bit of memory—hardly seemed worth repeating.

With a nod to myself, I decided to wait to see if more was revealed before speaking. It was encouraging to think my memories were returning.

Pushing my muscles that felt stiffer than dried out rubber bands, I stretched. It was hard to remember when I'd last worked out. Eons ago. I needed to get myself back into shape. Fighting shape. Preferably before the next attack. It would come. No doubt about that. Whoever had tried to kill me in the car accident in Mexico and then at the rehab place wouldn't stop until they'd finished me off.

The thought of what happened crashed through me. I scrambled through my memory, searching for more clues but found nothing but storm clouds.

Gabe's guttural yell as the car left the road and flew into a ravine jolted through my brain. My poor friend. To think he was dead.

Tears sprang up in my eyes, and I couldn't hold them back. Cupping my face, I tightened into a ball and cried, gut-wrenching, agonizing shudders that left me a quivering mess. My body shook as everything inside me curled up and died.

He'd been a good guy. He hadn't deserved this.

I felt guilty even if I wasn't to blame.

I roused to find Jax staring down at me from between the bed and the wall, his hands clenched into fists. His creased face suggested he wanted to commit violence on my behalf and, heaven knows, I wanted to be in on it when he did. Anger for whoever had murdered Gabe shoved aside my sorrow, making my heart blaze with an overwhelming need for vindication.

I'd remember what happened and then I'd track down the person responsible. I'd make them pay.

"You all right?" he said.

Nodding, I sniffed. I sat up and wiped my eyes with the edge of the bedspread.

Outside, darkness had descended. How long had I slept?

"About five hours," Jax said.

Could he read me that easily?

An overwhelming sense of vulnerability flashed across my skin, making it tingle. What else did he see?

I wasn't hanging around to find out. I'd already broken down in front of him. Hell, when I was in the hospital, I'd probably suffered unimaginable indignities in front of him while I'd been unconscious, like peeing in the bed or whatever. I needed to slink away and restore my composure.

Carefully edging to the side of the bed, I sat a second to catch my bearings before standing. My right leg screamed when I put weight on it, but it held me upright. Progress.

"I'm going to take a shower," I announced.

"I left a bag of things in the bathroom for you," he said. Out of the corner of my eye, I caught him scratching his head. His back. Was he uncomfortable that I'd broken down in front of him? Okay, I'd wailed.

Let it all out until there'd been nothing left inside me but an urge for revenge. Why would anyone be uncomfortable about that?

"Let me know if you need anything else," he said. "And I'll get it for you somewhere on the ship."

"Thanks." I shuffled past him, leaning more heavily on my left leg than my right. Yes, it hurt like the devil to walk on it, but I was moving. Soon, I'd be running.

Hobbling into the small adjoining room, I shut the door and flopped my back against it. With a groan, I scrubbed my face with my palms and took some deep breaths while staring blanking across the room.

"Get to it, Hay," I whispered, bumping off the door. "You're on your honeymoon! A hunky sex god waits for you in your cruise ship room." I rolled my eyes.

I decided I was grateful I wore a sundress. At least I avoided struggling to yank down anything over my sore thigh. Dropping onto the toilet I did my thing while staring at the tub/shower combo unit with its pristine white curtain pulled closed.

Internally, I berated myself.

Why couldn't I stop teasing Jax? It was like a part of me kept coming up with new ways to yank him around. I couldn't hold them inside.

I knew why I did it. I wanted him to notice me even if all I received was negative attention. Back at the shop, when he hadn't respond to my basic attempts at conversation like, *how are you doing,* and *do you want a muffin—I baked some and put them in the break room,* I'd kicked it into high gear with passive aggressive shit that rewarded me with nothing but his blank stare.

The stare hurt, because it meant he'd shut down. *Shut me down.*

I'd welcomed the assignment in Cancun because it pulled me away from Jax. I'd needed space and a chance to regroup. If I'd remained in his vicinity much longer, I would've said something I shouldn't.

Standing, I hiked up my underwear.

I limped over to the vanity, where I washed my hands and opened the supermarket bag to paw around inside. I dragged out a handful of undies and three more sundresses, a couple tees and elastic-waist shorts, and set them aside.

Jax knew how to shop for a girly-girl, though I wasn't sure that was me.

Mango body cream. Lemon-lime shampoo. Strawberry conditioner.

Jax had a thing for fruit.

A toothbrush, floss, and paste, thank heavens, which I used right away before digging back into the bag. I found a comb and some hair ties. Fancy bars of soap for *a woman's complexion*, a razor and honeysuckle-scented shaving cream, and a pink-flowered deodorant stick completed the mix.

Tampons. Yeah… I'd need those eventually.

Oh, and he'd included a bunch of bath bombs.

No wonder I liked this guy. He knew how to win a woman's heart.

And buried at the bottom, a big package of peanut butter M&Ms. How had he known they were my favorite?

My belly rumbling, I ripped open the package and

popped two into my mouth. Eyes closed, I savored the sweet, peanut-buttery flavor as it melted on my tongue. So freakin' yummy.

There were depths to Jax I'd yet to explore. Maybe it was time to keep my mouth zipped and let him spill a few secrets. I'd read somewhere that, when greeted with silence, people tended to speak when they otherwise wouldn't, as if they had to add words to make noise.

Might be worth thinking about.

I reached around the curtain and turned on the shower then loaded the shelf with the things I'd need. As I stripped, I tossed my sundress and undies onto the vanity beside the bombs.

My injured leg looked awesome. Outside of action heroes, not many women could boast about being enhanced with a titanium rod. The thin, pink scar would give me bragging rights when I was a grannie, assuming I lived long enough to have kids who could have kids to make me a grannie.

Once the temp felt right, I climbed beneath the spray and man, as it pummeled my skin, did it feel good. Bed baths had probably been my usual since the accident. I must be coated with acres of dead skin.

I scrubbed my hair twice then gooped it up with conditioner. My nose stung where that tube had been inserted. When I'd scrambled from the bed at the rehab place, I'd wrenched the tube out, tasting and smelling something that reminded me of nutritional drinks an old boyfriend used to make. Sticky, gloppy vanilla stuff that could not be better for a person than pizza and a beer.

My legs. Talk about a jungle. I shaved them then

scrubbed myself all over with the complexion bar, washing and rubbing until the last bit of my illness went down the drain with the suds. My ribs protested the action, but they'd get used to action. I was done being an invalid.

I was rinsing my hair when Jax knocked on the door and called out. "You okay in there?"

Like a virgin—not—I slapped my hands over my boobs, wishing I had a third to cover my crotch. Then I realized what I was doing. Did I really think he'd stroll in here and peek around the curtain?

"Haylee?" he said.

"Yeah," I croaked. My throat spasmed when I swallowed. There was something strangely intimate about talking with him while I was wet and naked and he stood only a few feet away. "I'm fine. Almost done."

"Good. I was worried."

That threw me sideways. Jax, worried?

A heroic rescue, tampons and bath bombs, my favorite M&Ms, and now expressing concern. If he kept at it, I'd fall in love with him.

Hell, I was partway there already.

"Thanks for all the thoughtful things you got for me," I said.

"No problem."

"Love the strawberry conditioner."

"It…reminded me of you."

I'd never worn fruity perfume around the shop, and I sure hadn't conditioned my hair with anything like the stuff Jax had purchased, so what was he talking about?

"Remember those turnovers Mia made?" he said.

Ah, yes. Strawberry. I'd teased him by snagging the last one off the plate before he could grab it, then dancing around the table, hoping he'd give chase. I'd been sorely disappointed when he hadn't, though I'd had fun eating it in front of him slowly, while moaning and gyrating my hips.

He'd pushed past me and stormed from the break room as if I'd pissed him off. Back then, I'd thought he was angry that I'd taken the last treat. Now, I wondered.

What if he'd been flustered by my performance instead?

"You wanted it, you know you did," I blurted out, unsure why my voice had gone husky. Maybe because…something was different between us. I couldn't define the heat I felt in his gaze or the message he seemed to be sending when his hands lingered on my body.

I shifted my feet, spreading my legs wider.

"I did want it." His voice came out just as deep and sensuous as mine. As if he'd run a 10k or wrestled for an hour on the dojo mat.

As if we were flirting. Through a bathroom door. With me naked beneath the shower. Him, only a thin panel away.

"How badly did you want it?" I asked as a surge of heat spread from my core and out to my limbs. I'd gone limp and was barely able to remain on my feet. Turning, I faced the showerhead. The spray hit me in the eyes, but I barely noticed.

"More than you know."

An admission? I wished I could tell by his tone. No, I

wished I could ask him. I wanted to demand he tell me what he meant.

With the water pummeling my back and cascading down my body like a heady caress, I braced my forehead against the tiles and clung to his every word.

"Tell me," I said.

"What do you want to know?"

"Everything," I breathed.

A long pause followed while I stood beneath the spray. My breathing had gone jagged as anticipation rose inside me.

Silence ruled on his side of the door.

"Haylee," he finally said.

I swallowed. "Yeah?"

"You're gonna run out of hot water."

Scowling, my eyes popped open. I stepped back, away from the spray.

Maybe I needed it cold.

"Not an answer," I said, barely resisting the urge to slam my fist against the wall.

"I ordered food. Should be here soon." I could almost see him yanking on the neck of his tee then running a hand across his tightly-cropped hair. Backing away from me both physically and mentally.

No, he was dismissing me as if we hadn't almost taken whatever was between us to a new level.

My growl slipped out, echoing around me.

This time, I wasn't teasing *him*. I'd turned it on myself, believing in a possibility that would never come to fruition.

"I'll be out in a few minutes," I said as calmly as I

could. I closed my eyes and took in a number of slow, deep breaths. Time to regain control, because letting myself run free with him wasn't an option. If I pushed too far, he'd shut me down like he had all the other times I'd subtly offered myself to him.

"Great," he said, his voice coming out normal. "I'll wait on the balcony." His footsteps shuffled away.

I turned off the water and yanked back the curtain.

Jax

My body had gone rigid when Haylee teased me earlier, asking me to tuck her into bed and give her a kiss.

Didn't come close to how my cock felt now.

Fuck. I'd stood about five feet from her, struggling not to think about her naked, with water sluicing across her skin. I'd wanted to storm into the bathroom, back her against the shower wall, and capture her lips with my own.

Touch every part of her body. Lick it, too.

I'd just about kill to kiss her, but I knew—again—she'd only been teasing. She'd meant nothing by her words.

I needed to let this go.

Like I weighed fifty thousand pounds, I dragged my feet on the floor as I crossed the room to the balcony. But my steps slowed as I passed the bed.

Teasing.

Were her words all for fun or did she actually mean

something by them?

Couldn't be.

Could it?

My hands shook badly enough I slapped them against my thighs to hold them steady. Nothing I could do about my racing heart.

Things seemed to be changing between us, but I couldn't figure out what it meant.

Growling about the hard-on I needed to suppress before she came out of the bathroom, I continued to the balcony door, whipped it open, and strode outside. I braced my palms on the railing and stared out at the endless sea. The moon had risen, and its light shimmered across the water.

Far beneath me, prop wash gushed away from the ship in swirling white caps as we cruised south, heading toward Key West. To my left, bursts of gold, pale green, and white peppered the shore, with larger residential areas glowing like huge nightlights.

A subtle rumble hummed up from the railing and through my body, a reverberation from the motors tucked away in the engine room below.

The briny essence of the sea filled my senses, and I closed my eyes and sucked in a breath then shoved it back out with a wedge of my tension.

This was something I'd learned to do when I lived on the streets. Anxiety could grab hold of a guy like a fist clenched around his heart. It wouldn't let go until you pried it off and pushed it away. Breathe in. Exhale. Center the mind in the moment.

My tension eased, as did other parts of my body. Things returned to normal, where they needed to be.

A hand touched my back, but I stilled my jump. I was on a cruise ship with Haylee, not sitting huddled on a scrap of cardboard beneath an overpass, wrapped in a threadbare blanket. She wasn't here to steal my stuff or beg cash for smokes or a bottle.

"Hey," I said in welcome.

"Shower's free if you need it."

"All set, thanks." I'd taken care of that this morning. Back then, I never would've thought I'd be on a cruise ship with Haylee within twelve hours.

Moving up beside me at the rail, she braced her palms on the smooth surface and stared at the ocean before turning abruptly and crossing to a chair.

"Tonight," she said as she dropped into the seat. She wedged her hands underneath her thighs and scuffed her bare feet across the tiles. "I'll take the sofa." Her head tilted in that direction. "You can have the bed."

"Not happening, Haylee," I grumbled, shifting away from the rail. I turned my back on the water and fully faced her. "I'll take the sofa." Or the floor, if it came down to it. It'd be more comfortable than many of the surfaces I'd slept on in the past. While I'd still need to sleep, half of me would be on watch no matter where I sought my rest. If nothing else, I wouldn't have to worry about rats or something worse crawling over me.

"You're too tall. Too..." Her gaze skimmed down my front, and her cheeks flashed pink.

What did the blush mean? I felt like I stood on a razor-sharp peak at the top of a very tall mountain. If I tumbled to my left, I'd find safety in green pastures. Clouds obscured the right, making it impossible to see. If I fell in that direction, who knew what I'd find? An oasis or a wasteland, maybe. Nothing good.

Leaning to the right meant taking a chance I'd crash forever. Did I want that?

"There will be more room for me than for you on the sofa." Her hands gripped the chair's armrests to the point her fingers blanched.

I blinked and watched her hands. Her gesture meant tension or nervousness, yet this was a regular conversation. Why would she be nervous about who slept on the sofa?

Maybe, instead of listening solely to her words and running from anything I found tempting, I should sit back and study her body language. It might give me an idea how to take her comments.

No reason for her to be afraid. We were relatively safe here. She trusted me. Hell, I hoped she trusted me.

"You trust me, right?" I barked.

She frowned. "What?"

"Trust. You know I'll do whatever I can to keep you safe."

Her hand flicked out as if she brushed aside my words. "Of course." Her lips thinned.

Irritation?

"I'm not sure what trust has to do with what we were talking about. Back to the sofa," she said firmly. "I'm sleeping there tonight. I insist." Her gaze fled from mine.

Evasive. What didn't she want me to see?

"Besides," she continued, her fingertip tracing the outline of a flower on her sundress. More effort to avoid my gaze. "The sofa must open up into a queen-sized bed. There will be blankets and pillows and sheets somewhere. Or we can call for them. There's plenty of room for me on a sofabed."

"No."

"There you go again, acting all alpha." Her teeth snapped together. "We're having a discussion, which means give and take."

"Not seein' much give on your part."

Reaching up, she yanked on her braid. The tip looked damp still, from her shower.

Did her hair smell like strawberries?

"If you're going to be like that," she added with a growl, as if shooting out a threat. "We'll have to share the bed."

"It's not about refusing. It's about…" Hell, had she just suggested we share the bed? My body shouted hell, yeah, while my gaze was yanked in the bed's direction. Sure, it was a king, but how did she expect me to sleep with her lying beside me?

Just realized I'd forgotten to buy her pajamas.

She wouldn't be wet but she might be almost naked.

"Jax?" she asked with concern shining in her voice. "Let me do this one thing."

I didn't need a degree in body language to catch the anguish in her voice. The sound dragged my brain back to where it needed to be, in the conversation, not in the bed with an almost naked Haylee.

Her shoulders slumped. "I'm a burden to you."

"Not."

"I can barely walk."

"You'll get stronger." We'd take walks that would turn into jogs then runs. Weights in the gym or using her own body as resistance. I'd help her get back to where she needed to be.

"I *am* a burden." Her arms flailed out, signaling her agitation. "I can't remember anything about what happened."

"Give it time." Maybe I was on to something with this body language thing.

Right side of the mountain or left?

Still undecided. Or maybe I wasn't brave enough to jump off and see where the unknown could take me.

She scowled. "You're not listening to me."

"Hearing you fine, sweetheart." In more ways than one.

She flinched at my use of the nickname.

Flinches were bad. They suggested repulsion. Like I'd offended her or pissed her off. She *had* asked me not to use the nickname. But I couldn't help it. It'd slipped out.

I'd try harder.

My gut sank all the way to the ship's engine room. For whatever reason, I felt like I'd tipped backward and had fallen down the wrong side of the mountain. Who wanted green pastures when the cloudy side might offer even a speck of a chance to be with a woman like Haylee?

She rose and limped over to stand in front of me,

staring up at me with her gorgeous eyes. Tears swam there, and I bet she hated knowing I saw them.

To survive in a military made up of too many bull-headed men, a woman had to perfect a sharp front. Any hint of weakness or vulnerability would be pounced on like a pack of hyenas on a quivering rabbit.

Since we'd left the rehab place, she'd shown a side of herself I hadn't seen before. She'd cried on the bed with such fury it had ripped my soul out sideways. Now she dared me to challenge her about her fresh tears.

"I need my dignity back, Jax," she said in a broken voice.

She'd hit rock bottom and was trying to find her way out.

I understood self-preservation. I had my own squishiness I was desperate to hide.

"Sleeping on the sofa will do that for you?" I asked.

"Don't act like you don't know what I'm talking about. It's not the sofa. You're treating me like a child."

"Am not."

"I want back on the team." Her hands clenched at her sides, showing me how important this was to her. "I'm not a woman who needs someone to take care of her."

Haylee had proven in the military and since that she could handle things herself.

She stomped toward the room before turning to face me. Her head tilted.

Easy to read her confusion in the gesture.

"Why do you do it?" she whispered.

"Do what?" I asked.

I imagined she could read the evasiveness on my part because I wasn't giving her a real answer. I knew very well what I was doing, acting dumb to avoid talking about how desperate I was to keep her safe, even if that meant doing everything for her. I was also trying to avoid talking about her and me sharing a bed.

"You know what I mean," she said. "Don't think you can hide from me, Jax." Coming back out onto the balcony again, she pressed up into my space. Her finger poked my chest. "I see you. Always have."

I crossed my arms on my chest, hoping she couldn't read me like I was reading her. "You only see what I choose to reveal."

"You think so?" she ground out, her finger digging harder.

I cupped her hand in mine and lessened the pressure. "Know so."

Her sigh rang out between us. "Why don't you want to share?" The crack in her voice mirrored the gap between us. Between me and everyone I'd encountered in my life. When you had to rely solely on yourself, you built thick walls. After all these years, it wasn't easy dropping them to let anyone inside.

When she complained about my not sharing, she didn't mean with everyone in general. She was asking me why I wouldn't share myself with her. As if she cared to know the guy I kept buried deep inside.

I did want to open up to her. More than anything.

But that cliff…

Once I started sliding down the cloudy side, there was no turning back. I could fall. Get hurt.

This woman could break me like no other.

She swiped her fingers down her face and when she stared up at the starry sky, her own mask solidified into place.

"You're not a burden," I said. "You're just down for a bit. You'll soon snap back and be the Haylee who decked me on the mat."

She sniffed and gave me a wavering smile. "Once."

"Once is enough to teach me not to turn my back on you again."

"I won't hurt you."

And there she went suggesting this conversation was about something other than combat on the mat.

Here I'd asked her about trust. If I expected to receive it, one of these days, I'd have to give it.

Did I dare risk offering it to Haylee?

"You don't really want to sleep in a bed with me," I said softly, almost afraid to let the words out.

"It's a big bed, Jax," she said in an equally quiet tone, focusing again on the world above and not on me.

"So's the sofa."

She growled. "Let it go, would you? If we shared the bed, you wouldn't even—"

A loud knock rang out on the door. "Room service!"

"Food's here," I said, shifting her gently to the side. I swore we both hissed when I touched her arms. "You win. I'll share the bed with you tonight."

And any other night if she held out her hand.

Haylee

When I laid down my challenge, I hadn't expected Jax to take me up on the offer.

We were going to share the bed.

How would I keep my hands to myself?

My mind returned back to the bags in the bathroom. Unless he'd tucked them someplace else, I was fresh out of PJs.

While the server jauntily pushed a cart inside the room and then shut the door, locking the three of us inside, I struggled to close my gaping mouth.

Watching my every movement, Jax's lips curled up slightly.

He was going to sleep beside me. Please tell me he hadn't been joking, because… Okay. Breathe. It was going to be all right. I'd stay on one side, and he'd remain on the other. The bed was big. We'd barely know the other person was there.

Dishes clanked as the server pushed the cart into the middle of the room. Plates with shiny covers were stacked on the top, and a white linen cloth draped down the sides, nearly brushing the floor.

Yummy smells filled the room, and my belly shouted hooyah. No vanilla nutritional gook for this meal!

Straightening, the server tugged on his cruise ship-emblazoned button-up gray vest. Underneath, he wore a starched white shirt and a deep blue tie. "Where would you like me to serve your meal?" the older man asked Jax, completely ignoring me

"On the balcony," I said with a lift of my chin. Hey, dude, two people eating, not only the man of the house.

Silver fox gorgeous, the server's smile widened to take in both of us. "Of course. I'm Stephen, by the way. I'll be happy to take care of all of your needs while you're on board the ship." With a nod, he wheeled the cart through the room and out onto the balcony, the dishes clanging. Ignoring us, he returned the chairs to their places. He then lifted and placed two of the plates on the table with a flourish, leaving them covered.

I could swear he was laughing, which didn't make sense. This was food. Not a candlelit, gourmet dinner.

Oh-oh.

From beneath the white linen cloth, Stephen produced two candles and a vase with a red rose. He arranged them carefully in the center of the table then lit the candles. Flames wavered and danced in the light breeze skipping off the ocean.

A bottle of champagne and two long-stemmed glasses followed.

With his hand low on my back, Jax urged me toward the balcony. "Let's go check it out."

Stephen's gaze briefly lit on the rumpled bed, and I resisted my urge to straighten the blankets as we passed.

"I understand you're celebrating your new marriage," Stephen said as we paused in the balcony opening. He held up the champagne bottle. "Compliments of the Captain."

While Jax and I shared a bemused look, Stephen popped the cork. It hit the ceiling and bounced onto the floor. Before bubbles could foam up and over the lip of the bottle, he elegantly poured champagne into each of the fluted glasses.

Jax shrugged and waved for me to go ahead of him outside.

Finished pouring, Stephen tucked the bottle into the silver ice bucket on the cart and strode around to hold out a chair. "Ma'am."

Nudging the guy aside, Jax held the chair while I sat. His hands briefly brushed against my shoulders before he rounded the table to take the other seat.

Stephen nodded in approval then lifted the lid off the plates in front of us, revealing our meals. "I will say, Spaghetti all' Astice, that is, spaghetti with lobster, is an excellent choice for your first meal on board. Maine lobster, of course."

I snorted. What cost $5.99 per pound off the boat back home in Maine probably cost five times that amount here.

I lifted my eyebrows in Jax's direction. Spaghetti all' Astice, eh? Fancy. While his cookie fetish was notorious, I'd always seen him as a meat and potatoes guy for his main meals.

Stephen added a bowl of crusty rolls and a little plate of butter pats to the table, plus a bowl brimming with green salad. "What would you like for dressing?" he asked. "I have Italian, ranch, blue cheese, thousand island, and balsamic cilantro. Or simple vinegar and olive oil, if you prefer."

"I'll have the balsamic cilantro," Jax said.

"Ranch for me," I said, scooping a roll from the basket and dropping it on the small plate Stephen had pulled from the second shelf of the cart.

Stephen paused, his fingers clinging to the dressing packages, and his brow narrowed.

Jax froze.

Then I heard it too.

Helo.

Incoming.

Jax rose and went to the railing. He leaned out to look toward the left, where the vehicle was approaching from.

The woop-woop-woop sound got louder as it came closer.

"Simply terrible," Stephen said softly.

"What's happening?" I asked, my attention drawn back to him.

"There must be a medical emergency on board," Stephen said, lowering the salad dressing packets carefully onto the table. He shook his head sadly. "A heart attack or a stroke. Perhaps a serious injury. They'll take the person to one of the hospitals on the mainland for treatment. I hope everything will be all right."

So did I.

But unease edged down my spine. It wasn't that unusual for a helicopter to land on a ship, but I couldn't keep my hands from clenching on my lap. Who wouldn't be nervous? Someone had tried to kill me more than once. There was no reason to think they wouldn't try again.

They couldn't have found me already.

The vehicle approached, the blades gouging through the air. The whooping sound grew in volume. From the pitch, the chopper was landing on the bow of the ship. As the engine wound down and the noise faded, Jax returned to the table and sat.

I read nothing but casual interest in the dinner on his face. But his flinty gaze met mine.

"Could you read the insignia?" I asked. In other words, was this a life-flight vehicle or someone else boarding the ship?

"No. Wrong angle," he said. He must've read the concern on my face. Or realized I still clenched my hands on my lap. "It's nothing. Don't worry about it."

"The person will be fine," Stephen said in a cheery voice, no doubt aiming for good customer service. Don't upset the guests. "So often when someone has chest pain, it turns out to be indigestion."

I was getting indigestion, and I hadn't eaten a bite in I didn't know how long.

Stephen waved to the cart. "For dessert, we've included something celebratory."

Please, no wedding cake. Although, I'd never met a cake I didn't enjoy.

"Your husband told us about your favorite," Stephen

said to me. He lifted a lid on one of the three remaining dishes on the cart. "Gingerbread cookies." He flourished the lid in the air. "We've included a complete array of toppings for you to use to ice and decorate your dessert."

Little brown men marched across the plate. Yum.

Yet I turned a wondering gaze toward Jax. First peanut butter M&Ms and now gingerbread cookies? "How did you know?"

His hands splayed out at his sides, and I swore his face darkened, though it was hard to tell in the candle-light. "Thought you'd like something familiar. Wasn't sure you liked lobster."

Stephen stood beside the table, grinning. "He's holding back the big surprise." Nudging Jax's shoulder, he chuckled. "Ready for the next reveal?"

Jax shrugged.

Shouldn't Stephen have left already? This was our honeymoon. We'd already messed up the bed—well, I had. He must know we'd want to be alone for our first dinner.

And this honeymoon thing was going to my head.

"Your husband is quite thoughtful," Stephen said, beaming a suggestive look Jax's way.

Don't get any ideas. He was already taken. Sort of.

I *was* Mrs. Jacobs.

"Last but not least." Stephen lifted the remaining lids off the plates on the cart, revealing one plate over-flowing with a thick slab of prime rib resting in its own juices, nestled beside a baked potato loaded with butter, sour cream, bacon bits, and then sprinkled with minced chives.

The other plate held a double bacon cheeseburger and a mountain of curly fries.

Jax obviously knew a lot about me. *He* might be into fancy stuff, but I was a meat and potatoes kind of woman.

"I'll leave you two alone now," Stephen said. "Is there anything else I can get you?" His intent gaze skimmed along the cart, the table, and then us. "Condiments and steak sauce are on the cart."

"Steak sauce on prime rib is a sin," I said.

Stephen shook his head and leaned in as if sharing secrets. His gaze skimmed down my front, focusing on the bare curve of my breasts at the top of my sundress.

No thanks.

"Some people," he said, agreeing with my comment about steak sauce. His gaze didn't move until he lifted his eyes and winked.

Sorry, not into threesomes, either.

"We're all set," Jax growled, his gaze flicking back and forth between me to Stephen. "Go." He rose, his chair scraping back loudly with his jerky movement. Facing Stephen, Jax puffed his chest. His arms rose to cross, and I didn't miss his hands clenching into fists.

Stephen was savvy, too. Straightening, he scooted around Jax and rushed toward the room.

If I didn't know Jax better, I'd believe he was acting jealous.

"My number is on the card by the phone. Give me a ring when you've finished," Stephen said. "I'll come back for the dishes."

"Don't come back," Jax growled.

Stephen frowned. "But the dishes."

Jax strode over to Stephen. He pivoted the server and pointed him toward the door.

"I'll put the cart in the hall," Jax said. "You can pick it up there."

"But…" Stephen sputtered as Jax guided him across the room.

I turned in my chair to watch. I'd never seen Jax act like this before. When we went out with everyone in the shop, he was polite if reserved. To the guys at Viper Force, he was friendly and joking. Me? Well, I'd caught him studying me on more than one occasion but could never figure out why he couldn't seem to take his eyes off me. The only emotion I could read on his face then was confusion.

Now, I wondered. Maybe he didn't take my teasing the way I'd intended. Here I was, trying to show him I liked him with my jokes, but maybe he couldn't read my signals. Did I dare step it up and push him in a way he couldn't read except as interest?

He could reject me. How would I meet his eye after that? We worked together. Hell, we were on the run together. I'd hate to make things awkward between us.

"No buts about it," Jax said calmly to Stephen. "Time for you to go."

Stephen wrangled himself away from Jax and wiggled his shoulders while yanking on the hem of his cruise ship vest. He wedged himself between the door knob and Jax, and his chin jutted forward.

Jax pulled some cash from his pocket and stuffed it into Stephen's hands. "Go. Don't come back."

Silver eyebrows lifting, Stephen huffed. But his eyes took on an excited gleam when he glanced down at his hands. His miffed expression turned into one of pure satisfaction.

"Thank you, Sir," he gushed.

How much had Jax tipped him?

"I'll check in first thing in the morning to see if you need anything else. Really. Anything! I want to make sure you enjoy—"

Jax shifted Stephen to the side and opened the door. He nudged Stephen through the opening while Stephen continued talking about all the things he could do to make our cruise a wonderful experience.

"Bye," Jax said.

"If you need anything else," Stephen called out, leaning around Jax to speak to me. "Just call. I'll—"

Jax shut the door in his face and pivoted on his heel. Face twisted, he strode through the room and back out onto the balcony to join me.

"Jeez, Jax," I said, my eyebrows high. "Stephen was just being nice."

Dropping into his chair, he shifted it forward. "He was too friendly."

"By offering to make our honeymoon wonderful?"

Jax's fingers stilled on his fork. "Honeymoon."

"Oh, yeah." My face grew hot. "Of course I know we're not *really* married."

But we were sharing a bed. Sort of.

"He stared at your breasts."

"Nothing new there. Guys do it all the time." Except

Jax. I hadn't caught his wandering gaze once. I wouldn't have minded if it had been him.

"Not with me watching out for you." He lifted his fork and stabbed a lobster claw and brandished it. His steely gaze met mine across the table. "We'll eat at the buffet from now on."

Some might suggest Jax was just being protective.

But I had a feeling there might be more to his behavior than keeping me safe.

Jax

"It's time to go to bed," Haylee declared as I wheeled the cart off the balcony. Behind me, she slid the door shut with a bang, leaving us alone in the room that suddenly felt the size of a shoebox.

Had I heard excitement or anxiety in her voice? No way to tell.

She'd offered me a place in the bed, I couldn't have heard anxiety. But excitement? That didn't sound like the Haylee I'd interacted with for months back at the shop.

Unless she was teasing again, which meant… Hell, I didn't know what it meant. Not any longer.

I paused beside the bed, my hands twitching on the cart's handle. Grimacing because I couldn't figure her out—again—I picked up my pace, clanking the cart across the floor to the door.

My brain spun. A bed. With Haylee.

How the hell was I supposed to sleep? Had a feeling I'd lie awake all night long listening to her breathing.

And trying to keep from accidentally groping her or crowding her off the edge. 'Cause I had a feeling my body would seek hers the second I let down my guard.

I hated that I might do something stupid that would drive her away.

This wasn't about sharing a bed to have sex. We needed the rest because we'd be on the run again soon.

My brain kept rationalizing while other parts of me shouted hell, yeah.

One bed in the room. No reason either of us had to be cramped on the sofa.

After I'd parked the cart in the hall, I locked the door and leaned against it.

Haylee puttered around the room. Straightening the bedspread. Lining up the paperwork on the desk. Fidgeting with the balcony curtains she'd already closed to block out the lights.

Like a guy on a real honeymoon, my heart had to be galloping a thousand miles an hour. My breathing hitched.

Nerves made my limbs twitch. I shouldn't feel anxious about this. Nothing would happen other than sleep.

Except…I'd climb into bed with a woman I'd been crazy about for months.

"You napped for hours this afternoon," I said. "You sure you want to go to sleep this early?" A quick glance at the clock on the desk showed me it was a little after ten p.m. I guessed it wasn't too early for bed.

"That was…" She tweaked the brochures on the desk again. "You'd think after I slept for weeks I wouldn't want to lie in a bed again for the rest of my life." Her jerky shrug suggested she was as unsettled about this as me. "But I'm tired. I guess my body got used to doing nothing."

"We'll take a walk tomorrow. Begin strength training. We can build from there."

"That's a great idea. There must be a gym somewhere on this floating resort."

"Gotta be." I advanced toward her, my hand twitching, wishing I could find a way to reassure her. "I'll…" I shook my head. "You don't need to worry about a damn thing happening while I'm in the bed with you."

An odd expression crossed her face, one I couldn't define.

She backed up a step. Another. Her gaze flicked to the bed and steel filled her eyes when she looked back at me. "I won't touch you, either."

…*even if you were the last guy on Earth*, her expression suggested.

I didn't like how my heart took her comment, as if a spear had hit me square in the chest, but there it was. Laid out for both of us to chew on.

Her lips tight, she waved toward the bathroom. "I'll go get ready so you can have the room after for…whatever."

What did she think I planned to do in there? Jerk off?

Fuck.

Time to shove aside my irritation along with my interest in Haylee. It was clear as day she'd never look at me the way I wanted her to.

"Sounds good," I said, to fill the silence.

Brushing past me, she limped into the bathroom and pretty much slammed the door.

I'd angered her, and I had no idea how.

About the norm for me with women but especially with Haylee. No matter what I said or did, I seemed to irritate her.

While I tried to tell myself otherwise, I'd never been good at reading cues, which was why I avoided social situations. I was more apt to say something offensive than something pleasant. And then I'd worry everyone would pick up on my shaky hands. While in the military, when asked to attend a big event, I'd stay as long as I had to then bolt.

I dealt best with small groups and in situations where I and the other person could be upfront. Blunt, some might even say. No messing around by hinting at one thing while meaning another.

Haylee emerged from the bathroom, still in her sundress. "I hate to sound like I'm complaining because you've done so much for me already but—"

"Pajamas. Sorry I forgot them." Reaching into my backpack, I pulled out a clean tee. "You can wear this if you want."

She took it from me, and our hands brushed.

I couldn't hold back my hiss. Haylee was fire, and I was something combustible. One spark, and I'd explode.

Color rose in her face and she blinked a moment, staring at my hand.

What did she mean by the stare?

Hell, I'd never figure this out.

She turned back toward the bathroom. "Thanks."

"I'll wear boxers, by the way," I called out, trying to ignore how husky her voice had sounded.

Touching that simply couldn't have meant anything to her, could it?

Once she was inside, she shut the door. Water ran. Things went bang. Didn't have a clue what the bangs meant and wasn't sure I wanted to find out.

My turn to twitch the drapes and make sure the brochures were neatly stacked on the desk. Eventually, I slumped in the too-soft chair in the corner and waited, my hands braced tighter on my knees than I liked and my pulse thumping wildly in my throat. The sweat tickling down my spine told me I'd need to shower before climbing underneath the covers after all.

Haylee emerged from the bathroom and…

Closing my eyes, I counted to ten, but I couldn't erase the image imprinted on my mind.

She was slender—extra since the accident—and my tee hung on her frame. Since she was about six inches shorter than me, the hem swept along her thighs, brushing against the puckered scar on her right side.

Legs that went on forever, ending at bare feet with cute toes. She'd unbraided her hair and created a wild, black cloud on her shoulders that spiraled down her back. Her face had been scrubbed until her cheeks blazed bright pink. And her eyes…

Had she been crying? The red rimming them sure made it look that way.

The idea I'd somehow hurt her hit me like a fist in the gut. I stood and stretched a hand toward her before

I realized what I was doing and yanked it back. She wouldn't welcome my touch or my comfort, especially if I was the one who'd caused her pain.

Would I sound weird if I apologized?

"All yours," she said softly, tilting her head toward the bathroom.

"Thanks." I snatched up my pack as I passed it then angled myself around her, being careful not to brush against her smooth skin. As if we were a couple on the brink of divorce, determined not to show the other even a hint of vulnerability.

Or give the other a weapon.

"Do you want me to leave the light on for you?" she asked as I entered the short hall.

Only the glow of the lamp on the desk lit the room; we'd turned the others off already.

"Nope. Might be a while. Don't want to keep you awake. I'm going to shower." Do my teeth. Shave. Count to five million. In other words, I'd remain in the bathroom long enough to give her time to fall asleep. Then she might not feel as uncomfortable with me climbing beneath the covers beside her.

"All right."

"Yep." No agreement needed but it felt safer to give it. As I'd learned, body language could be misinterpreted. Back on the balcony, I'd thought... Well, who the hell knows what I'd thought. I'd misread her if I believed she might be showing interest in me.

I wouldn't make that mistake again.

Inside the bathroom, I dropped my pack on the vanity then braced my palms and forehead on the back of the door. Deep breath in. Heavy exhale out. Pushing my tension away along with the air.

Once centered, I took a long shower, savoring the satisfaction I got from getting clean. As a teenager, I'd washed up too many times in gas stations. The few times I'd sought out a shelter—mostly when it was too cold to sleep outside—I'd washed quickly in the open shower room, too nervous about people watching to think about scrubbing every crevice.

Shelters weren't a home but they gave a guy a chance at decent meals, new(er) clothing and, if he had a job, a way to save some of the money. A guy could hand over his check, they'd give him an allowance, and the rest would be placed in the bank to help him get his feet underneath him.

I'd left all that behind when I joined the military after passing the GED. It wasn't a home, but it had given me a place to rest my head at night.

After dressing in my boxers, I turned off the light and creaked open the door. Blackness greeted me. Plus soft breathing that suggested Haylee had taken the time to fall asleep.

Good. Wouldn't want her nervous.

I padded barefoot across the room, realizing I hadn't cleared a side with her first.

I paused at the foot and waited for my eyes to adjust.

A lump on the balcony side.

Crossing around to sit on the bathroom side, I rubbed my face. My hair. My chest. Then realized how wound up I felt. I'd never sleep unless I let this go.

But she would lie beside me…

Never thought this opportunity would come into my life and, if it did, never thought it would mean nothing.

Shifting the covers back, I lay down and drew the blankets up over my body. I lay stiffly, struggling not to move or disturb her.

Beside me, she shifted. Sighed.

She rolled over and her leg hitched up over my thighs. Her arm flopped onto my chest.

I ground my teeth and stared at the ceiling.

Haylee

I woke up sprawled on top of a warm, too-sexy body.

Jax.

With his arms wrapped loosely around my waist, he wasn't exactly shoving me away. I wanted to stay right here forever, maybe pretend I was still asleep, that I'd climbed all over him while I had no clue what I was doing.

A hard-on poked my thigh.

Like someone had shoved a big spider in my face, I scrambled off him and leaped onto the floor.

Ouch. Watch the leg, girl.

Huffing and groaning about how sore and stiff my body was, I backed toward the balcony doors.

The thought of me bailing on the opportunity to lounge with an almost-naked Jax made me laugh. But the homo erectus? I couldn't remember the last time I'd woken up to one of those.

Definitely needed to find my way back into the dating scene.

All guys got morning woodies. It didn't mean a damn thing. He hadn't been, like, turned on because it was *me* draped all over him. The stiffy would've made its "point" known no matter who was in bed with him. Probably without *anyone* in bed with him.

His eyes opened and his smoky gaze watched me like a predator with prey.

Since I'd never been one to back down from a challenge, I hobbled over and stood beside the bed. "I'd like to report rogue Navy steel underneath the covers. You could be court marshalled for something like that, Sailor."

One eyebrow lifted. "Navy steel?"

I snickered. "Twig and berries?"

He winced and shifted his hips on the bed. "Not a twig." Utter disgust filled his voice.

A branch, then. But should a girl point out something like that? It could make a guy's brain… "Swellington?"

He placed his palms behind his neck, relaxing as if watching a show. "Think you can do better than that, sweetheart."

When had the reserved, quiet Jax been replace by this bold, sexy god-like being? And could I ask him to hang out awhile longer? I was loving this new, playful Jax.

We needed to wake up in bed more often.

But he'd just issued me another challenge. I'd be stupid to ignore it, and no one outside my stepmom had ever called me stupid.

"Personally, I'm kind of fond of stimulus package," I said, inching closer to the bed.

His laughter snorted out.

"Rocket on deck?"

His grin only encouraged me. Didn't he know that? "Vagina miner. Chicksickle. Thrill drill." When a woman worked almost exclusively with guys, some of their cruder humor sunk in. To compete, I'd had to dig deep. Hence, I had a complete repertoire I could pull out at any moment. "Cock-a-saurus rex. Full salute, which, by the way, works well in the military, as you very well know."

"Where did you…" He shook his head. "Don't really want to know."

Not telling, either.

"Mammoth mountain." I lifted my finger. "No, wait. I know! What we're dealing with here is a one hit wonder."

He growled and tossed back the covers.

Okay, now I was going to get it for implying he wasn't good for more than a single show.

Hell, I hoped I'd find out one day if he was good for more than one show. I also hoped I was going to "get it". My friends always said my mouth would land me in trouble one of these days. Never would've thought it would be Jax trouble.

Pivoting as fast as I could on my wobbly legs, I raced —limped fast—toward the balcony, giggling. I couldn't remember the last time I'd giggled, but Jax was chasing me, and that was a record-setter, too.

What would he do when he caught me? And, shit, why was I running? I kind of wanted to be caught.

Definitely wanted to be caught.

He snagged me at the curtains, his arm gliding around my waist when I was caught off balance and stumbled.

It was hard not to read anything into this. To Jax, this would be the same as Viper Force team wrestling, nothing more. Might as well have a mat underneath our feet and the other guys cheering us on.

Jax *had* said we'd be working out today.

Yet while he might see this as joking around with the "boys," I saw him catching and holding me in a different way. His warmth and scent surrounded me, and that was awesome. I turned in his embrace and stared up at him, breathing faster than I should be.

His breathing was ragged, too. And he wasn't pushing me away.

His heat sunk into my skin. Dressed in only his boxers, he was practically naked. My senses overload, drowning me in everything Jax. Heat burst inside me and it spread from my core out to my limbs like liquid gold.

Stilling, his gaze met mine, and something I couldn't define flashed in his dark blue eyes. They dropped to my mouth.

"Yesss," I breathed, cupping his shoulders and rising up onto my toes. He was so close, so appealing. I couldn't resist. I'd never be able to resist. "Jax." His name slipped from me, the word husky with anticipation.

As if he read the need in my voice, he answered, his mouth crashing down on mine.

The room, the curtain behind me, and the hum of the engines deep inside the ship disappeared. I clung to him, savoring the feel of his kiss.

Finally.

As if he expected me to wrench away from him and scream "what the hell are you doing?" he held me loosely, giving me an out.

None of that. I wanted more. I leaned into him, giving him permission to do whatever he pleased. Groaning, he tugged me flush against his body. His erection hadn't gone anywhere, and I wanted it. Wanted him. I rubbed against him, my hands trailing down his muscular back to cup his ass. Damn, these boxers had to go.

His tongue slid along the seam of my lips, and I opened my mouth to welcome him inside. His hand moved from my waist, trailing along my abdomen and up to a breast. I arched my back and moaned. I wanted to wrench off his t-shirt and give him full access.

He shuddered, and his mouth stilled on mine. His hand dropped away from my breast, leaving me wanting. Unlooping my arms from around his neck, he scooped me up.

I should be yelling about him going all alpha on me again, hauling me around like a doll, but I couldn't. It felt good.

He dropped me on the bed, and I thought this was it; we'd finally be together.

I scooted back to make room for him, and my ribs

spasmed. My hiss of pain slipped out, and I cradled my chest.

Jax's expression slackened. "Fuck. Did I hurt you?" As if he realized he'd been tossing me around, he backed away from the bed with his hands lifting. "I… Crap. Sorry, Haylee. I shouldn't have…" His hands raked across the top of his head. "Never should've touched you."

Like a ninety-year-old virgin flashed by a trenchcoat-wearing dude in the park, his face went scarlet and he fled. The bathroom door banged shut behind him.

My hiss had been made more by reflex than true pain. Yeah, I ached, but not badly enough to hold us back.

I flopped back on the bed and stared at the ceiling.

This was a side of Jax I'd never seen before. Fun, flirty, and beyond-sexy.

And his kiss…!

I liked it.

He wanted me. Why was he holding himself back?

I propped my palms behind my neck and lounged on the pillows like he had a short time ago.

What could I do to get a "rise" out of Jax again? He might believe this was a game for me, but it wasn't. My heart was involved. It had been for too long. I'd never thought I'd stand a chance, but now?

I had hope.

Which was tromped on when he came out of the bathroom.

"Let's talk about that kiss," I said, getting off the bed while he putzed with his backpack, tucking a shirt inside then taking it back out. He folded it and laid it on the end of the bed. Then stood there staring at it as if he expected it to flip around and make itself messy again.

"Don't want to talk about it." Finality filled his voice. His fingers clawed at his hair again. "It didn't happen."

"Sure it did." I paced slowly up to him. "We kissed."

"Shouldn't have. Won't again."

My heavy sigh slipped from me. Why wouldn't he look at me?

"Get dressed. Then we can go eat." Pivoting sharply, he strode to the door. He leaned against it, his arms crossed on his chest, staring down at the floor.

Growling, I grabbed some clothing and walked to the bathroom, slower not just because of my leg but because my bubble of excitement had burst. He'd popped it.

After shutting the bathroom door, I stood on the rug and pinched my eyes shut. Had I misjudged this entire situation? Now I was second-guessing everything. I'd thought he was into the kiss but what if I'd essentially thrown myself at him and he hadn't wanted it?

Talk was impossible once we left the room, and not only because I couldn't think of anything to say. My gut had sunk all the way to the bottom of the ocean. And people crowded the halls, the elevators, and everywhere in between. Like sheep, we all streamed toward the food.

When the elevator doors slid open, we stepped inside and were packed in so tightly, he and I jostled together. His arm went around my waist to hold me steady, and he shifted us so I was against the wall with his body standing between me and everyone else. I refused to read anything into his actions this time. He was being protective, nothing else.

As much as the realization hurt, I had to accept that what went on back in the room had been standard Viper Force buddy stuff on his part. Wrangling with the guys. Maybe even tossing me on the bed.

Except for the kiss. But I'd obviously been the only one involved in that.

The elevator stopped and some people got out, only to be replaced with twice as many. Jax maintained his position, keeping me isolated in my own, sheltered bubble. Isolated from him, too, due to his stoic expression and his stiff posture that gave nothing away.

He went out of his way not to touch me, bracing his hands on the wall on either side of my shoulders but shifting them when I moved closer. Was I that repulsive to him? The idea stung worse than the time I'd stepped on a bee.

"I'm sorry," I said. Couldn't help it. Silence killed me. I had to fill it with words.

"For what?" he murmured, and I swore a hint of frustration came through in his voice. Was he still beating himself up for supposedly hurting me?

My quick glance up only threw more confusion onto my smoldering self-berating fire.

He stared down at me as if he couldn't figure me out. And his gaze had locked onto my lips again.

"Don't do that," I whispered, my heart sinking. How much more of this could I take?

"Do what?" His voice lifted, perhaps to make sure I heard him above the elevator music piping in from the speaker overhead. I should be worried about blowing our cover, but couldn't hold myself back. It wasn't as if we'd see any of the others here again.

"Stare at my mouth like you want to kiss me when I damn well know you don't." There, I'd named it. I *had* offered to talk about this in the room, because, jeez, who wanted to hash something like this out in public?

"I… I know you don't want me," I added, to make this completely clear. Might as well get it all out in the open. "You're never going to want me." My shoulders slumped with defeat. "I won't push it any longer."

My attention was drawn to a woman standing next to Jax. She watched us, and the sympathy on her face made me squirm.

"I won't…you know. Try to kiss you," I offered to his continued silence. "Not again, since this whole thing—" I waved my hand between us. "—is obviously one-sided."

The woman clucked her tongue. "Aw, honey." She shook her head, and her dreads brushed across her shoulder. Her sharp gaze fell on Jax. "You sure this guy's worth it?"

He was, but if he wasn't into me, I had to find a way to let go of my feelings.

"What the hell are you talking about?" he practically shouted. "I never said I didn't want you."

The woman's eyes widened, and she turned to fully face us. Her hands flicked toward me as if urging me on.

"What else am I supposed to think? Jeez," I said, my hands fisting. "Running into the bathroom rather than climbing onto the bed with me kind of gave it away."

"Whoa," the black woman said. She reeled away from Jax. "You actually did that?"

Two guys standing next to the woman, snickered. "Dude," one of them said. "Maybe take this back to your room?"

"Yeah," the other said with a grin. "Crawl on her if that's what she wants. Hell, I would."

Jax, his face florid, whirled on the guy. He lifted his fists.

"You shut up," the woman said to the guys, stepping between them and Jax. "Can't you see they're working this out? Leave them alone to do it."

The guys collapsed under her glare and slunk behind a gray-haired couple who stared forward, watching the numbers click on the elevator digital display, seemingly oblivious to the drama going on behind them.

Two other couples watched us avidly, and three teenagers scrolled through their cell phones. A little girl hummed and danced in place, and a boy who must be her brother intermittently poked her. Another woman jostled a fussy baby while the woman with her fumbled with a bag, maybe looking for a pacifier or a bottle.

"The one-sided thing is me, not you," Jax growled, facing me. His hands braced on either side of me again, penning me in.

Under normal circumstances, I'd be okay with that.

But hold on. What had he said? "Wait. What?"

"You're doing great, girl," the black woman said. "Men." She shook her head. "Sometimes they're completely clueless, amirite?"

Not just men. It seemed I might also be somewhat clueless about relationships, as well, though I'd never admit that to Jax.

"What did you say?" I said, pressing up into his space.

Jesus, did he have to smell so good all the time?

"I said—"

The elevator doors opened again.

"Our floor." Pure relief came through in his voice. "We've got to get to the buffet."

"Food can wait," the woman said. "Romance is more important than a muffin."

We'd arrived at the floor with the buffet. No! I wanted to keep talking, because maybe… Again, was I reading this situation incorrectly?

"Food can't wait," Jax said to the woman. He took my hand, and I would've snapped if he hadn't squeezed it and murmured, "Later? Please?"

I nodded, because I really didn't want to go through this with an audience.

"If you two want a referee or maybe just general input," the woman said with a grin. "Say so. I know a thing or two about relationships."

Jax cringed.

I grinned. "Thanks."

"Go for it, girl," she said softly as she passed us, heading in the opposite direction than the buffet.

"Let's eat then we'll go to the room and talk, okay?" he said.

"Sure." I stumbled beside him, my brain whirling. I

hadn't misheard him, had I? He'd said he thought things were one-sided on his side, not mine.

So why the hell wasn't he acting on it?

We entered the restaurant, and Jax guided me to the start of a long line of food.

After shuffling around, filling our plates, we took chairs at a table outside, near the end of the deck. Since it was out of the way, we'd remain out of view of the main entrance. Standard precaution.

We'd barely sat when a server appeared beside our table. "Coffee? Tea? Mimosa?" She winked at me.

"Coffee," I breathed. "Gimme all the coffee." A jolt of caffeine should make it easier for my brain to process Jax and whatever was going on between us. Assuming there was anything going on between us.

She laughed and poured me a cup then turned to Jax. "You, Sir?"

"Coffee, too."

"I assume they weren't injecting it into me while I was..." I darted a glance at the server who seemed solely focused on filling Jax's cup with the brown liquid gold. "While I was indisposed."

"'Fraid not," he said.

"No matter. It's here now, and I can drink all I want." I added two creams and three sugars to my cup and stirred before taking a sip of the smoky deliciousness. As it slid down my throat like melted ice cream, I closed my eyes and wiggled in my seat. Yum.

As he watched me, the look on Jax's face could only be described as stunned. Or blindsided.

I *had* to be on to something here. All this time, I'd

assumed he didn't like me, that this was why he didn't respond to my teasing like he responded to Mia or Ginny when they joked around.

Now he'd led me to believe he might like me. What was I going to do about it?

So many possibilities.

"What's up?" I asked when he continued to stare without saying anything. "Never seen anyone enjoy coffee before?" When in doubt, fall back on teasing.

His gaze dropped to my plate. "There's nothing wrong with enjoying coffee."

"Good. I'd hate to think the coffee police were around, cuffing whoever drained the pot."

"You… In the elevator, when you said…"

"Why did you kiss me, Jax?" There. I'd said it.

"You kissed me."

"You kissed me back. Then threw me on the bed. I swore you were about to bring on the good stuff, but then you—"

"I hurt you. Shouldn't have done any of it."

My shoulders drooped because it felt like we were spinning in circles. Perhaps I needed to return to the start and work forward from there. "We kissed each other, didn't we?"

A little girl raced past our table, followed by another. Both wore frilly pink dresses and their giggles filled the air.

This might not be the best place to hash this out with Jax. But I wouldn't put it off for long, because oh, my freakin' God, he'd implied he did want me. I'd really heard that, hadn't I?

"We, umm…" He watched the kids before turning his attention back to me. His face went pink again. "What's with the bacon?" His fork flicked toward my plate,

Here I was, wanting to say something like, *how about you drag me off to bed* or *tonight, don't wear any undies*, and he wanted to talk about bacon.

I did a quick comparison of our plates, and whoa. Jax took healthy eating to the edge of a precipice and then dove over the other side. His plate was carefully sectioned with sliced fresh fruit taking up one third, a half a slice of dry, whole grain toast taking up another third, and an egg white omelet made with mushrooms and colored peppers almost overlapping the rest of his plate.

"You forgot to ask for cheese in your omelet," I said, pointing my knife toward it.

He carefully cut it with his knife and fork. "No, I didn't."

"Are you lactose intolerant, because that would be a tragedy. Imagine, never being able to eat cheese, butter, or ice cream."

"Those with lactose intolerances take an enzyme, but I chose not to have cheese in my omelet."

"Who'd do something like that?"

He blinked as if I'd stunned him all over again. "Someone careful with their diet." As if that explained everything.

Healthy, huh?

I, however, had seriously looked for a platter before sadly taking a regular plate and loading it up with goodies. I'd scored in the pastry section with two chocolate croissants. Then I'd waited in line for the chef to make me a real omelet, one loaded with both parts of the egg. I'd "egged" the chef on, encouraging her to add a triple serving of cheese. It oozed yellow goodness from the sides. As the pièce de résistance, I'd stopped where a chef was carving a whole ham and, while I'd passed on a slice, I'd loaded a mountain of bacon on top of my plate from a nearby platter.

"Are you really going to eat all that bacon?" he asked.

Funny how he only focused on the bacon and not the mounds of yummy things underneath.

Lifting a slice, I munched on it, folding it into my mouth until I'd stuffed it all in. I spoke around it. "It's good. Salty. Bacony." The best thing I'd eaten in months.

"It's loaded with nitrites."

"They taste good, too." I picked up another slice and ate it.

"There's nothing nutritional about your meal."

"You're saying that as if that was a crime, but you're wrong."

His eyebrows lifted.

"I got fruit!" I waved to the little bowl I'd filled.

"Cocktail cherries isn't fruit."

Tossing one up into the air, I tried to catch it in my mouth but four weeks, three days, and more than twenty minutes recovering from my wounds had thrown me off my game. I'd need practice to get back into the swing of things.

My cherry agreed as it bounced off my forehead and bailed over the railing beside me. Cool.

"That one's for the sharks," I said with a smirk, tilting my head toward the water.

He scowled.

"Come on. Why so cranky?"

"I'm not cranky," he grumbled.

My laughter rang out. "Dude," I said. "You need to lighten up."

"Haylee."

I lifted my eyebrows and took a big bite of a croissant.

Huffing, he shook his head and lifted a delicate bite of his anemic omelet up to his mouth.

"So is this how you stay so ripped?" I asked, plowing through the rest of my croissant and wondering what Jax would say if I went up and got a third.

"What do you mean?"

I waved my cheesy, egg leaden fork at him. "You have muscles. Lots of delicious muscles." All over his body. I'd spent most of the night trying not to brush my fingertips across his abs, his thighs, and whatever else I could reach.

Sputtering, he stared down at his plate.

Had my cousin, Mia, been right about Jax after all? He'd always come across as aloof but self-confident to me. Yet Mia insisted he was shy and a true introvert. She said he didn't like crowds or social situations to the point he'd avoid them. That he had a hard time talking about emotions.

What if he really did like me but assumed I didn't

feel the same? If he was shy, he might be waiting for me to make the first move.

I thought I'd already done that but I could do it again.

"I like to work out," he finally said dropping his fork beside his plate, leaving his egg only half eaten.

"Jax," I said. "You do know you're gorgeous, right?"

"What?" Shock came through in his voice.

"You heard me."

"Guys aren't gorgeous."

All humor fled my voice, because this was it. It was time to test my does-Jax-actually-like-me theory. "You're the hunkiest, sexiest man I know."

His breath whooshed out.

A man of few words, I'd assumed he was quiet because he had no interest in talking to me. But what if he was one of those people who stumbled because he didn't know how to give voice to what he wanted to say?

All this time…

Mia said she thought Jax liked me. I'd blown her off, never dreaming it could be true. But dreams like this were meant to be explored.

"Life's about living." If anything had taught me that, it was my recent, near-death experience. "Imagine you died tomorrow. You'd miss out on all the fun foods."

"I can live with that," he said dryly. "There's nothing wrong with being careful about what I eat."

I shrugged. "I suppose not."

This wasn't solely about food. A tiny, excited part of me suggested this conversation was also about *us*. Because he seemed determined to take this cautiously.

"Sometimes, you have to take risks." I leaped out of the plane, unsure if I had a parachute or not. I'd either smack on the ground or maybe, Jax would catch me. "What if you're missing out on something—someone—who could make your life complete?"

His gaze focused on my mouth again, but he didn't say a damn thing.

I lifted a strip of bacon and held it out to him. "Sure you don't want to try a bite?"

"Maybe I do want a bite," he said gruffly. My skin tingled when he took my hand and guided it to his mouth. He nibbled on the end then took a regular-sized bite, chewed, then licked his lips as he sat back in his chair.

With my attention solely locked on his mouth, my hand plunked on the table.

Hot. While the sun might be shining on the other side of the boat, casting us in shade, I was sitting in a sauna.

"You're much better than me at teasing," I said.

"Not true." He studied me with more intensity than I'd seen before. Well, except for this morning, before we kissed. "You're the tease."

"Maybe I'm not teasing."

He blinked as if processing my words. "Some-times… I just don't know how to take you."

He could have me any way he wanted me. He just had to name it.

"Does my teasing mess with your mind?" Done eating, though my plate was still more than half mounded with food, I pushed it away.

"Always," he whispered hoarsely.

Heat poured through me. We were close to something I couldn't define. As if we skated on thin ice. We'd either make it across the lake together, or it would split down the middle and send us in two different directions.

It could be wrong of me to push this, to lay it out in a way he couldn't mistake my meaning. A big part of me suggested I pull back, protect myself. Because he could reject me like he had in the room.

Like I'd been rejected before in life.

Our waiter appeared as if by magic beside us, and I jumped.

"Finished?" she said.

At our nods, she started to gather up our plates.

We stood and tossed our cloth napkins onto the table.

As we walked toward the elevators, I leaned close to him. "Just so you know. It's never been teasing. I've been trying to show you I want you."

11

Jax

She couldn't mean it. Not Haylee. For months, she'd poked and prodded and done everything she could to drive me out of my mind.

It had all been a joke. Nothing she'd said was real.

She'd only wanted to get a rise out of me.

Now she expected me to believe she wanted me?

"Jax?" she asked, hobbling beside me. "Slow down, will you?"

"Jeez, I'm sorry." I held back my pace.

Fuck. I'd been running. From her? Maybe. Could anyone blame me for being spooked by this entire situation?

I'd spent a hell of a long time telling myself she'd never be mine.

Stopping in the middle of the hall, I turned to her. "What do you mean you want me?"

A teenage girl walking past us in a bathing suit and cover up ran her gaze down me then grinned at Haylee. "You go, girl."

Haylee smiled and gave the girl a thumbs-up. Her smile wavered when her gaze fell on me. "Seems pretty simple to me. I want you."

"As in want, want…"

"Lots of want."

"I…don't understand."

She shrugged, and her words came out soft, hesitant. "Don't worry about it. *I* understand." Pivoting, she started hobbling down the hall. "You're not into me the same way."

I followed. Stumbled mostly, trying to absorb what she was saying.

After going only a few feet farther, she stopped and turned to face me. "I promise I won't make this awkward. I know we'll be together for a while still, because whoever was trying to kill me probably hasn't given up yet. But I'll stay professional. I won't try to kiss you or touch you or do anything to make you uncomfortable."

Pivoting, she walked toward the elevators again.

What was she saying? My brain felt like it was coated in molasses. I'd been barraged with concepts I'd never dreamed could come true.

But one thing was clear. She was putting herself out there, making it clear she wanted something between us.

I'd be a fool not to be all over this.

I strode after her, right up to her, and placed my hands on her shoulders.

When I turned her, I took a sledgehammer in the gut.

Tears shimmered in her eyes and it ripped through my insides like shrapnel.

I pulled her into my arms. "Haylee."

"I'm sorry," she sniffed. "I promise I'll let this go. From now on, we'll be buds. We can wrestle and fling each other on the floor and I won't take it the wrong way."

My chuckle burst out. "What if I want you to take it the wrong way?"

"That's the problem. You don't want me."

"What if I do?"

Leaning back in my embrace, she stared up at me. "I'm not hearing you right. 'Cause I could swear you just said—"

"I like you. I want you. Thought I made that clear in the elevator."

Her jaw dropped.

"I'm not one of those guys who's good at sharing feelings."

"No shit."

"But I'm laying it out here for you because you're right. Sometimes, you have to take a chance."

"Did you just say you want me?'

"I did."

"Really?"

"A whole hell of a lot."

"Whoa."

I grinned. "Whoa."

"Why didn't you tell me before?"

Taking her hand, I tugged her toward the elevators. "I never thought you'd be interested."

"All that teasing didn't give me away."

"I'm clueless?"

A snort of laughter made her tears disappear. "You're doing pretty good at the moment for a clueless guy."

"I think I can do even better."

She rocked up onto her toes. "You mean there might actually be another kiss in my future?"

Growling, I backed her into the wall then nipped at her neck.

She went limp in my embrace. Body language. Shoulda been watching her months ago.

Her hands braced on my shoulders, but she didn't push me away. "Jax."

"You want something, sweetheart?"

Peering up at me, a half-smile rose on her face. "Who are you and what did you do with the other Jax?"

"Maybe I'm letting my inner Jax shine through."

"Don't ditch him too soon, okay?"

I gave her a quick kiss, enough of a taste to make it a promise. "I have a feeling he's not going anywhere."

"Room," she said, taking my hand and dragging me toward the elevators.

Following, I couldn't keep the grin off my face. Who would've thought Haylee liked me?

We stopped to wait for the elevator, and other tourists crowded around us, including a guy I hadn't seen before. I'd find it easier to forget about him if he didn't stare.

Haylee leaned against my side, and I put my arm

around her waist. A casual gesture that meant every-thing to me.

"I think we should work out in the room," she said.

My mind dropped into the gutter, picturing all the dirty ways we could "work out".

She didn't mean that, Soldier.

"Weight resistance?" I said, meaning using your body as the weight. Lunges, squats, pushups, abdominal crunches, and pullups.

Rising onto her toes, she tugged my head down close. "I was thinking you could do the working out and I could…lie back and watch."

Fuck. If I wasn't careful, my body was going to embarrass me. Thankfully, the doors opened. We stepped inside, joining a bunch of other people, most dressed in tropical clothing. What was it with the palm trees and flowers?

The guy who'd been staring backed against the back wall and crossed his arms on his chest. His gaze never left us, and it made me uneasy.

It never paid to let down your guard.

"Well, there you are!" someone said from behind us, providing a distraction.

Haylee side-eyed the older woman we'd run into outside the bank of elevators yesterday. Middie.

"How's the honeymoon coming along?" Middie's face went red. "Oops." While her hand slapped over her mouth, her smile leaked past her fingers. "Coming is a poor word choice on my part." Her flip-flop clad foot reached out, smacking her husband in his shin. "Francis! Why aren't you keeping me in line?"

"Now, Middie," Francis said. "You know I never order you around."

"Sometimes, I wish he would," Middie said to me. "That's EDSM, right?"

I frowned. EDSM?

My attention returned to the guy, and my pulse rate dropped when I saw him chatting with a woman dressed in capris and a pink top. They might be together.

But I'd keep an eye on him.

"I can't imagine the thrill of whips or chains, but I'd be open to a little alpha domination every now and then." Middie wiggled her gray eyebrows at me.

Ah. BDSM.

Haylee's eyes sparkled, and she leaned close to me. "They're so cute."

"Please, Middie," Francis said.

"I suppose I can hold myself back." She turned to Haylee. "What are your plans today in Key West? Francis here is keen on the pub crawl but personally—" She scrunched her face, creating a profusion of wrinkles. "I'd like to try the mangrove kayak eco tour."

"I didn't exactly say I was interested in the pub crawl," Francis said. "I said I wanted to go deep sea fishing. You took that to mean beer."

Middie leaned close to me. "Silly man. He's allergic to fish!"

"I wouldn't need to eat my catch, Middie," he said patiently. "I could throw it back."

"Bait," Middie said with a shiver. "They make you touch the guts and tiny fish, don't they?"

"I think so," I said.

"We're not sure what we're going to do yet, right honey?" Haylee linked her arm through mine and blinked up at me through her lashes. "We might just lounge around in our room."

Middie snickered and elbowed Francis. "Maybe we could lounge around in our room today, too."

Francis rolled his eyes. "That pub crawl doesn't sound so bad, after all."

I couldn't drag my gaze away from Haylee's face. Lounge around. Did she mean in bed? She was teasing, right?

She'd said her teasing wasn't really teasing.

Last night, while we were sitting out on the deck having dinner, her body language told me something. I wasn't completely sure what yet, but she'd been nervous about sleeping with me in the bed. Ready to take on the sofa to avoid it.

I was beginning to believe she hadn't been trying to avoid it. She'd been nervous because she wanted to be there.

Like the biggest epiphany smacking me in the head, it all started to make sense.

I was a second grader, spending too much time passing notes through friends, not enough time asking the girl to speak her mind.

And her heart.

She'd just said she wanted me.

She liked me.

"What about the butterfly conservatory?" Middie asked Haylee. "Though you still seem to be limping, dear." She tapped Haylee's arm. "Did you twist your ankle? That happened to me on my first cruise. Hurt like the dickens. Perhaps you should consider doing something less strenuous when you go into town."

"Like the hop on, hop off trolley," Francis said. "Personally, I'd hop on and encourage others to hop off."

"Francis!" Middie smacked his arm but her face split with a huge smile. Leaning close to him, she tugged on the front of his palm tree printed, button up shirt and then kissed him.

Francis, despite the joke about bailing on Middie, placed his hand on her ass while he kissed her back.

Whatever they had together seemed to work. When we first met them and I heard they'd been married for fifty years, I'd assumed they'd stayed together because it was a habit. But now I wondered.

What would it be like to be with someone that long? To share combined jokes. To feel confident grabbing my woman's ass in the elevator.

Bet they knew what the other person was going to say before it came out.

Ending the kiss, Francis took Middie's hands and squeezed. "You know what? We can do the kayak tour, if you want."

"And then we can do the pub crawl together!" She clapped her hands and bounced on her toes. "Unless you'd truly want to go deep sea fishing? I guess I could bait your hook."

The elevator came to a stop and the doors swept open. Our floor.

"Have a nice day, you two!" Middie called as we exited and turned left.

Fortunately, the guy who'd been staring remained in the elevator, his attention still on the woman beside him.

"Thanks," Haylee said, linking her arm through mine and leaning against my shoulder. "Ready to go to our room, Sailor?" Humor shone in her eyes. "I think my hook is already baited."

I pushed the guy on the elevator from my mind. It had been nothing.

And maybe it was time to do a little of my own fishing.

12

Haylee

T he hint of mystery in Jax's eyes stirred up something wild inside me. I wanted to shout hooyah. Skip down the hall.

No, run.

My damn leg was holding me back.

For the first time in forever, I had hope for a future. I wasn't sure where this thing between me and Jax was going, but I had a feeling I'd soon find out.

As we approached our room, a gray-haired house-keeper was coming out. Back to us, he ensured the door was locked then pushed his cart down the hall, toward his next assignment.

Great timing.

Jax opened the door and encouraged me to enter ahead of him.

The curtains had been pulled and the bathroom door was shut. But the housekeeper had left the desk light on, which gave the room a muted, even romantic atmosphere. And he'd crafted a swan out of towels and left it on the bed. Cute!

It was nice to see the room tidy and the bed made. I kind of wanted to toss the swan on the floor and mess the bed back up, but that was pushing things. Jax and I had finally started talking. Talking didn't mean diving beneath the covers.

"I don't think we should go into Key West today," he said as he shut the door. "The less time we're exposed in public, the better."

"I agree." Hobbling over to the in-room coffee maker, I got things ready to make a pot. One cup would never be enough for me. Passing him with the carafe I intended to fill at the bathroom sink, I stopped where he stood in the hallway. "Since we're sticking to the room other than for meals, maybe we can play cards or…something."

His pupils dilated, telling me I might be taking my teasing too far.

But I was the one surprised when he said, "*Something* sounds good." Pivoting, he strode toward the balcony and pulled open the curtains to let in the sunshine, while I collapsed against the wall.

I'd unleashed the krakens and they were ready to conquer the world. Or me. Who would've thought I'd ever be joking with Jax about sex?

After dumping the water into the coffeemaker, I joined him on the balcony. Behind me, water trickled as it filtered through the grinds. The smoky aroma wafted through the room.

We leaned against the rail side-by-side, saying

nothing but settling into a moment filled with comfort and promise.

The boat had pulled into dock, with the town to our left. People streamed from the ship and out onto the enormous parking lot that served as the gateway to Key West fun. Tropical music carried faintly in the air, probably from town.

I didn't mind missing out on kayaking, the pub crawl, or even deep sea fishing. Spending time with Jax was enough fun for me.

"For a long time, I've wanted to tell you how I feel," he said, staring forward. While it would be great if he looked at me while he spoke, I understood why he didn't. It would be hard for a shy person to share feelings. Eye contact would increase the intimacy, as well as the risk. He couldn't know he could trust me, that if he fell, I'd catch him. "But whenever I tried to speak up, the words jumbled around in my mouth. I couldn't get them out."

"I think it's natural to worry about rejection. That's why I kept joking and teasing with you," I said. "I realize now this was my own, clichéd twelve-year-old boy move, like yanking on a girl's braids to show her I like her."

"And I…" Turning, he faced me, leaning his hip against the rail. He still wasn't making eye contact—his gaze seemed focused on his hands—but I wouldn't trade him opening up to me in this way with any other. It was pure Jax. "You might've already guessed, but I'm not a bold kind of guy."

"I've heard you're shy."

He nodded. "Mia."

"I hope you don't mind that my cousin and I talked about you."

"Not really but…" He cocked his head. "What did she say?"

"You can call her the leader of your fan club." I chuckled but sobered fast. "She said you're really uncomfortable in social situations." To the point it was almost painful to watch him, but I wouldn't say that; it felt too personal. And I wanted to hear how he saw it, not just take Mia's word for how he behaved.

Jax eyed the open balcony door behind me and I wondered if he'd run like he had earlier, after we'd kissed. But him relaxing back against the railing suggested he might be done with running. "Whenever I'm in a big crowd, I break out in a sweat. Can't stop my hands from shaking. Hate that about myself."

"It's a part of you. We all have things we don't like about ourselves."

His brow wedged together. "Not you. You're ballsy, kickass, and I'm jealous of how confident you are all the time."

"It's a front." I crinkled my eyes at him. "Inside, I'm actually squishy." Squishy for him. Would a time come when I'd be able to declare that to the world? I hoped so. "Mia also said you've been crushing on me for a long time." Which, maybe I shouldn't bring up. However, I wanted to know where I stood with him, if this truly was one-sided on my part.

"Also true." He raked his fingers across the back of his neck, the movement jerky.

"It is?" I breathed, still unable to believe we were finally having this conversation, that this wasn't him letting me down easy. Breaking my heart. "When did this happen because, from where I'm standing, you haven't shown me you were interested."

"I've been into you pretty much from the first time I saw you."

"At Viper Force?" While I wanted to stand strong in front of him and show him how open I was to hearing whatever he wanted to tell me, spasms shot through my leg and I worried it would give out. Yanking a chair closer, I dropped onto it and propped my feet up on the rail.

"While you're there," he said, nudging the tip of my sneaker with his own. "Stretch the hamstring on your bad leg."

"Is that one of the exercises recommended by physical therapy at the rehab place?"

"The first of many. If you want, I'll write down the plan. Then you can follow it."

"Hey." I pushed out a laugh. "I was hoping my own, personal physical therapist was going to walk me through each exercise." Give me a massage after, but I didn't feel brassy enough to go there yet.

However, he was right. I needed to do whatever I could to get back into fighting form.

"I'm happy to help however I can." The gleam in his eyes that had gone smoky-blue, stirred fire inside me.

"I'm going to take you up on that offer." Straightening my leg, I leaned forward and grabbed my toes, pulling them backward, moaning and groaning at the discomfort shooting up my leg. I hated how I could barely straighten my knee in this position or touch my toes. My thigh muscles twitched and complained, atrophied from the long lack of activity. It was going to take considerable sweat and tears to get myself where I needed to be.

"Not sure you know it, but I was assigned duty at the Embassy in UK a few years ago," he said. "You were there with your father, for a party. That's when I first saw you, when…" His hand flicked out. "When I realized I wanted something with you. Just wasn't sure what it was yet."

"And you're sure now?"

"Sweetheart," he said, his voice deep and husky. "I've been sure for a very long time."

My fingers stilled on my thigh. I'd been rubbing where it ached most, without truly realizing what I was doing. The pinch in my chest was worse. "I… I don't know what to say." All I could do was feel. My heart slammed against my ribs like I'd run fifty miles, and my throat clamped tight with emotion.

"No need to say anything." Reaching out, he stroked a few strands of hair off my face. His fingertips trailed down my cheek. "Me telling you, opening up to you, is important. I've held things back but I don't want to do it anymore."

"You said a party?" I frowned, trying to remember when… "The only one I went to at the UK Embassy was when my stepmom was sick and couldn't be there for Dad." I huffed. "Would you believe my father actually called my commanding officer and told him he needed to borrow me for a few days? I was active, deployed, and he hauled me out."

"I can't imagine having a family who cared enough to know where I was, let alone want to be around me."

That was a different way of looking at it. And sad. "Sounds like you had a crappy home life." I tried to picture the boy he might've been, the teenager. Cocky, full of energy, but all heart.

"I had no home life after I turned fifteen." Turning partway away from me, he stared out at the sea again. Not shutting me down but trying to turn off the conversation? I wouldn't push it, push him. Not if it made him uncomfortable.

"I do remember you from the Embassy Ball." The totally hot guy outfitted in double-breasted, service dress blues with gold buttons marching down the front of his chest. Three gold bands on his left sleeve. He'd stood at attention near one of the doors leading to the gardens, and while his gaze kept darting to the main entrance often enough I wondered if something weird was going on outside, the warmth of his gaze had also settled on me. His heat had scorched my skin. "I actually started to work my way around the room. I wanted to talk to you but by the time I got free of Dad and everyone who wanted to say hello, you were gone."

"I cut out as soon as I could," he said. "But I would've hung around if I'd known." He yanked on the collar of his tee. "Never felt comfortable with frilly people. I was homeless from the time I turned fifteen until I went into the Navy." From the sharp way he watched me, I got the feeling he was testing to see how I'd respond to his revelation.

All I felt was pity and frustration for the scared kid he must've been back then.

"How did it happen?" Here I was bitching about my longing for my stepmom to like me when he'd been worried about where he'd sleep and what he'd eat.

"Like most people who end up on the streets, it just kinda happened. My parents never hooked up more than a few times, so I didn't know my dad. He took off and we didn't hear from him again by the time I was five. My mom tried hard to be everything for me, though." Emotion made his voice crack. "She was awesome, you know? Did all she could for me. Worked three jobs. Made my favorite cookies. She'd sit me down and make me do my homework every night. And reading. She was big on reading, sometimes to me but otherwise handing me a book I'd read myself and then we'd talk about it. Classics but fun stuff, too." His attention drifted to the horizon and a pall of sadness settled over him. "She was killed walking home after a late shift at the supermarket where she worked as a cashier. Some asshole shot her and stole her purse for all of three bucks."

"God, Jax." It hurt to push the words out. I kept picturing a vulnerable kid trying to turn himself into a man overnight. "What did you do after that? Did you look for your dad?" Probably not if he was soon homeless.

"No one seemed to know. Dad was… Who the hell knew where he was. Mom didn't."

"There wasn't anyone else? Grandparents? An aunt or uncle?"

"I did call my mom's folks and they wanted me to come stay with them in Florida, but that felt weird. And I knew, if I left, I'd never feel my mom again. I stayed in the apartment as long as I could, going to school because education was important to Mom and hiding when the social service folks came around snooping. I worked after school as a dishwasher at a Chinese restaurant, but couldn't make enough for the rent. Mom had a little money in the bank, but it went fast. Got evicted and that was that." He pulled out his wallet and, opening it, carefully slid out a picture he handed over. "This and a few things I put in storage, is all I've got left of her."

In the photo, his mom wasn't looking at the camera. Instead, she'd tipped her head back and a hint of what I believed was her burst of laughter echoed in my mind. She had deep sapphire eyes that sparkled with life. He'd gotten his dark hair from her, too. His burly build must've come from his dad, since his mom appeared small when compared to the surroundings.

I handed it back to him. "She was pretty."

"Gorgeous." He blinked fast as he stared down at the picture in his hands before tucking it back into his wallet. "I miss her."

My eyes stung with tears. I'd lost my mom when I was little, but I barely remembered her. At least I'd had my dad. "How did you survive?"

"Any way I could. With my wits. My determination to make something of myself so my mom would be proud." He lifted his clenched fists. "With these whenever I had to."

"You joined the Navy."

"It gives guys like me a sense of belonging. I've always been the one standing on the outside, looking in."

My chest ached to think he'd never felt he had the comfort of home.

"I got my GED and joined up. The rest is history."

"I admire you so much." Some women would've been turned off by what he'd gone through, what he might've had to do to survive, but not me. It only made me care for him more.

"Now you know my worst," he said.

"Not your worst; your strength." I wiped my eyes.

"Hmm. I guess?" His jaw tightened. "I fully understand if this makes you change your mind about me."

"You need to know right now this only makes me admire you more. Everything you've been through has helped make you the awesome guy I...."

He flashed me a grin. "I'm not awesome."

"There's no denying the truth."

"I..." His chest rose and fell with a big breath. "Anyway. I thought you should know that about me before we..."

"Sleep together?"

"I meant do things like sit here on the balcony, maybe hold hands." His gaze fell to my lips, and I parted them in anticipation. I knew very well what he meant and the idea of spending time with him like that was as awesome as he was.

"Sleep together." Chuckling, he shook his head. "You have no filter, do you?"

"I prefer to think of it as being honest."

"I imagine being honest has gotten you into trouble on more than one occasion."

"Especially with my stepmom. My dad… I guess you could say he put up with me." I held up my hand. "Don't get me wrong. He loves me. I know that. But…"

"You said he put your stepmom first when you were growing up."

And it still stung. No denying that. "They got married. It made sense he'd want to make her happy."

I could see why my stepmom might've asked him to choose, but I'd never fully understood why he'd picked her. The idea was toxic and how hurtful to a kid who'd lost her mom and still needed her dad. No one should be asked to pick between a wife and a kid.

"Might've made sense to her, but you're the one who paid the price," he said.

I shrugged. "Probably. That was a long time ago. I've…put it behind me."

"You've grown harder. Take it from someone who knows what he's talking about. It's natural to build a wall for protection, to shut everyone out. Keeps you from being hurt."

"Damn squishy emotions. They grabbed hold of me too often while growing up. I tested my stepmom all the time. Must've driven her out of her mind sometimes. But looking back now, I can see I was doing it because I wanted her affection, something she refused to give me all on her own. I needed to feel like she cared for me even if only a tiny bit. She must've, in some ways, because she wasn't mean. It wasn't *that* bad. But she sure didn't show she cared all that much for me." My childhood and teen years had been filled with frigid Christmases with her sitting on the sofa while I opened my presents, making sure I took care of the shredded paper before enjoying my gift, then chastising my dad for spending too much on my presents. Summers shipped off to camp to get me out of the way, though she'd called it "enrichment". She'd encouraged me to play sports, an instrument, and do charity work on the side. Not because it was good for me and it kept me busy, but to get me out of the way.

"I'm sorry," he said.

"Thanks." I stiffened my spine. I was an adult. Time to ditch my teenage longing for a mom who probably rejoiced when I joined the military, because it removed me from her life. The mom ship had sailed eons ago. "I don't need her. Or my dad, for that matter. He chose. I've accepted that."

"Have you?"

"Yup." But I couldn't hold his gaze.

Reaching for my toes, I kept my leg straight and pulled the front of my foot back, tugging on my hamstring. I did it over and over, ignoring the sting in both my leg and my heart. Hard to tell which hurt the most.

"Now I know why you push people's buttons," he said softly.

Scrunching my lips, I squinted up at him. "That, I prefer to call teasing."

"You're trying to get a response, even if it's negative."

I wasn't sure I liked him seeing this deep inside me. It cracked me open wide and made me feel unsure about everything, even myself. Yet I wanted to be honest with Jax, to share myself with him, especially the things that made me vulnerable or sad.

"How did your stepmom handle it?" he asked.

"With anger." I winced. "Which made me try harder."

"Did it work? Did she eventually soften to you and let you inside?"

I rubbed my chest, where it smarted most. "You tell me, since I've been using a similar technique whenever I'm around you. Did it work?"

"In some ways."

"Not with her. Never with her. The harder I tried to make her see me, the more she shoved me away."

"I'm not going anywhere," he said. "You test me. Most of the time, it drives me out of my mind. I feel a burst of excitement because you're paying attention to me, but it's often followed by…" He twisted his lips. "Okay, so I was bummed, because I assumed I couldn't take you seriously."

The opposite of what I'd intended. "Why not?"

"I wanted to. Hell, there were times when you drove me so close to the edge of my patience, I wanted to back you against a wall and…" His growl slipped between us. "Better not go there."

I stood and walked right up to him, not stopping

until our bodies brushed together. "Go there. What did you want to do to me when I teased you?"

"Kiss you," he shot out. "Pin you against a wall and love you until all you could think about was me."

This man. He twisted my insides into a knot then unraveled them.

"You're right," I said because being honest, naming it to him was important. "I push, push, push, until I get a reaction. I'm still seeking…"

"Validation."

"Why do I need it? I'm twenty-nine freakin' years old. I shouldn't need anyone other than myself."

"Because inside, you're still the scared little girl whose mom left you. I get it."

"How do you balance it in your mind? You lost your mom, too. And you didn't have anyone to step in and give you the security you needed."

"I told myself I could go it alone, that I didn't need anyone else."

"Is that still true?"

"I need you," he said softly.

And I needed him. More than I had anyone in my life.

"What would you do if I teased you now?" My limbs had locked into place. Dizziness clouded my vision, leaving only me and Jax on the balcony. The ocean could be sucked down a drain and leave us stranded here, and that was the only place I wanted to be.

One of his hands slipped beneath my hair and he cupped my neck, while the other slid around my waist.

"Do you want me to kiss you, Haylee? Is that what you're saying?"

Tentatively, I reached up and stroked his hair and his stubbly face. I trailed my fingertips down his neck to his shoulder that I gripped tightly. "I do."

"Any time you want me, you just tell me."

"I want you, Jax. I have for a very long time."

His fingers slid down to my hands and squeezed them. "I'm going to kiss you, but I don't know if I'll be able to stop there. I haven't been with anyone for a long time, not since I met you."

"At the Embassy or when you joined Viper Force?"

His chin ducked. "What do you think?"

"Tell me."

"Sounds stalkerish but since I saw you at the Embassy."

When he'd lit a spark inside me. I couldn't believe he'd waited for me to catch up.

"I don't want to wait any longer," I said. "Life's too short. Someone's determined to kill me."

His chest rumbled. "They'll have to take me down first."

And I'd do everything I could to protect him. But sometimes, no matter what you did, bad things happened. Like with Gabe.

"Kiss me, but don't stop there," I said in a fever. "Make love to me, Jax."

Tugging me close, he cupped my face with his palms and stared down at me. "You sure? Because I'm okay holding hands." One side of his mouth quirked up. "For a little while."

"Two seconds of knowing you want me but not being with you is about all I can stand. We've already held hands. We've kissed. It's time to try something more." Whatever he wanted, I wanted it too. Taking his hand, I tugged him toward the room.

He strode to the closet, pulled out his backpack and then rifled around and stuffed something into his pocket. Joining me at the bed, he tugged me around to fully face him. "If you don't like something I do or you need me to stop, you tell me. There's nothing I want more than to bury myself inside your body and stay there forever. Love you all day, if I can. But I want you with me every second it's happening."

"Same goes for you." I winked. "I could do something you don't like. Say, taste every inch of your body."

"I plan to do some tasting myself." He pressed me against the wall, and his mouth captured mine.

Fire burst inside me, an inferno only he could put out. His tongue parted my lips and plundered deeply while his hands slid along my arms to my waist, my belly. My breasts. He ran his thumbs across the nipples, and I moaned and arched into his touch.

Trailing kisses down my neck, he came to the top of my sundress.

"This is in the way, isn't it?" I said with a teasing smile. "How about I take it off?"

Stepping backward, he grinned. "Take it all off for me, sweetheart."

"Would you like a show?"

"Hell, yeah." Dropping into the stuffed chair in the

corner, he kicked back and put his hands behind his neck.

The sizeable bulge in his shorts urged me on.

It seemed like today I was good for a *different* kind of tease.

"Tell me what you like and what you don't, Jax," I said, my voice gone husky with desire. Teasing him was going to bring me to the edge; I could tell that already.

I sauntered close to him, bunching the skirt to my sundress up in my fists.

"I'm enjoyin' everything so far," he said, his hawk-like attention on my thighs.

Moving in a circle, I slowly swirled my hips as I tugged my skirt up over my hips. I bent forward in front of him, glad I'd opted to wear no panties. I assumed Jax hadn't felt confident enough to buy me anything sexy. And the white undies, while decent enough, hadn't felt right after I got out of my shower.

He groaned and his hands clenched on his thighs. "You're killing me already. Why did you…?"

I peeked past my arm while shimmering my hips, then spread my legs enough to give him a better view. Creases appeared on his face, and the cords in his neck stood at attention.

"I could drive myself into you right now," he growled. His fingers traced along my butt cheeks, moving inward until his thumb stroked down the crease. "Fuck. Wet."

"Do you like it wet?" I asked in a coy voice. "There's more where that came from." While it killed me to do it,

I stepped forward and straightening, swiveled my hips, moving around in a circle until I faced him.

His shorts tented up with something rigid I ached to feel sinking inside me.

But not yet.

I pulled my skirt up to my waist, and his guttural moan rang out. The muscles in his arms stood out in sharp definition when he grabbed the arms of the chair. "This tease is gonna kill me."

"I'm planning to die along with you, so don't let go yet."

His eyes smoldered when they met mine. "I guarantee complete satisfaction. I'm going to make you come a thousand times."

"I'm holding you to that promise." Fuck, I burned for him between my legs. My breasts ached for his touch, his mouth, the feel of his tongue moving across them. If the ship went down this moment, I wouldn't have it in me to jump overboard. Not until I'd felt him driving himself inside me.

I slid my dress over my head then stood in front of him completely naked. Going without a bra wasn't always a bad thing.

"Shit, shit," he said, his eyes gliding down my body like a heated caress.

I dropped to my knees, ignoring my protesting thigh. This had to count as PT, didn't it? Inching forward, I undid the button on the top of his shorts then slid down the zipper. "Commando? You've been holding out on me."

He was glorious. Thick and long enough to satisfy,

with veins bulging along the sides. His cock bobbed as if reaching for my touch.

Leaning forward, I licked him from the base to the tip. While he stretched out and tipped his head back, his muscles going rigid and his body flexing upward, I took him into my mouth and sucked.

My fingers climbed up beneath his tee to stroke his abs while I moved my mouth up and down on his cock, tasting and stroking and doing all I could to bring him pleasure.

His fingers fisted my hair, holding it back, pressing me in place. He pumped his hips and groaned. "Fuck, Haylee. You've gotta stop or…"

Lifting my head, I released him from my mouth with a wet pop and smiled. "Am I teasing you enough or do you want more?"

Nudging me aside, he stood and shucked his shirt and shorts fast.

My god, he said he liked to work out, and it was clear he worked all his muscles. I drank my fill, taking in his tanned, broad chest with a light dusting of hair, his narrow waist and thick thighs. And his jutting erection.

No twig in sight.

"Your turn," he said eagerly.

My grin came out pure tease. "But I haven't finished. There's so much more I can do if you—"

Growling, he turned me around and bent me forward, leaning me across the end of the bed.

"Yes, like this," he said hoarsely. Dropping lower to the floor, he nudged apart my thighs. "Show me everything." His palms, calloused and rough, rubbed along my legs, teasing closer and closer to the core of me that ached for his touch. His breath was hot when he pressed his face between my thighs and licked me.

I bucked and moaned because it felt better than anything I'd experienced in my life.

Bracing me still with his forearm, he dipped his thumb inside me.

We both groaned.

While his fingers pumped in and out, reaching deep within me, his tongue stroked my nub.

I couldn't stop shrieking. The blankets I'd buried my face in muffled my voice but he heard, because he chuckled low and deep.

"Come for me, sweetheart," he murmured. "Fall apart for me."

His fingers dove in farther, all the way to the hilt, while he sucked and laved and stroked me with his mouth and tongue.

Damn. I couldn't hold back. I wanted to feel him driving inside me, but I was spiraling apart from the inside out.

Guttural cries erupted from deep within me as I flew all the way up into the sky.

13

Jax

I sheathed my dick in a condom then centered myself at her core.

One hit wonder, eh? Time to show her everything I'd ached to give her for a hell of a long time.

While she quivered and whimpered into the blankets, I pushed myself forward, burying myself to the limit.

"Jax," she moaned.

She'd be sensitive, almost in pain if I took this too far, too fast. And I wanted her with me all over again.

"Relax," I said. "I'm just foolin' around." Drawing myself all the way out, I stroked inside her again, then repeated the movement. Slow and deep and driving me insane. Hopefully taking her along with me.

She felt too good. Tight and wet. Soft and rigid, all at the same time, her inner walls cushioned my cock. Stroked it.

I reached forward, bending over her while pumping in a steady, deep rhythm.

While I ached to take her nipples into my mouth, to suck them while she writhed beneath me, I'd have to be satisfied—and satisfy her—with my fingers while she lay face down.

Her nipples pebbled as I stroked them, the weight of her chest pushing them into my hands.

"Jax," she yelped. "Damn, man. That feels so good."

Her hips started to twitch then lift up to my pumps.

While my fingers rolled one nipple, I slid my other hand down and lightly stroked her clit, taking the firmness between my thumb and index finger. I rolled it.

She quivered and thrust toward me, moaning.

Though it just about killed me, I kept my pace slow. We had time. All day, in fact. I wouldn't stop until she screamed she'd had enough.

Kinda hoped she'd never scream she'd had enough.

Pulling myself back, I shoved forward, harder, deeper this time, because she was with me now.

She shrieked, the sweetest sound I'd heard in my life.

I stroked her folds and rubbed, driving her closer to the edge, aching to give her the best orgasm she'd ever had. Then I'd start all over again and give her another.

"Oh, God, go faster," she said. "You... I can't..." Her words dissolved into a moan.

"Like this?" I groaned out, diving hard within her. I drove myself into her over and over, so fast, the front of her body indented the bed.

"Yessss."

While I stroked her with my fingers and pinched her nipple, she bucked beneath me, spreading herself wider and jutting her hips up to take me as far as I could go.

"I can't. Jax…" She shuddered and moaned while I plunged faster.

Sweat trickled down my forehead, and my muscles bunched tight. I strained to give her everything while holding myself back.

When she dissolved around me, her inner walls spasming and gushing, I couldn't hold back.

My body corded harder than steel. As my muscles strained and twitched, I jerked deep inside her, pumping as a burning heat rose from my core.

Bellowing her name, I burst into flames. While she quivered and moaned around me, I rocked against her and came.

I collapsed on top of her, spent.

We lay together, though I slipped out and nestled beside her to give her room to breathe.

She rolled over to face me and smiled. I stroked her back while she traced her fingertip down my chest and around a nipple, which tightened and sent heatwaves to my cock all over again.

A quick trip to the bathroom, and I returned to find her still lying on the bed, her eyes closed, pure satisfaction blazing on her face.

Knowing I'd put that expression there made me puff up inside. I couldn't believe this woman wanted me, wanted to be with me. I'd ached and longed for her for a hell of a long time.

I would've been happy just to stand in her shadow.

We'd left the door and curtains open. Sunshine and the sultry air swirled through the room, combining with the musky scent of sex. An aphrodisiac for my body, which responded to her nakedness.

I eased her up fully onto the bed then climbed over her, bracing my thighs on either side of hers with my palms planted on the bed on either side of her shoulders.

Leaning forward, I drank from her welcoming lips. She tasted sweeter than honey. Nectar. If she let me, I'd keep on kissing her forever.

This morning, I swore I'd woken up to her fingers lightly tracing along my shoulders, my chest, then moving down to glide along each ridge of my abdomen. While I'd ached to have her hand go lower, it hadn't.

I'd opened my eyes to find her standing beside the curtain and decided I must've dreamed of her touch.

"You okay?" she said with a grin.

I couldn't keep what had to be a sappy smile off my face. "I am awesome."

"I hope you have a lot of condoms," she said boldly, her fingers teasing across my abs then going lower. "Because I think I'm insatiable where you're concerned."

"I've got more than enough for that one-hit wonder." Impertinent of me, but I'd picked up a box when I'd been at the big box store.

She climbed up onto me. "Where are they?"

My laugh slipped out, low and husky. Because heat was building inside me all over again. My cock bobbed against her thigh, and she wrapped her fingers around it and pumped.

I groaned. Couldn't hold it back. "Some are in my

backpack. I put a few in my shorts pocket before we got started."

Lifting up and off me, she smiled and shook her finger. "Naughty boy. You were hoping to screw me today, weren't you?"

With a growl, I leaped off the bed and stalked her until her back nudged the wall.

Her giggles dissolved to moans as I cupped her breasts then, bending over, took one of her nipples into my mouth.

"Please tell me you put lots of condoms in your shorts," she said.

"Five."

"Whoa." She laughed. "I like how you think."

I snatched my shorts up off the floor and dug into the pocket, pulling one out. Okay, so I *had* hoped to screw her today.

She took the condom from me and, with a grin, wrapped me up for her pleasure.

As I lifted her and backed her against the wall, her legs went around my waist and her arms wrapped around my shoulders. "Show me everything you've got, Sailor."

14

Haylee

Gabe and I waited in an alley near a seedy bar on the outskirts of Cancun. Latin-infused pop music spilled out from the club to our right, and the air smelled like sunscreen and tacos.

Our new contact had promised to meet us here, but...

"He's late," Gabe said. He stomped back and forth, his shoes crunching on things stuck to the pavement. Probably trash, though I wasn't going to turn on my phone light to find out.

Night eclipsed the world around us, but lights from the hotel strip speared in our direction from across the bay behind us.

When our contact called and said he had a lead on the Maestro, he'd picked this location, saying it was out of the way enough we wouldn't be seen, yet public enough we'd be safe.

Ha. As if anything was safe about this mission?

Someone had already taken pot shots at us from a vehicle last night when we left a restaurant. And the scorpion in my bed the other day sure hadn't made me feel warm and fuzzy.

The crunch of tires at the head of the alley sent us both spinning in that direction.

Headlights blinded me. While an ominous feeling swept through me, making my muscles cramp, the car door opened and footsteps rounded the vehicle. A man stopped between the beams, facing us, saying nothing.

He reached for his weapon...

Startling awake, I gulped back my scream. I stared around blindly for a moment before everything sank in.

The accident. Waking up in rehab. The cruise ship.

Jax.

I slumped back onto my pillow and turning, curled against him. He continued to sleep, completely unaware I'd had a nightmare beside him.

It hadn't been a dream, had it? The scene had felt so real.

My head pounded like a herd of horses were stomping through it. If only I could remember...

Pinching my lips together, I slid over to the side of the bed and sat for a second to catch my bearings. Jax inched over to cup me with his body. He stroked my back, and I closed my eyes and leaned into his touch.

"You okay?" he asked, his voice barely louder than the hum rising from deep within the ship that told me we'd left Key West and were steaming toward Cozumel.

"Yeah. Just have to go to the bathroom."

Darkness had fallen while we slept, and the only light came from the neon blue bands ringing the balconies around ours. Beyond the ship, a few small boats zipped across the water, heading for shore, with red lights winking on the port side and green lights on starboard.

"I think I'll take a bath while I'm there," I said.

"Soak my muscles. *Someone* has given me a solid workout today."

His chuckle shouted complete satisfaction. "A bath sounds fun," he rumbled. "Want company? A massage?"

Warm water. Lying back with my eyes closed. Jax's hands sliding across my skin. Sounded like heaven.

Turning, I smiled down at him. He was cute when he was sleep-rumpled. Cute when he wasn't rumpled, too. "Maybe? I'm going to try one of those bath bombs. Let me lounge in the tub for a few minutes then join me. Bring your shorts—and what's in the pocket—with you."

I'd dived into a relationship with this guy, and I was falling fast. And while my brain shouted caution, my heart knew I could trust him. He understood me, and he wouldn't hurt me.

Sliding off the bed, I turned and stood staring down at him.

The sheet loosely covered his thighs, plus something that was stirring underneath. Damn, with his broad shoulders and narrow waist, his muscular chest and rippling abs, he was the hottest guy I'd ever seen.

Pass out hot.

I fanned my face, unable to believe Jackson Ramsey wanted me.

No one else.

Me.

My heart pattering about the whole thing, I walked slowly into the bathroom. Parts of me that hadn't been active for a long time protested the movement. Never thought I'd say it, but I might have to ask him to slow down.

One-hit wonder? Not even close.

I shut the door, not sure why I bothered. I wanted him to follow me into the bathroom, right?

Yeah. I did.

Standing at the vanity, I grinned at my reflection. Razor burn tinged my chin. My skin tingled. And my hair was a wreck after Jax had run his fingers through it. I'd been well loved, something I wasn't sure I'd ever experienced in my life.

Jax could break me. That thought smacked me in the head. I clutched the edge of the vanity and blinked back my fear. He wouldn't die like my mom. He wouldn't choose someone else instead of me like my dad.

Was I a fool for handing my heart to a guy who could toss it aside?

No, Jax wouldn't do that.

"Jeez, Haylee," I whispered to myself. "Talk about spooking yourself. You've started something with the guy. Had your best sex in months." My lips twisted. "Okay, the best sex you've had ever. But the point is, it's new and wonderful. Enjoy it for what it is instead of trying to read anything else into it. Stop analyzing it."

Time to soak in a tub infused with a bath bomb. That would cure my unease. I could let my cares—and my aches—slip away, down the drain with the water.

And soon, Jax would join me.

The only question for the moment was which bath bomb to use tonight.

Hmm. Lavender? The purple flower was supposed to help you relax and calm emotional stress. It was also good for headaches, per the wrapper. Not a bad option.

Rosemary. A pick-me-up that helped fight off exhaustion, headaches (I sensed a trend here). It also was purported to relieve aches and pains. Good choice there. I nudged it ahead of the lavender.

But Jax had given me others, which meant I didn't have to decide yet.

Peppermint. Considered the best for mind stimulation. An energy booster, it invigorated the skin, promoted concentration, and stimulated the senses.

It might also cause unpleasant tingling in all the wrong places. I set that one aside for another time.

Vanilla. Thought to promote relaxation and reduce stress. Its sedative effects could reduce anxiety and calm the soul.

Sounded good to me.

I'd turned and reached toward the shower curtain, prepared to tug it aside when a slithering sound came from the tub.

Frowning, I paused, my hand tightening on the creamy white bath bomb. I couldn't quite place the sound.

Another rattle.

Nah. I was on a cruise ship, partway between Key West and Cozumel. In the middle of—sort of—the Gulf of Mexico.

This sound couldn't be a…

The slithering sound was followed by crunching like boots scuffing through fall leaves.

It couldn't be. There was no chance I'd pull back the curtain and find…

My heart thumping in my throat, I stepped forward and latched onto the plastic. The screech of the curtain sliding along the rod was followed by a gasp I bit off before it slipped past my lips.

A rattlesnake lay coiled in the bottom of the tub, its tail shaking, its beady eyes focused on me. One wrong move, and it would strike.

Inane details flew through my mind.

Untreated, a rattlesnake bite would kill a person within six to twenty hours. Did the ship's clinic carry anti-venom? Rattlesnakes were meat eaters, enjoying rats, mice, and small birds. They didn't eat people but had been known to strike if disturbed. They have thermal receptors they use to detect warm-blood creatures, a.k.a., their prey.

Me, if I moved too fast.

Their rattles were made up of bits of keratin within their tails. The pieces knocked together and produced their well-known buzzing sound. Each time a rattler shed its skin, it added another segment to the rattle.

While this wasn't the first deadly snake I'd encountered—tours overseas had introduced me to more creepy-crawly things than I liked to think of late at night—a rattlesnake in a cruise ship bathtub was a first for me.

No one would ever call me a snake handler but I had, once, moved a snake. A nonvenomous variety, but I wasn't completely lacking in experience.

Some people would've screamed or called for the

hunky, muscular man waiting in the room outside the bathroom.

Not me.

Yes, saliva pooled in my mouth and my breathing jerked in and out of my chest. I'd be foolish not to feel scared shitless. But I couldn't leave it here.

I reached up and carefully pried the shower curtain rod out of its socket. The soft clicks made the rattler shake its tail faster.

Sweat trickled down my spine as I tucked the shower curtain to the side and slowly slid the pole toward my snake. Maintaining my position with the rod close to the snake, I eased toward the door and pulled it open.

"Don't come in here," I said in a soft monotone.

"You change your mind about that massage?" Jax asked from where he must've been waiting in the narrow hall. "I'm happy to give you longer if you want more alone time."

"That's not it." On any other occasion, I'd quip something that I hoped would come out witty. Or dirty.

With a snake problem to handle, this wasn't the time for joking around. Sadly enough, teasing Jax would have to wait.

"Can you go open the door to the balcony?" I asked.

"You want to sit outside on the balcony?" he said. "Sure, I can open the door. We can open that bottle of wine the concierge left, if you want." His footsteps shuffled across the room.

I edged back into the bathroom, pleased to see the snake's rattle lay silent, though the creature still watched my every move. As long as I did everything in a non-hurried, careful manner, I wouldn't stir it up too badly.

I bent the end of the curtain rod over to make a hook then, keeping the tub surround between me and the snake, inched the tip close to the snake again, creeping toward the upper part of its body. From what I'd learned, as long as I didn't irritate it too much, it might rattle but it wouldn't strike.

No need to call Jax to handle this. Doing it myself would prove something. I'd been injured but I wasn't out of the battle yet.

Teeth clenched, I tucked my hook about six inches back from the snake's head. The beastie reeled back and its rattle rang out, but when I held the pole still, it settled again, not considering me a threat. Yet.

Keeping my movements slow and easy, I lifted the snake, holding it close to the tub. I carefully slid it up the smooth tub surface, then headed toward the door.

"Nice and slow," I whispered. "No jerky motion that might heat it up."

So far, it wasn't rattling again, a good sign on any day of the week.

When its tail hovered on the edge of the tub and I had its head and upper body draped over my hook and extended out in front of me, I bent down and loosely grabbed the tail. If I clamped onto it, it might feel threatened. But the stability would help keep it relaxed.

Jax appeared at the door. "You know what, sweetheart…" His jaw dropped. "What the…?"

"You might want to get out of the way," I whispered. It was hard to sound perky when my teeth chattered.

Was this fun? No. Did I still feel I needed to do it? Yes. "My friend here would like to go swimming."

"What the fuck are you doing, Haylee?" He backed away, his hands raised.

"What does it look like?" I glided across the floor tiles, aiming for the hall.

"Put it down," he said. "Move away from it, and we're outta here."

"Thanks for opening the balcony door," I said as I floated toward the opening. "I wouldn't want to jostle this poor thing while trying to do it myself." Moving like this made my thigh spasm. Okay, any movement made my thigh spasm. My ribs weren't happy with me right now either. They suggested I lie down, put my feet up, and have a big glass of wine. Soon, babies, soon.

The snake's tail still snug in my grip and my arms shaking more than I liked, I extended the pole forward with the creature's upper body lounging across the hook. With the end near, I picked up my pace. No time for dancing or playing around. This snake needed out of our lives for good. Later, we could speculate about how it had found its way into our tub.

I didn't like the idea that we'd been outed already.

Passing the bed and then the squishy chair, I hustled out onto the balcony. Good thing the ocean was beneath us

"Watch out lounge chairs," I whispered, catching them out of the corner of my eye. "Snaky coming through." To Jax, I tossed over my shoulder, "Wine sounds nice but is there any beer in the fridge? Because I think I'm going to need a brewskie after this."

"Haylee." He chewed on my name.

"Yeah, Jax?"

"Fuck," he said from so close behind me, I had the impression he'd like to snatch me up into his arms, whirl me around, and put himself between me and the snake.

I felt the same.

"That's a rattler," he hissed.

The snake's tail trembled in my hand, shouting out a warning.

"Hey, don't piss it off," I said.

"You think it likes being carried?"

"I didn't ask."

"You…" He shook his head, edging out onto the balcony behind me.

"Pretty, isn't he?" I asked softly. "Nice size, too. I'd say about three years old, based on the number of rattles."

When I reached the balcony, I lifted the snake and flung it over the railing. I kept hold of the shower curtain rod, knowing I'd have some explaining to do for ripping it away from the wall, but for the moment, my limbs felt like they were on fire and adrenalin surged through my veins. Damn, it felt good to be alive, to do something like this. Like I'd come out of hibernation roaring.

The snake dropped away, falling toward the water. Fortunately, rattlesnakes could swim, because I wouldn't want to kill it.

As the curtain rod slipped from my hand and clattered on the balcony floor, I drooped against the railing. My legs trembled, and my damn hands weren't any steadier. So much for adrenalin and feeling empowered.

"Think I'm gonna pass out, Jax," I whispered as the world darkened around me.

"I've got 'cha," he said, scooping me up off my feet and into his warm arms. "Hang in there, sweetheart."

"Thanks," I whispered, my eyes sliding closed against my will. I nuzzled my face against his chest. He smelled good. Like guy but also something spicy-citrusy.

And a bit of us.

"Woman," Jax said in a husky voice as he carried me into the bedroom. "You are fuckin' badass."

15

Jax

Haylee was going to be the death of me. Watching her carry a rattlesnake through the cabin and toss it off the balcony had to have stripped ten years off my life.

Forget putting her down on the bed. Still holding her in my arms, I dropped down into the too-comfortable chair parked in the corner, before my legs gave out.

Her eyes had rolled back in her head. Had she passed out? She mumbled and snuggled into my chest, seeking my warmth. I liked that.

"Haylee?" I asked softly. If she was out cold or sleeping, I'd leave her where she was. At least I'd know nothing would harm her while I held her in my arms.

How had someone found us so fast?

No doubt, the snake had been planted in the bathroom to put one or both of us out of commission.

I needed to get us off the boat as soon as possible. Which was going to present a problem until we reached Cozumel tomorrow. My skin itched at the thought of being trapped on this floating hunk of metal. Water all around us and no way off.

If we'd been outed, it could mean our IDs were compromised. We needed to disappear, which meant we had to avoid being tracked the second we hit our next location.

We'd hide in the room until we hit Cozumel. The honeymoon cover and a *do not disturb* sign on the door would work best with the staff. As long as someone didn't try to break down the door, we'd be safe.

But shit, I hated not knowing where the next threat would come from.

"Jax?" Haylee asked, stirring in my arms. "I'm dreaming, right? I didn't just drag a rattlesnake out of the tub with the shower curtain rod and throw it off the balcony, did I?"

"Did."

"Crap." Easing away from me, she shuddered. "Someone knows we're here."

"Yep."

"What are our options?"

She shifted on my lap, reminding me we were both buck naked. No time for fun, now, however.

"We can..." Hell. My body had other plans. What were we talking about?

Haylee wiggled her butt as if testing things out. "I suppose the bath is out," she said with regret in her voice.

"Jax?" she whispered, easing off my lap.

"If you still want that bath, go for it." I stood. "I'm

going to call Dwayne. Make sure things are set up for tomorrow."

"We're bailing in Cozumel, I assume." Her lips twisted. "Mexico. Love the food. Love the people. Most of them, that is. Except for the ones determined to kill me. I assume our snake friend was brought in by the housekeeper we saw in the hallway."

"My thought, too."

"Not a true housekeeper." Her arms wrapped around her waist, and she shivered. "Which meant the snake has been waiting for hours, while we—" She tilted her head toward the bed. "And while we slept."

Striding to the door, I slid the do-not-disturb tag over the knob, checking the hall and finding no one, naturally. The guy who'd done this wouldn't be waiting around for me to tackle him. I shut the door and engaged the dead-bolt. I could drag the chair over and prop it under the knob tonight, though it wasn't much protection.

I didn't like this situation. It made me feel antsy. I needed a weapon but it was doubtful I could talk anyone in security into handing over a firearm. They'd probably lock me up and call the cops.

Was there somewhere else on the ship we could hide?

"It's gonna be okay," I said. "Promise."

She sniffed. "I believe in you. I believe in us. But I'm scared. And I hate admitting it."

"Nothing wrong with admitting it. I'm scared, too." Afraid I couldn't protect her. They weren't after me. This was solely about Haylee.

I'd lay down my life to keep her safe but it might not be enough.

"I'll feel better once we're off the ship. It's a floating trap. Whoever is after me could knock down the door or even come in through the balcony, if they need to. We can't put up barricades everywhere."

"An alternative is to find somewhere public then remain there all night, but the idea is problematic."

"They'll surround us. Separate us." Her voice broke. "It would kill me if something happened to you, Jax."

Tugging her into my arms again, I dropped my chin on the top of her head. "Feel the same, Haylee."

I hated feeling helpless. It was time to take control of the situation. I just needed to figure out how.

"Tell you what," I said, leaning back in our embrace. "I'll clean the tub and then you can take that bath."

"I wouldn't dare. What if something happened while I was lounging in the water?"

"Don't let someone stop you from enjoying this one thing."

She sniffed. "I imagine they think I'm hovering in the corner, shivering. You're right. I don't want to give them that satisfaction." She hefted the shower rod. "I'll smack anyone who dares come at me."

"You do that. I'll stand guard out here. Between the two of us, they don't stand a chance."

Big tears rolled down her cheeks, and I wiped them away with my thumbs.

She followed me into the bathroom, where we both made sure no other surprises waited. I'd scour the main room once she'd locked herself inside.

Without a brush, I used a washcloth and shampoo to scrub out the tub. I plugged the drain and turned on the hot water. She could balance the temp with cold as it filled.

"Bath bomb?" I said, my gaze falling on them lined up in a row on the sink.

"I'd decided on vanilla. The package said something about helping me relax and reduce stress. Seems like I need that now even more than I did before." Unwrapping it, she held it close while watching the water pour from the faucet.

"You make that call," she finally said, lifting her chin. "I'll be okay here by myself."

"You don't need to be alone."

The half-smile she gave me held equal parts joy and sadness, and it hit me in the chest like a boulder. "I wanted you to join me in the water." She barked out a rueful laugh. "To give me a massage."

"Still can give you that massage." And anything else she asked of me.

"Later?" She leaned over the tub and dropped the bomb into the water. It fizzled, and a sweet scent filled the air.

When I'd walked through the store trying to decide what I should get her, I'd stopped in the beauty section. Never heard of bath bombs but they sounded fun, like something the Haylee I remembered from before the accident would enjoy.

"Right now, I'm going to soak," she said. "I need to close my eyes and pretend…" Her voice choked off to a whisper. "Pretend we're safe. That nothing will harm us. But I don't know, Jax. I don't… I'm tired. So, so tired."

And I was part of the reason why. I'd been hot to prove I wasn't a one-hit wonder and hadn't considered how exhausted she still was from the accident. She should be resting, healing, not foolin' around with me.

"Don't even think that," she said, straightening. She sauntered over to me, reminding me we were both still naked. Although, my body hadn't forgotten. "After I'm done soaking, I'm going to drag you off to bed."

"I thought I should get some food. We missed lunch. And dinner."

She sighed. "We can't order room service. Who knows who or what might arrive?"

An open door was an invitation inside. Or an invitation to poison.

"The only food I trust is stuff from the buffet," I said. A quick glance at the clock on the desk said it was after eight. The buffet would still be open another forty minutes or so. "Once you're done here, I'll go fill a few plates and bring them back. That'll hold us until morning."

"Sounds good." She trailed her fingertip down my chest. "Still plan to take advantage of you later."

My body responded to her touch but my mind remained solid. I'd need to remain on guard 24/7, not give into my urge to love her all night long. Someday, a time would come when we could be together without fear weighing us down. I'd make it up to her then.

"Unless you're going to join me…" She cocked her

head toward the water. "Go make that call. I'll be out in a few."

I kissed her, long and slow and full of promise, cursing the tenuous situation we found ourselves in. We'd barely found each other, and I refused to let anyone tear us apart.

After I shut the door, I turned off the lights then, using my penlight, made sure the room was clean. I didn't find anything to be concerned about, but that meant nothing. Then I made that phone call.

A chair under the knob wasn't much of a deterrent but it would present a challenge if someone tried to gain entry. Worst case, it would make noise if someone tried to force their way inside.

I needed to booby trap the balcony. Reaching into the closet, I pulled out the bag Dwayne and Eben had brought when we met up in the parking garage.

Had that only been yesterday? It felt like it had been ten years.

Dwayne had done some shopping for me, outfitting me with devices like those we tested at Viper Force. Some over the counter, others he'd picked up… I hadn't asked. We'd been limited with what we could get through cruise ship security, even with a checked bag.

I removed a spool of thin, nylon wire and some cutters.

After removing the furniture from the balcony, stacking it off to the side inside the room, I strung the wire about eight inches up from the floor of the balcony, tight enough to trip someone.

If someone rappelled from above or found a way up from one of the rooms below, they'd be eager to maintain the element of surprise. Short of waiting for them on the balcony where it could turn into a gun battle with me the first victim, the best thing I could do was try to trip them up. Then we'd have notification they were there.

These people were sharp. We were former military, so they'd know we could protect ourselves. They'd be cautious, wary, and conniving.

But like my buddies at Viper Force, I'd go simple.

The lights on the ship could be an issue, pinpointing our location and outlining us if we stood on the deck. I took a screwdriver and, removing the cap on the outside light, I unscrewed the bulb. That was the easiest solution to that problem.

Then I locked the balcony doors. With brute strength, I broke one of the deck chairs. If maintenance didn't like it, they could charge the cost of the chair to my WOW bracelet. I placed one of the main supports, a long metal bar, between the screen and the door, making it infinitely harder for someone to open the slider even if they found a way to break the lock.

Haylee emerged from the bathroom with a fluffy white towel wrapped around her body. She'd created a high ponytail with her hair, and she looked all of seventeen. But the girl who dropped the towel and advanced on me was one-hundred-percent woman.

I held my arms out to her, and she stepped inside my embrace. She nestled against my chest, smelling sweeter than honey.

Damn, she made my eyes ache. My heart, too.

"How about I get us something to eat?" I asked, my voice croaking.

The odds of someone striking so quickly after leaving the snake were…probably the same as them deciding to lull us by waiting. But we needed food.

"I am hungry," she said. "I'll get dressed then let you out the door."

"Block it again with the chair." I really didn't need to remind her, but I couldn't help it. She was military trained, as savvy about this as me, if not more.

"I've got this, too." She hefted the bent shower curtain rod. "It's not much but it'll have to do." She pulled on underwear and then tossed on shorts and a tee, and slipped her feet into the sneakers I'd purchased for her. With a nudge, she encouraged me toward the door. "Go. I'm fine here alone. Come back fast. Like, two seconds ago." While her voice came out cheery, tension tightened her spine.

Before I left, I ducked into the bathroom. "What's your least favorite scent?" I called out.

She appeared in the doorway.

"I'm looking for a weapon," I said.

Her face cleared. "A bath bomb. In a sock. What a great idea."

"Simple yet effective." Swung through the air, it could break bones on impact. Who says a man needs a knife or a gun to defend himself?

"Honestly?" Crinkling her face, she lifted and handed the lavender bath bomb to me. "Not to be unkind, because I imagine you put some thought into it, but this one smells a bit too perfumey for me." She grabbed one of the others and tucked it inside a sock. Hefting it, her smile contained grim satisfaction. "Between my shower rod and this, I'm going to teach anyone who tries to invade our room a lesson."

I was for damn sure determined to make sure it never came to that.

"Keep your rod and sock handy," I said hoarsely. I didn't want to leave, didn't want to leave her alone. But to heal, she needed to eat. I wouldn't be gone long.

"I could kill someone at least fifty different ways with my pole." Her eyes gleamed with humor, but she wasn't lying. We'd engaged in hand-to-hand combat more than a few times, and she'd provided a solid challenge.

Her comment made a grin rise on my face. Haylee —the spunky woman I was crazy about—was back. She might've been knocked down a peg, but she'd scrambled back up to the surface.

"You see it, too, don't you?" she said.

I nodded. "You're back."

"Better than ever."

"Solid. Strong."

"Undefeated." Tears shimmered in her eyes. "I'm not letting anyone hurt me ever again."

"I'll stand beside you through it all."

She dipped her chin, staring down at the sock-encased bath bomb hanging from her hand. "Thanks."

After stroking my knuckles across her cheek, I moved around her to the door, where I lifted the chair away from the knob. The peephole in the door allowed me to see the hall directly outside. I hadn't expected anyone to be standing there, waiting for me to open the door, but you never knew how people would behave.

"On three," I said softly.

She nudged my back. "Just go."

The deadbolt clicked open.

"Get some good food, will you? None of that nutritious crap. Bacon, if they have it. Lots of bacon. And a cream horn, if you can find one."

"Yes, Ma'am."

"Don't forget cheese."

"Cheese?"

"Smoked cheese. Swiss. And wedges of nice, sharp cheddar."

Turning, I leaned against the door. "Should I make a list?"

She pursed her lips. "Now you're the one teasing." Her quick kiss was followed by a smile. "Thank you."

"For sharp cheddar?"

"For being here for me. Without you, I'd be dead."

Gathering her close, I kissed the top of her head. "I won't be long."

She sniffed. "I'll be waiting."

We separated, and I reached for the doorknob.

"Lock up behind me," I said, eager to get to the buffet, load the plates, and hurry back.

"Already planned to," she said with steel in her voice.

"I won't be long," I added, knowing I needed to leave but hating the idea. I'd find the first restaurant accessible with this WOW thing and demand two full meals. "Maybe ten minutes tops." Hopefully.

After another look through the peephole, I opened the door and, ducking down, tucked a fraction of my head out into the hall and pulled back fast. Nothing and no one moved. Didn't mean someone wasn't lurking around a corner, waiting to strike.

I hefted my sock, wrapping the loose end around my hand.

My first priority once we'd eaten would be rigging a better weapon. Shower curtain rods and bath bombs would only do in a pinch. I hated feeling vulnerable. Defenseless. Whoever was after Haylee had started with a snake but things would escalate fast. We'd be dead by morning if I wasn't careful.

I stepped out into the hall and pulled the door shut. The click of the deadbolt rang out, followed by a dull thud as she stuffed the chair beneath the knob.

At the elevator bank, I pushed the button. Again. Hurry up, hurry up. Should've taken the stairs.

A middle-aged couple joined me to wait.

The elevator arrived and we stepped inside. Two families with kids and an older couple already inside the car. I pressed up, since our suite was on the seventh floor and the buffet was above us.

The elevator came to a stop on the ninth floor and the two men and the families got out.

We reached deck ten, and I hustled around the families, down the hall toward the buffet restaurant.

Things were fancier at night than at breakfast. Romantic lighting, too, but it was late. They could gear this seating time toward those without small children.

Didn't matter to me. I planned to be in and out before anyone knew I'd been there.

Plates. Best would be paper, but I didn't see any around.

"Where can I find paper plates?" I asked a server rushing past me.

"No paper," she said, pointing to stacks at the end of one of the buffet lines. "We use the real thing, over there."

"I want to take a few plates back to my room."

She frowned. "Have you considered ordering room service?"

"Don't trust it not to be poisoned."

"Excuse me, Sir?" Her spine stiffened. "I can assure you that any food delivered to your room will be completely safe."

"I didn't mean anything the cruise ship delivers." I meant whatever potential murderers delivered.

She faced me fully and I could tell by the creases on her face, she was gearing up to defend the entire cruise line. "The kitchen prepares it fresh and it's piping hot when it arrives. They'd never bring you something that has sat around for any length of time."

Each second I spent arguing with this woman was one more I wasn't protecting Haylee.

"Where would you like to sit?" she asked, glancing around the room. "We don't have many tables available inside, but there are plenty of them free out on the deck, overlooking the water."

"I'm not sitting. I'm filling plates and taking them back to the room."

"Everyone is seated before they collect their food." She lifted a smile. "How about on the deck? It's beautiful outside tonight."

"My…wife is waiting in our room. She's injured; can't get around well. I'm collecting and bringing a meal back for her."

"Aw, that's so sweet." She glanced around as if making sure no one would overhear. "Tell you what. Let's seat you out on the deck." Her finger lifted when I started to protest. "Load your plates and wait at the table while I go out to the kitchen and find containers for you. Then you don't need to worry about walking through the halls with open plates. Accidents happen!"

"Okay. I can do that." Nothing more.

"Lovely. Follow me."

Weaving around tables with guests enjoying drinks, food, and each other's company, we eventually arrived at a table on the deck, near where Haylee and I had sat and eaten breakfast this morning.

She dropped a small placard on the table that said, *reserved*, and she'd barely started toward the kitchen when I left the table and rushed toward the buffet.

Hustling up to the end of a line, I grabbed two plates and started moving around the buffets, taking chicken and beef and a couple vegetables because I wanted them even if she didn't. I added thick slices of crusty bread and a bunch of butter packets.

Cream horn. Where the hell would I find one of those?

I spied a section near the salad bar that held platters loaded with various cheeses, and added those to the pile.

I finally located the dessert section.

The server stopped beside me, her arms loaded with containers. "I'll fill one of these with a variety of sweets for you, if you'd like?"

"That would be awesome."

"Let me put the containers on your table. You can load your meals in them while I'm collecting the dessert."

I gave her a wan smile but planned to grab some desserts on my way out, because I couldn't trust anyone, even this random server.

Drinks? There must be water bottles in the fridge. Worst case, there was tap water.

Following her, I returned to the table, which was adjacent to the railing and overlooking the water ten stories below. On any other day, I'd sit, kick my feet up on one of the other chairs, and savor the view.

Tonight, I scrambled to open the containers and then carefully arranged the food inside. No reason to bring Haylee a mess. She wanted a ton of food but I didn't imagine she wanted it all thrown together.

A thump below, off the edge of the deck, drew my attention, but I didn't see anything down there to be concerned about. They'd strapped the lifeboats below where I stood, in a neat row.

I'd turned and was lifting the covers onto the containers when two guys rushed around the table, arms extended. They bowled me over, shoving me backward, and my hip bit into the rail.

People nearby leaped to their feet and a few shrieked

and pointed. Probably thought this was a fight, not a murder attempt.

Bellowing, I fought them, swinging my fists and kicking. One guy dropped to his knees, holding his nose that squirted blood. The other screamed when I twisted his arm.

Rising to his feet, the first grabbed onto my legs while the other one took my arms, as much as they were able to hold onto me while they were wounded and I was flailing.

I struggled and hollered, and the other cruise ship guests rushed our way to intervene, but the guys heaved me up and over the side.

I plunged down toward the ocean churning below.

16

Haylee

Jax should've been here by now.

My guts in a knot, I rose from the squishy chair where I'd sat to wait. In the dark. Alone. And scared.

But not defenseless.

My arsenal lay on the floor by my feet as well in strategic locations around the room.

Two socks with bath bombs. The shower curtain rod. Three chair legs. A throwing disc made out of the base of a lamp I'd unscrewed. A plate left over from the meal last night. Plus a few other assorted items.

If someone came after me tonight, they wouldn't find me helpless, not like the last time, when I'd been lying in a rehab bed.

Something heavy thumped on the balcony, and I froze in place, my fists white knuckling against my sides.

Jax had strung wire out there. Unless a big bird had landed on the deck, the thump would've come from someone tripping over the line and falling.

An early warning didn't stop my pulse from jumping.

As if they thought I might not have heard them, whoever was out on our balcony lightly tested the door. A flimsy thing, the lock wouldn't hold long. And if someone had made the effort to climb up or down to our balcony, they wouldn't give up easily.

After setting things in place, I climbed up onto the chair, the curtain rod snug in my right hand, the bath bomb sock in my left.

My heart thundered behind my ribcage, and sweat trickled down my spine. I'd aptly defended myself against multiple challenges during my military career, even when attacked by men one-and-a-half times my size. But back then, I hadn't been four weeks out from multiple rib and femur fractures. A newborn kitten could knock me over.

To defend myself, I'd have to use my wits instead of the strength I'd relied on for much of my life.

The door didn't give, partly due to the lock but mostly because of the chair leg Jax had wedged into place to add resistance.

Would they give up? There were limits to what someone could do to break into a room, especially when they must know I could hear them. They might find the main entrance an easier challenge.

As if on cue, the door knob clicked. Back and forth. No hiding their intent now.

My mouth flashed dry. They were coming at me from both directions.

Where was Jax? The fear bolting inside me

suggested they'd already gotten to him. Hurt him. I bit back my cry of outrage and pain.

Lifting my chin, I tightened my grip on my weapons. I wouldn't go down without taking a few of them with me.

A pop and beside me, the safety glass in the French door shattered, hit by a bullet from a gun with a silencer. Bits of glass rained down on the carpet.

I hefted my weapons.

When a head poked into the open doorframe, I slammed the rod down on top of it. I followed it up with a hefty swing of my bath bomb, smacking the person in the neck. With a groan, they toppled onto their knees and fell onto the broken glass inside the room.

I climbed off the chair and backed away from the person lying silently on the carpet.

Behind me, the door rattled in the frame. The chair wouldn't keep them back for long.

The guy on the floor groaned and, like a terminator, rumbled to his feet. He pawed around on the floor. Looking for the gun?

I should've grabbed it when I had the chance. Why hadn't I? My senses had been dulled by inaction.

He staggered to his feet and he squinted around, his gaze honing in on me.

I hobbled toward him, my guts rising up into my throat and adrenalin setting fire to my veins. My sneakers crunched on the glass as I flicked the plate at him like a Frisbee. It hit him square in the chest, and he stumbled backward a few steps before shaking and then rushing toward me.

I threw the base of the lamp at him next, and he ducked. The brass fitting flew through the open French door and disappeared over the railing.

The chair legs would work best for close combat.

"Just come at me asshole," I huffed. See what a wounded Seabee could do.

His fists swung out, and I deflected it to the side with my forearm. I dodged his leg when he kicked out then tucked my foot behind his knee and yanked. He staggered sideways but regained his balance.

Pulling a knife, he swung it up, aiming for my throat. With a twist of my wrist, I levered his arm to the side, and the angle of his shoulder forced him to bend forward at the waist. I jerked my knee up, impaling him in the belly, and he grunted and fell toward the floor. The knife fell beside him as I drove him onto the carpet with a clenched fist in the upper part of his spine.

He scrambled around and gained his feet then plowed toward me with a yell. I struck out with one of the chair legs while swinging the bath bomb with my other hand. It connected with his jaw, and he grunted.

And kept coming.

On any other day, I'd be good for a long bout of combat, but I was tiring fast. My body, still recovering, had no stamina.

The main entrance door slammed open, and the chair was shoved into the room.

Crap. Flagging already, I couldn't handle two.

Where was the gun? And that knife? I needed to locate them and end this before they did it for me.

Jax burst into the room, his wild eyes taking in the scene.

With a roar, he barreled forward, hitting the man in the back and taking both of them onto the bed. They tumbled across the end and onto the floor on the balcony side. Glass crunched beneath them as they wrangled for purchase. Jax reared up above the guy and his fists descended, smacking fast and furious, connecting with the guy's flesh in meaty thuds.

The man bucked and dislodged Jax, sending him sideways, into the stationary balcony panel. With a bang that reverberated through the room, he hit the glass and bounced off.

I rushed in their direction, armed with my bath bomb and chair leg. I speared the leg out at the guy, gouging him in the side. Grunting, he swung the knife toward me. Yelping, I reeled backward but hit his upper arm with the bomb while deflecting his hand away with the chair leg. Airborne, the knife clattered into the wall and thudded on the floor.

Jax loomed behind the man, breathing rapidly, his face florid in the dim lights filtering in from outside.

Grabbing the guy, Jax spun him out onto the balcony. He followed with a roar, and his roundhouse kick sent the man back against the railing.

Jax raced forward and with a mighty grunt, lifted and heaved the guy over the side.

Jax

I gathered Haylee into my arms. Glass crunched beneath our feet and a stiff wind blew in from the ocean. She trembled with what had to be rage and fear, because I shook for the same reasons.

"You okay?" I shot out. What if I hadn't gotten here in time?

"He didn't hurt me. I fought him off until you arrived. I'm just glad you got here when you did, though. It was getting tough." Leaning back in my embrace, she frowned and smoothed her fingertips across my brow. It stung, probably from where I'd scraped it while falling off the ship. "Your forehead."

I was bumped and bruised-up, but I barely felt a thing. All I could think about were the feelings that had poured through me when I'd latched onto a balcony railing and hauled my ass back up onto the ship. I'd been worried about Haylee. Horrifying scenarios had spun through my mind, none of them ending well.

They'd tried to eliminate me to make it easier to get her, and I wasn't sure I'd get here in time.

"I imagine I'll have a shiner," I said. "I was attacked at the buffet."

"While that sounds like something from a comedy, I have a feeling someone wasn't fighting you for the last slice of prime rib."

"Two guys jumped me and threw me over the railing."

Her gaze darted to our balcony. Had the guy I'd thrown over grabbed something on the way down or was he shark bait now?

My heart wouldn't stop thundering. After crawling onto a room balcony below the buffet deck, I'd banged on the door until the guy inside opened up. I'd raced through his room, startling a little boy playing on the bed, and dashed out into the hall. After that, I'd taken the stairs to this floor rather than wait for an elevator.

"Someone was trying to get in from the hallway. I assume you took them out?" she asked, looking in that direction. Her nostrils flared. "While I was fighting off the one from the deck, I could hear the other trying to break in."

"He won't be bothering us again," I said, having no interest in telling her what I'd done with him. Since he was one of the dudes who'd thrown me off the buffet deck, I'd taken grim satisfaction in driving my fist into his face. "One man down, the other overboard."

"Let's hope they were working alone." Backing away from me, she collapsed on the bed. She dropped onto her back and stuffed a pillow underneath her bad leg.

"The one I ran into in the hall looked like our snake-planting housekeeper, and our swimmer was the one we saw yesterday in the hall when we arrived."

"So they could be the only ones onboard. Do you think we're safe until we reach Cozumel tomorrow?"

I shrugged. "I'd like to think so."

"I hear a but in there." She bolted upright, her head turning toward the balcony. A moan of distress slipped from her mouth.

I stilled.

"Incoming," I said. The whoop-whoop-whoop of an approaching chopper raked its claws down my spine.

We went out onto the deck and watched grimly as the helo coasted past the ship, heading toward the landing pad on the bow. The engines soon wound down.

"What are the chances it's someone injured or sick?" she asked, breathless. Any hope she might've drummed up at the realization we could've eliminated all threats fled her face, turning it sallow in the muted lighting.

"Twice in one cruise? Hard to say." I couldn't lie to her but I sure couldn't tell her the truth. While whoever was running this shit show couldn't know what had happened to the two on board, they'd be stupid to take chances. Better to drop a few more people in to make sure the problem was taken care of. They probably guessed we'd disappear again once we reached Mexico. It would be harder to track us once we'd hit the ground.

"You know they're sending in backup." Her voice cracked and her hands shook so badly, she dropped the sock with her bath bomb. It hit the tile floor, creating a dull smack. "They'll keep coming until they overwhelm us. In a short time, whoever just arrived will find their way into our room no matter how much we barricade it. Forget blocking the balcony. Might as well put up a sign with an arrow pointing in this direction. Even if we could secure the entrances, we can't stay awake all the time. We have to eat and that means leaving the room or taking a chance on them bringing us poison."

"I'll figure this out." I had a plan but couldn't put it into effect until we arrived at the port in Cozumel.

"We need to find a way off the ship," she said softly. "They'll get me no matter where I hide."

My growl of frustration erupted in my chest, and I put my arm around her shoulders. I was unable to offer her more than physical comfort, because she was right.

I hated that I couldn't think of a way out of this situation.

"What are we going to do?" The hint of defeat in her voice socked me in the chest all over again. "Is there any place we can go where they won't find us? There must be, oh, I don't know, closets or isolated hallways in the bowels of the ship where no one would think to look for us."

Doubtful. The Maestro seemed determined to eliminate Haylee and if he or she brought in enough people, they'd finish us off before we reached Cozumel.

Disguises were not an option; they'd see right through them even if we could rig something with what we had on the ship or from the stores on board. We couldn't tell anyone about the damage to our room or ask for another, not without them locking us up. Even if we could hide until morning, the Maestro's gang would grab us the second we tried to leave the ship.

It appeared we'd run into a solid brick wall.

But when you can't climb over or dig your way underneath, sometimes, you had to blast your way through the middle.

"Can you pack up your things?" I asked. Maybe we could…

"Sure." Curiosity and a spark of excitement lifted her voice. "You have an idea?"

"Yeah." I rushed to the closet. "We've got to be fast."

"I'm not up for swimming," she said, and I was happy to hear her sounding hopeful.

"No swimming." I shot her a grin. "But can you run?"

"Watch me." She hobbled into the bathroom and started tossing things into her bag.

Dragging my pack from the closet, I made sure I still had the bag from Dwayne then stuffed the rest of my clothing on top. I hadn't brought much, and I was ready as quickly as Haylee. I added her bag to my pack then swung it up onto my shoulder.

"Ready?" I asked, holding out my hand.

"Always," she said with utter relief. "Where to?"

We wove around the chair still waiting by the door.

The first thing I'd done after we arrived on board yesterday was study the layout of the ship.

"We're going down in the world, sweetheart," I said.

She hurried beside me as we headed toward the elevator banks. "Are we hiding in the engine rooms?"

"Even better."

Three teenagers were waiting and they joined us in the elevator car when the doors opened.

I pressed five.

"That's not where the engine room is," she said.

"We'll save the engine room tour for another day."

One of the teenagers side-eyed me.

The doors opened, and we stepped out.

"This way," I said, urging her to the right. "You up for bullying our way past a few crew members?"

Because her breathing was coming fast already, I slowed my pace. Creases on her face told me how tired she was already. She'd need to rest soon, if at all possible, but I'd just put a new plan into place.

She cocked one eyebrow my way. "Where are you hiding us? I assume that's where we're going."

"I'm hiding us where no one can touch us."

"I have no idea where that could be other than Mars, but I'm eager to find out."

We hurried down the hall, around a corner, and then strode out into the night. Not a star or the moon in sight, and a stiff wind from the southwest suggested a storm might be coming this way. The idea made my skin pepper with unease. We'd be heading in that direction.

Out on the open deck, a crew member stepped in front of us, tugging his blue jacket down over his tailored pants. "Excuse me, Sir, Ma'am." He nodded to Haylee and eyed my pack with a frown. "I'm going to have to ask you two to wait inside a bit longer. Once the pilot's finished inside, the helicopter will be taking off again. After it's air bound, you're welcome to come out and check out the landing pad for as long as you'd like."

"Crap," Haylee hissed, shooting me a startled look. "How are you going to pull this one off, Jax?"

"Bonus that the pilot's inside the ship," I said with a grin that didn't sink past my face. How *was* I going to pull this off?

"Sir?" the crew member said, nudging us backward as politely as he could. Must be tough trying to move guests without risking offending them. "Please wait inside. I'll be happy to let you back out in just a few minutes."

"You ready, Haylee?" I asked, my muscles tensing, my heart racing already.

Eyes wide, she gave me a nod. "Give the word, Jax."

"No need to count."

The half-smile she sent my way made my chest ache. Please, let this work.

"Counting's for kiddies," she said.

"Go," I growled.

We rushed forward, and I shouldered past the guy, knocking him to the side. Arms flailing, he emitted a shriek, but I didn't stop. As we ran across the open deck, footsteps thundered behind us. The guy had recovered and was right behind.

Had to hand it to Haylee. When she said she'd be able to run, she meant it. Yeah, her gait wasn't smooth or pretty, but her uneven rocking motion covered the ground quickly.

We took the stairs and rushed toward the chopper.

18

Haylee

J ax was freakin' crazy, and I loved that about him.

Love.

What an epiphany to have at a moment like this!

Maybe I shouldn't have let myself care. While I knew I was more than a good time to him, we hadn't exactly discussed feelings.

We'd have to do that soon.

Once we were sure we'd survive.

"Thought we'd fly out of here," he said as we raced up to the chopper. "Any chance you've flown one before?"

"You're kidding me, right?" Panic burst inside me, and I skidded to a stop. *This* was his plan? "Please tell me you can fly."

"I can."

Fool. He was joking. I hoped.

"Phew," I said. While he yanked open the driver's side door and started climbing inside, I ran around to the passenger side and did the same. My butt smacked onto the vinyl seat, and I yanked the door closed.

A quick glance into the back showed me there was no medical equipment on board, telling me this chopper wasn't being used for a medical emergency. As awesome as Jax's escape plan was, I wouldn't have wanted to steal the ride from someone in grave danger.

No medical equipment on board meant *I* was the one in grave danger.

The ship's crew member hadn't followed us up onto the helo pad. Must've run inside for help, because more crew erupted from the boat, waving their arms and shouting. I had a feeling it wouldn't be long before the pilot appeared, plus whoever the pilot had dropped off.

"Buckle up," Jax said, doing the same.

My fingers scrambled for the belt, and I locked it into place. We put on noise reduction headsets that would let us talk to each other, and I centered my feet on the floor mat and looked around again, taking in the back. Bench seats for passengers said this was a no-frills operation. Probably not VIPs, then, but regular transport.

While Jax fiddled with the stick used to control the helo's forward, backward, and sideways tilts then the collective, which was the emergency brake-like thing on his left side that controlled lift, I did the rest of the usual safety check. I'd flown in quite a few choppers before and this was standard protocol.

Jettison latch to open the exit hatch. Check.

Leaning forward, my fingers encountered the life vest underneath the passenger seat.

No life raft I could see but they might not have one on board.

As crew members rushed toward us from the ship, Jax hit the battery button and then the starter, which engaged the blades.

Whoop-whoop-whoop. Gotta love that sound.

The crew skidded to a stop, their faces displaying a mix of scowls, anger, and shock.

"No time for the usual takeoff procedure," Jax said. "Time to get this baby into the air."

Fear clawed down my spine.

Crap. Crap. Crap.

This was wild and foolish and I shouldn't be having fun with the entire thing, but there it was. As long as no one shot at us, this might actually work.

"Go," I shouted.

Overhead the blades picked up speed, a roaring, grinding sound that chewed through my bones.

"Hold on, sweetheart," Jax said, his knuckles blanching on the stick. It took a delicate touch but he wasn't jerking it.

Three guys ran from the ship, weapons in hand. Shit, we'd been right. The Maestro had sent them to finish me off.

"Guns," I shrieked. "Get us out of here!"

He carefully pulled up the collective and the helicopter jolted up. And up some more, as he carefully maneuvered the stick.

In seconds, we were airborne, hovering over the helo pad.

A popping sound like a stick being poked through foil told me the guys were firing on us.

"Fuck," Jax shouted, cords standing out prominently on his neck. He stared forward, through the windshield. "Hold on!"

We tipped and spun, and the whirling blades sent dirt and random debris flying around us. The guys covered their faces with their arms and backed away from the chopper. It was either that or be hit by the crud stirred up by the blades. Bold of them to keep waving their guns, though. If we were lucky, the ship's security team would confiscate them.

The craft shuddered and tilted left then right, bobbing down before zipping back up into the air.

My belly roiled, telling me it was eager to ditch whatever might still be down there.

"Thought you said you knew how to fly," I said, horror filling me up inside to overflowing. If he didn't get us up and level out, I was going to start hurling. At least we hadn't eaten.

"Simulators are the same thing, right?" he said, his hand carefully maneuvering the stick.

"Holy shit." I latched onto his shoulder as the helicopter dove over the edge of the ship, almost taking out the railing on the way by.

"Maybe don't do that?" he said wryly, tilting his head toward his shoulder.

Wincing, I yanked my hand back and latched onto the oh-shit bar hanging from the ceiling.

Pulling up on the collector, Jax took us higher, away from the water. With light pressure on the right foot pedal, he turned the craft in that direction, then pushed the stick forward.

We flew away from the ship, heading southwest.

"Where would you like to go?" he asked me. "I was thinking Disney."

I reeled around and stared at him. "I thought you had this all worked out."

"I have a few ideas."

"They don't involve the states." If he took us back there, there was a good chance we'd be arrested before we could call Flint and engage Viper Force protection. Whoever was after me would walk into the jail, grab me, and finish me off.

Our best chance was to continue toward Mexico, where we could step into the plans his friend Dwayne had already arranged for us.

"The ship was just a quick getaway," he said. "I had to get us out of Miami, and a cruise ship with fake IDs should've been a great way to hide."

"The Maestro always seems to be one step ahead of us." My gut sank. "Do you think they've got someone inside? Not at Viper Force but maybe someone who works with my father?"

"Hard to say but I know Flint's already going in that direction. Too many coincidences add up to something bigger going on here."

"Mexico it is."

"Dwayne cooked something up that'll make us disappear. Then we can give Flint time to gain control of the situation and bring us home safely." He darted his gaze to the dials then nodded. "We've got to get to a small town on the southeastern side of the Yucatan."

"So, no Cozumel. Can't say I'm disappointed. I wasn't looking forward to the ferry ride to Playa del Carmen. A small ferry with the Maestro one step ahead of us isn't my idea of a fun time."

"Nope. We'll land this baby in an isolated location, walk into town, and hitch a ride from there."

We'd only flown about forty-five minutes before we hit the storm I'd seen from the ship. Like we rode a bucking bronco, wind gusts jerked the chopper in every direction. I white-knuckled the oh-shit bar and braced myself with my legs to keep from slamming into the door or worse, into Jax.

"How much farther?" I shouted. I didn't need to yell. With the headset on, he'd hear me fine. But being rocked and buffeted around with my body yanking on the seat belt made me feel as if I was tied to the bow of a ship, a carved figurehead facing hurricane-force winds.

"A while." He glanced toward the gauges again.

"What aren't you telling me?" I asked, studying the gauges myself, though I couldn't tell what might be his focus.

"Nothin."

"Not buying that, Jax. What's wrong?" I'd never flown before and the only times I'd been in a chopper had been while serving in the military. I'd sat in the back, though it hadn't looked anywhere near as palatial as the squishy seats behind me.

"Fuel," he said.

"We're losing fuel? Did one of those bullets hit the tank?"

"I don't think so. But these things are only good for three hundred or so miles."

"And we've got how far to travel still?"

"Fifty minutes or so."

A bolt of anxiety shot through me. It was mirrored by a flash of lightning to our right. Thunder boomed within moments, telling me the storm was right overhead.

"This thing goes about one-sixty an hour, right?" I asked.

He nodded.

"We're cutting it close." Leaning into the window, I tried to locate land or anything that might tell me where we were. "Have we reached the Yucatan yet?"

"Passed the northern tip about five minutes ago."

"I missed Cancun's lights." I didn't miss Cancun. Nothing against the vacation destination, but I'd lost a friend there and nearly lost my life.

Though I strained, rain drizzling down the window obscured everything else. The ocean was below us, but there wasn't a white cap in sight; we were too high to see them. Or the complete darkness hid them. I could only imagine how furious the sea must be in the storm.

"Shit," Jax hissed.

I whirled around to face him. "What?"

"It's… Crap."

"We're almost out of fuel and we're not there yet, right?"

"You got it."

"I hate being right all the time."

He snorted. "I hate that you're right *this* time. Don't mind all the other times." Reaching out, he tapped the fuel dial, though that wouldn't make a difference. "We're going to have to land."

"But we're not there yet."

"Close."

"How close?"

He growled. "Not close enough."

"So we'll land wherever and get there eventually. We must've lost the Maestro's men by now."

The helicopter shuddered.

"Hold on," Jax said, carefully nudging the collective down. The vehicle followed, and the ocean suddenly appeared below us, a furious mix of swirling tides and crashing waves.

"I don't see land!"

"No time. I thought we had more fuel but…"

The blades seemed to gulp as they lost torque. Like a car sputtering as it ran out of gas, the chopper bucked.

"What are we going to do?" I asked in full-blown horror.

I kept seeing the cliff approaching.

A smack from the SUV behind us sent our tires squealing. Gabe and I shot forward against our seatbelts.

The car roared toward the edge, out of control.

My hands tightened on my seat.

"I can't…" Gabe's hoarse cry echoed in my mind.

We went airborne…

"Gabe!"

"Haylee. Haylee!" Jax's voice broke through the flashback, calling me back to the situation at hand.

We tumbled down the cliffside, the tires slamming into rocks and trees, making us jerk sideways.

Rolling.

Over and over until I couldn't tell which way was up and which way was…

"Haylee." Jax's warm hand stroked my face. "Come back to me, sweetheart. I need you."

I shook my head, ridding myself of the memory for now.

Gabe.

My heart broke all over again, because I'd relived his last moments of life.

"I'm here," I said, hoping he wouldn't call me on the shake in my voice. I needed to put the memory behind and focus on the moment.

"We're going to impact the water soon," Jax said. "I'll do my best to keep us upright."

"Flotation devices on the side will deploy, right?"

"They're required by law, so they should. If they don't do their thing…"

"We'll flip. The blades are the heaviest part of the craft." They'd drag us down before we could escape.

His lips thinned. "Get that life vest out from underneath your seat and put it on."

I yanked mine out then his. In moments, I was clipped into my vest and somehow maneuvering him into his while he kept us aloft.

"I'm bringing it down now," he said as I fastened the last clip on his vest.

We skimmed only forty, fifty feet above the water. Air currents pushed us in one direction then another.

Stats showed that the odds of surviving a helo crash were much better during the daylight hours than at night. With a storm surrounding us, our odds were dropping by the second.

The most frequent cause of death was drowning. Just awesome.

"I'll get us as close to land as I can," he said.

"Where are we?" Dummy. I should read the gauges. They'd show longitude and latitude. But my brain kept spinning away, dragging me back to the scene of the car crash back in Cancun.

"We're south of Cozumel. Not exactly sure how close we are to our original destination, however. We're meeting up with my guy just north of Belize."

"Belize."

"We were heading in that direction."

As he got closer to the water, the vehicle bucked and swayed. Helos weren't known for their gliding capability, which meant we wouldn't have much time to ditch the craft. Then we'd be in the ocean. Warm water would increase our odds of survival, but our best chance of living would come from finding land. People.

Not those directed by the Maestro.

"We'll stay with the chopper," I said as I dragged my vest on and secured it.

"That's... not the best idea."

"You're right." I swiped my sweaty palms across my thighs. My heart was a drum in my throat, stomping out an unsustainable beat. "They'll track us." Should've thought of that, too.

"If we swim, we'll reach land eventually," he said. "We're not that far from shore."

"Too far to make it?"

Silence.

"Jax?"

"Yeah." He swallowed. "I'm sorry. Should've known the fuel would go fast."

"How could you know that?"

"I thought we'd have enough to squeak by. To reach our destination. Hoped so, anyway."

"It'll be okay." It had to be. A primal scream kept rising up in my throat. Stats for our survival kept racing through my mind and our odds were not good.

I braced myself as best I could. There wasn't much to hold onto.

"I'll try to angle it so we land upright, but with the storm, it'll be tough. Get ready to ditch the craft as soon as possible."

"Together."

His gaze—filled with concern—met mine. "I'll be with you."

Our movement slowed as he manipulated the stick to put the vehicle into position. Then he slowly lowered the collective, all while the storm buffeted the chopper.

The water rose up to meet us, an enraged beast made up of huge waves and endless, swirling darkness.

We spun to our right and Jax corrected as best he could with the left pedal. Then with the right, struggling to hold us somewhat steady. But it was a losing battle.

With high gusts from the storm smacking into us, Jax was barely holding on.

The water rushed up toward us, and the wind from the blades added to the churning mass.

Seein' white caps now!

"Hold on," Jax yelled.

We slammed into the ocean, and I was thrust forward. My teeth jarred together and my ribs screamed as the belt snapped, keeping me in place.

A wave crashed over the front of the helicopter, and we bobbed around like a big buoy in rough seas.

The helicopter tumbled to the left.

Why weren't the flotation devices keeping us upright?

As the few things inside the helicopter not tied down flew through the air, Jax's shoulder smacked against the side of the craft.

His head, driven by gravity, impacted with the glass.

We jolted fully onto our side, and I prepared for us to flip over. With the blades in the water, we'd go down fast. We'd need to unbuckle and ditch the chopper as quickly as possible.

But the ride wasn't over. While the ocean grabbed us and flung us around, the flotation equipment kicked in, and the chopper bobbed upright again.

Jax hung limply against the seatbelt, his chin resting on his chest.

He wasn't moving.

"Jax?" I yelled. "Jax!"

19

Jax

Someone called my name, pulling at my consciousness and bringing my mind to the surface.

Water shifted me back and forth, back and forth, as if I sat on a swing or was being rocked in a cradle. A solid, rough thing had clenched itself around my chest. When my body surged up, the…life vest bit into my chin.

"Jax," Haylee said softly from behind me. "Please. Wake up." Her fingertips stroked across my face. "Stay with me. We didn't get a chance. We didn't… Come back. I need… I need to tell you I love you."

I must be asleep. Only in my dreams would Haylee say she loved me.

Her arms, wrapped around my waist, dragged me through the water until my ass hit solid ground. Releasing me, she dropped down and tugged me up onto her lap. Her fingers stroked my forehead, bringing me further awake.

When she choked on a sob, my eyes burst open.

My arms flailed out, and I shuddered. Bright sunshine brought tears to my eyes. A thousand elephants had decided to stampede through my skull, and my left shoulder felt like I'd slammed it into a concrete wall.

What happened rushed through my mind. I'd brought the chopper down into the sea during a storm. I vaguely remembered the helo smacking into the water then flipping toward the left side with me tumbling along with it. My body had hit the door, and the rest was a blur…

Haylee urging me to move… Taking my hand and shouting for me to jump. We'd dropped from the chopper and were submerged in water… Waves crashed over us… I was drowning! The change in temp sent shockwaves blasting through me…

Then swimming… Sort of. Floundering, not knowing which direction was up and where the hell I was. Hell. Yes, I was in hell.

Haylee turned me onto my back. She inflated my vest and supported me with her own body, her arms holding me secure from behind.

"I won't let you go." She'd said those words over and over.

Rough water raged around us…

Then nothing.

"Please, Jax." Her voice cracked. "Come back to me."

Groaning, I rolled off her, falling into water that was probably only a foot deep, but deep enough to submerge my face. I propped myself up on my palms, but a wave hit my back and drove me forward. I came to a rest in a few inches of water and flopped over onto my back.

Haylee rushed over and stood above me, blocking

the sun, thankfully, because my eyeballs kept screaming about the light. "You're awake!"

"Kinda like Snow White, sweetheart." Even though my brains kept trying to dig their way out of my head with a jackhammer, I had a compelling need to reassure her. Make her laugh. "Except… you didn't wake me up with a kiss."

Choking on a sob, she dropped down on top of me and wrapped her arms around my chest. "I was so worried about you. You've been unconscious for hours. I couldn't wake you! All night, while the current dragged us south. The storm ended and then the sun came up and I hauled you here and—"

"Crap. Whoa. Wait. I'm sorry, Haylee." Blinking, I rubbed my face. Gritty sand scratched my cheeks. "I was joking. I wanted to make you smile."

Rising up over me again, she shook her head. Her lips did quirk up, reassuring me somewhat. "If it only took a kiss, I would've given you a thousand." Her salt-encrusted hair hung around her shoulders and her cheeks had pinkened already from the sun. Sand coated the left side of her face and shoulder, and one of her hands had an inch-long cut across the back that still seeped blood. If I could make my body work, I'd get up, find a bandage, and take care of it for her.

"Where are we?" I asked.

She shrugged. "Somewhere. This was the first bit of land I could find. It looked like an island from farther out, but I won't be sure until I do some recon."

I lifted my upper body onto my elbows, groaning when my shoulder and back protested the movement.

She helped me to a sitting position, and I stared around blankly. The ocean rocked against my feet, burying them in fine, powdery-white sand. Ahead of me, waves crested on a reef that Haylee must've dragged us past. Beautiful teal water with darker shadows stretched for as far as my eyes could see.

Paradise on a good day.

Isolation and possible death for us on every other.

Haylee straightened and shoved her hair off her face, then squinted around. "I think we're somewhere off the coast of Belize, but it's hard to tell. After I got you away from the chopper, the current grabbed us and swept us south, which was a blessing as I wasn't sure how far I could swim for both of us, and I wanted to leave the scene before the Maestro's crew arrived."

It would be nice to think rescue teams would've found us first, but the odds suggested whoever was trying to kill us would get there ahead of anyone else to finish us off.

"When the helo tipped, I hit my head." I carefully tested the skin on my left temple. It stung and I had a lump the size of an egg, but the skin was unbroken.

"The blow knocked you out. I was able to wake you enough to get you off the helicopter and into the water. You passed out after that."

I staggered to my feet and when I would've fallen like a baby taking his first step, she grabbed my arm and steadied me.

"Hold on there," she said. "Not so fast. You've got a head injury. You need to take it easy."

"Woman, my skull is harder than concrete."

"Except today," she said placidly. She guided me out of the water and up the beach, and I was glad she hung on to me, because the world kept spinning. Or I was spinning. I had a feeling the problem was me.

She'd brought us to a narrow strip of sand with dense jungle encroaching almost to the water. We moved into the shade of a palm tree, and our sneakers crushed shells and squish-squish-squished as water was pressed from them. More water dribbled off our clothing. We'd have to change.

"My pack!" I whirled around and was relieved to see it sitting above the waterline. "How did you get both me and that out of the chopper?"

"It wasn't easy." She sighed, and her eyes welled with tears again. "Rescuing you was a given. But I knew your bag held all our stuff, and we'd need it no matter where we ended up."

"It's one of those rafting packs. Waterproof."

"And it floats, so it kept us from drowning."

Getting up, I staggered across the sand and latched onto a backpack strap. Rather than lift it, I turned and dragged it up the beach. Haylee hovered beside me like I'd seen nurses do back at the hospital with unsteady patients while walking in the halls. As if she expected me to swan dive onto the sand in front of her. My wobbly knees suggested the chances were pretty good that would happen.

We took off our life vests and tossed them into the vegetation, out of view, then dropped down onto the ground again beneath the palms and scooted backward until only close scrutiny would reveal us.

Haylee snuggled closer to my side and dropped her chin onto my good shoulder. "How's the head?"

"It's been better." My body ached like I'd fallen down a cliff, but this was nothing like what Haylee had gone through in the car crash a little over a month ago. Yet here she was, four weeks out and rescuing me.

She held up fingers. "How many?"

"Two."

Her frown deepened. "Now?"

"One."

Rising up onto her knees, she held my face still and studied my eyes. "Pupils look even. Your speech isn't slurred."

"That's a relief." I tugged away.

She scowled. "Let me finish checking you out."

I stroked my hands along her waist. "You can play doctor with me anytime you want."

"Later," she said, all business. "Any nausea?"

"I'm hungry."

"So, nope." Her sigh bled between us. "We've already seen that your balance is off, but you don't seem confused."

"I'm gonna be okay."

"And I'm gonna keep an eye on you."

"I'm doing the same with you."

The smile she released this time shouted pure relief. "You're back. You're here." Her arms wrapped around my shoulders, and she gave me a quick kiss before leaning back. "We *are* a team, aren't we?"

"Always." My mind could be playing tricks on me, but I swore she'd said she loved me not long ago. Did she? Though I was dying to know, I wasn't sure I dared ask. This wasn't the right time or the right place, not when our lives were in danger.

She settled back on her heels. "As your doctor, I diagnose you with a concussion, and I recommend rest, plenty of fluids, and no strenuous activities, all of which may not be possible, depending on where we've landed. We'll just have to see how this plays out."

The shadow we both feared—a brain hematoma—loomed over us, but we were wise not to name it. By the time I lost consciousness again from something like that, it might be too late. Only a CT could diagnose a bleed, and they were scarcer around here than high rises. I'd have to pray my luck held. And try to take it easy.

Which…wasn't happening.

"Before we do anything else, I'm going to check out our surroundings." Rising to her feet, she brushed sand off her legs. "Like I said, this looked like an island from a distance, but it could connect to a larger land mass on the other side. It's small, but there seemed to be higher elevation in the center."

I might have a concussion, but my mind was still working, plotting out various scenarios. If we'd found ourselves on an island, there might be people living here. Houses. Boats. We could be on our way to the mainland within an hour.

Or we could be stuck here until we could find a way off.

"I'll go with you." I'd started to get up when she pressed down on my shoulders with both hands.

"Rest. I'm not going to do full recon, just check out the general vicinity."

"Don't go too far. I…" I hated that I couldn't be at her side, protecting her. After the horrific accident, she was the injured one, the person who should be sheltered from harm. Yet here I was, down and out, barely unable to defend myself, let alone her.

"It's okay." Her curt nod acknowledged my unspoken thought, and her fingers traced the scar on the thigh where she'd had surgery. "I can't go far on this leg, though it held up to swimming last night and this morning, long enough to get us here. I don't plan to push it, just make sure we're not lounging on a beach two hundred feet away from a nice old couple with a speed boat sitting at the dock in front of their cottage."

"If you find something like that, bring the boat back, okay?"

"You'll hear me coming." She pivoted on her good leg.

I watched as she headed down the beach, taking my heart along with her. Her stride hitched to the point it was painful to watch. Pausing, she bent forward to lift a long piece of driftwood from the sand. Then she rounded a bend using the stick to support her wounded leg.

After she'd disappeared, I dropped down onto the sand and groaned while rubbing the back of my neck. Shit, I hurt all over. And my head wouldn't stop pounding. Haylee was right. I probably had a concussion. If everything I'd read about head injuries was correct, it would take weeks if not months to a year before I'd be back to normal.

Sitting around and waiting for her to return was gonna drive me out of my mind.

While I couldn't do much, I could do a few things for her that she'd welcome when she returned. I got up and, struggling to ignore my pounding head, dug through my pack.

Too much time passed before I caught her movement to my right. Walking much slower and with a heart-wrenching limp. Instead of using her stick to give her a boost, she leaned on it heavily.

I rushed down the beach to meet her. She swayed into me, sweaty, sand-covered, and completely worn out. Still as gorgeous as the day I'd met her but as limp as a strand of spaghetti.

While most people wouldn't call my gesture restful, I lifted her off her feet and into my arms.

"Jax," she whispered as her arms wrapped around my shoulders. "You shouldn't be doing this."

"I don't imagine the physical therapists would think a three, four hour walk in the sand was the best thing for your leg, either, but here we are. Right now, I'm the strong one. Lean on me. Let me help you."

She dropped her head against my chest and sighed. "Sometimes, I do enjoy alpha."

"I'll keep that in mind." I strode up the beach and, reaching the shady spot we'd staked out, I lowered her carefully onto the space blanket I'd taken from my pack. She leaned against a nearby palm tree and crossed her legs.

"I imagine you're thirsty," I said. "Hungry."

"Miles of water surround us, and not a drop to drink." Desperation clung to her voice, and the sound socked me in the gut, reminding me again how tenuous our situation might be. We'd become the wounded taking care of the wounded.

"How about this?" I lifted a plastic container and offered her the rainwater I'd collected inside the jungle and purified with tablets I'd taken from my pack. It wasn't much, only a few cup's worth, but I could get more. "That storm last night was a godsend."

Her eyes widened as she took it from me. "I'm not going to ask how you found this." She drank deeply but stopped before finishing and nudged it back my way. "You, too."

"Already drank some. This is yours."

"Cool." She drained every drop then handed me the container.

"And this?" I held out a protein bar.

She eyed it like a banker would a bar of gold. "We'll share it."

"I've got twenty. Well, eighteen now." This woman had rescued me last night and kept us both afloat, then walked for hours today. Without proper nutrition, she not only wouldn't heal, she'd collapse.

Peeling back the wrapper, she ran her tongue across her upper, chapped lip. "I'm salivating already." She took a big bite and, closing her eyes, moaned while chewing. "This is better than bacon." Her eyes opened. "I know you didn't find this lying on the beach."

"Back in Miami, I gave Dwayne an extensive shopping list but he outdid me, adding things to my pack I couldn't imagine we'd ever need. But I had told him we might be roughing it for a while in Belize."

She finished off the bar and even licked the chocolate off the inside of the wrapper. Carefully folding it, she handed it to me. "Let's not trash the place any more than everyone else already has."

I tucked it into one of the outside pockets of my pack.

Yanking her hair out of the ponytail she'd created while she was gone, she raked loose strands off her face then re-secured it, holding up the scrunch tie before doing so. "Found this during my walk. This is the only time I'll express even a speck of gratitude to the people who dump their shit in the ocean. A lot of it has washed up here."

"I assume you didn't find a sweet old couple with a dock or a power boat."

"Sadly, no. As I suspected, we're on an island. I'd say eight or nine hundred acres total." Squinting, she studied the ocean. Waves lapped the shore, like they'd done a thousand years ago and would do so a thousand years from now. Humans were the transient part of the equation. "No signs of habitation. We must be quite a distance from the mainland, because I didn't find evidence anyone had been here for a long time." Her arm swept out. "This place is gorgeous. A dream vacation destination under any other circumstance."

"Less exciting when we're stranded."

"The only good things about it are the reef, which means fish, the jungle—" Tipping her head back she studied the coconuts suspended above us. "And there appear to be plenty of places to hide."

In addition to a few hiding spots inside the jungle behind us, I'd also noted the coconuts. When ripe, the inside would provide liquid, though too much could give a person the runs. The flesh was rich in minerals and had a high fat content. With coconuts supplementing our diet, we'd be able to make the protein bars last longer.

"You went inland?" I said.

"Not far. Only in enough to get a lay of the land. There are cliffs and hills maybe a couple hundred feet in elevation deeper in the jungle."

I'd only walked a short distance into the dense vegetation, enough to locate water, but since we were stuck here, I'd do a better survey before it got dark. I hadn't wanted to be gone long in case she returned. She'd be frantic if she couldn't find me. Hell, I'd practically gnawed off my nails, worried about her the entire time she was gone.

Tugging my pack up between my parted legs, I unzipped it.

"We won't be writing S.O.S. in the sand," she said.

"It'll draw them right to us. And they'll be searching for us already."

"We'll have to set something up to hide us from thermal imaging," Haylee said, squinting toward the horizon. "I haven't heard a chopper or plane, let alone seen a boat since we left the helo, but it's only a matter of time."

"If we're lucky, we'll see fishing boats passing and

can signal them. Our odds will be best if we can get to Belize, where my friends are waiting." I pulled a small mirror from my pack and tossed it onto the sand by my feet. "This should work if we spot a boat." I added a small set of binoculars.

"Let's not signal the guys who shot at us last night, huh?"

"We'll be very careful not to draw the wrong attention." As best we could. The binoculars would help us identify the good guys from the bad.

She tapped the side of my bag. "What other surprises are you hiding inside there?"

"We can expect drones with infrared, but we can lie underneath this." I pulled out the four pack of camo space blankets and laid it on top of the mirror.

Thermal cameras picked up the heat from a body. If heat couldn't reach the camera, our chances of being seen would drop substantially. We could hide underneath the blanket, but we'd have to be careful not to touch it or our heat would transfer through the material and the cameras would identify the change in temp.

A boulder would also work well but a quick glance around told me we were fresh out of boulders. As would the deep vegetation behind us. The more barriers between us and the camera, the better we'd remain hidden.

"Thanks, Dwayne," she said, flicking the package of blankets with her finger. She nuzzled closer and kissed my jawline.

Even a sweet gesture like this made me come undone.

I pushed aside the pack and cupped her face. Then sunk my lips onto hers, drinking in her heat, her affection.

Had she really told me she loved me?

"Wish I had some of the stuff we were testing at Viper Force," she said as we pulled apart.

I settled back into my spot and continued to rifle through the backpack. "Right now, we have the advantage. You said we floated some distance from the helo?"

"The current caught us, and we drifted for hours. So we're maybe fifteen, twenty miles tops from where the chopper went down."

"Not far enough to hide for long but it's better than bobbing around beside the chopper."

"First thing we should do," she said. "Is set up camp inside the jungle. The more vegetation we have overhead, the better we'll hide. We can come back to the ocean before sunset and look for shellfish." She pulled her t-shirt away from her chest. "I'm sweaty and would love to take a quick swim, too." Standing, she extended her hand to give me a boost.

"Here," I said, handing her the wrist slingshot Dwayne had packed. I'd reassembled the nondescript parts he'd scattered among our possessions. I'd been grateful the weapon made it through security, especially now. The odds were better something like this would pass if it was packed in a checked bag, but cruise ships took security differently than airplanes, where a person wouldn't collect their bag until the trip was over.

"Awesome." She slid it onto her wrist. Stooping down, she selected a stone and placed it in the pouch.

She turned and stood with her legs nicely spaced apart and lifted her arms as if sighting with a bow and arrow. Using her index finger and thumb, she pulled back the pouch. She took a deep breath, then using her chin as the anchor point, released the stone. It smacked into a piece of driftwood lying in the sand about thirty feet away. "Cool." When her gaze met mine, she grinned. "I think I'm falling for Dwayne."

I snorted and rose to my feet. "I'd like to point out that I assembled the slingshot."

She sauntered over to me and traced a finger along my jaw. "And a fine assembly job you did, darlin'."

My arm went around her waist. Yes, we needed to get into the jungle and start building a tiny fortress, but hell, I'd never be able to resist Haylee.

"What else did Dwayne—I mean you…" The smirk she fed me lit me on fire. "Put in that pack for me?"

After a satisfying kiss, I stooped down beside my bag. I pulled out the exercise bands I'd added to the list. "Originally thought these would be great for your PT, but I'm thinkin' there are other uses for them now."

She slid her finger along one of the elastics. "We can make a bow with the bands. And we'll find a way to make arrows."

I held up my jackknife.

"I wouldn't think that could make it through security," she said.

"Surprisingly enough, you're allowed to bring them onboard as long as they're less than four inches long." I peeled back the blade. "This baby barely squeaked by."

"We can make arrows," she breathed.

"Love how you think." Hated that we had to focus on defense before anything else. But we could be stranded for some time, and it never hurt to be prepared for the worst eventuality.

"First up is a shelter." I studied the sky. "It rained last night, and it looks like we'll see more rain tonight."

"Water to collect for drinking, but it's dangerous for us to get wet. During the day, we'll be moving, which will keep us warm but if we're wet all night, we'll be cold and could get sick."

"Which we can't afford to do." Bad enough we were both injured. Adding illness on top of that could be lethal. I hefted my pack onto my back and nudged my head toward the jungle, encouraging Haylee to go ahead of me. "Let's see if we can find a location off the ground to build a shelter." Worst case scenario, we could build on the ground but that would expose us if anyone searched on foot. On the ground, we'd also be more apt to encounter insects. Bad enough the mosquitoes would eat us alive. We didn't need to play with ants or...

Haylee yelped and came to a stop in front of me.

20

Haylee

"If you've got snakes," I said in a tight voice. "I'll wrangle them. I'm the girl to call if you want to be hauled through shark-infested waters. Hell, I'll even dodge assassin's bullets with a smile on my face. Mostly." Shuddering, I stepped backward and bumped into Jax. His arm went around my waist for support. "But I don't do spiders."

"That thing?" he said, moving around me. He nudged it out of our way with the stick he'd collected from the beach. "Only a little tarantula. It won't cause any harm."

Little? It was the size of my palm. "Spiders crawl on you."

"Then flick it off."

"They bite."

"Not any worse than a bee sting."

"I'm not horribly fond of bees, either, but I'll take a hive any day over that beastie."

"She's beautiful." He stooped down to study the

spider. "Leave her alone and she'll do the same. Look…" He pointed. "See? She's already moving away. I imagine she doesn't want us stepping on her."

I grumbled because, okay, I might've been tempted to do that.

"Tarantulas are the least of your worries. Now, Brazilian wandering spiders? They can be lethal."

"Thanks for the tip," I grumbled, my skin flashing with goosebumps. "What do they look like?" So I could avoid them.

"Big," he said, coaxing the tarantula into the bushes. "Leg spans can reach up to six inches."

"Ugh." I backed up another step, my feet sinking into the soft sand.

"They're brown. Hairy. With black spots on their bellies."

"Lethal you said?"

"Only if you're not carrying antivenom."

"Which we don't have."

"Yeah." His gaze shot toward the sea, but when he squinted up at me, I didn't catch even a hint of mocking on his face. "You okay with this?"

This, meaning trooping through a tropical jungle. Like I had a choice? "Yeah. I'm good. Remember? I shot out that tire. Beat off the guy who broke into the room." Sort of. "I'm one tough chick."

"Toughest woman I know." Rising, he strode past the spider as if she was no different than the tiny, benign daddy long-legs I'd encountered back home in Maine. He moved ahead, into the jungle, swiping vegetation aside with the stick. Nice ass. Not that I was watching.

All right, I was.

"You know how it is in the military," I said, watching where I put my feet as I followed. "I've lived in extreme climates, and I've been in situations that would make your hair stand on end." I smirked and jumped up to swipe my hand across the top of his high and tight haircut. "Not you, but everyone else."

He shook his head, but grinned.

"I can handle a few spiders," I said, trying to act brave while also trying not to be spooked by every tiny movement in the vegetation around me. Where there was one tarantula, there could be a whole bunch of them. "Do they run in packs?" I asked.

"Not usually." He glanced around. "Don't worry. I'll slay all your dragons."

"Appreciate it."

"Since our best chance of survival is getting off this island, we'll build our shelter inside the jungle far enough that we're not visible to anyone passing by, yet close enough we can draw the attention of someone friendly."

"We'll spend the days on the beach, watching for those friendly beings."

"Whenever we're not foraging for food."

Which...

"What kind of food might we find here?" I pushed aside a clump of palm fronds and caught up to stand beside him. He studied a cluster of trees then grumbled and moved through the jungle again, staying parallel to the beach. "We might find avocados. Breadfruit if we're lucky, though it's not originally from this region."

"Avocados are yum." Actually, anything edible sounded yum right now.

"Apra might be an option. It's a fruit. There might even be wild oranges or limes here."

"We may not need to go fishing."

"We'll need the protein. You in particular, to heal."

Valid point.

"I thought you could fish tonight, before the sun goes down, while I look around in the jungle. I want to set up a secondary, simpler shelter, plus get a lay of the land."

"And arrange for some booby-traps, I assume." I hated to think we had to worry about anything like that, but it never hurt to be prepared.

"Yeah. In case…"

"They find us." Dread coiled tightly inside me. My skin itched, and it wasn't solely from the pesky mosquitos that kept landing and biting. "I'd like to think we're far enough away from the crash site to make it impossible, but I imagine they'll slowly widen their perimeter."

"I would."

Me, too, which meant our time was limited. "We need to get off this island."

"A raft isn't an option. It's not like we could get away if they came across us."

"Maybe a bunch of beer-toting tourists will stop by on one of those catamaran cruises. We can hitch a ride to the mainland with them."

"While that would be awesome, the odds are slim.

You said you didn't see evidence anyone had been here for a while."

I hadn't other than scattered bits of old campfires. And trash that had washed up on shore.

"So random fishermen are our best hope," I said, my gut sinking. If the island wasn't a tourist destination, what were the odds fishermen came to this part of the sea? "You think we're on anyone's fishing route?"

Jax stopped to study another cluster of trees. "I hope we are."

"Under any other circumstances, I'd love to be stranded on a deserted Caribbean island with you." I could barely inject any humor into my laugh. "Well, I'd enjoy it if we had a cute little cottage to retire to in the evening. You know, running water, squishy bed, screens on the windows, a deck, and plenty of food. Oh, and rum."

He took my hand and tugged me close. "We'll see this through then we'll do that. Promise."

We kissed then moved through the jungle again, keeping the water within sight through the vegetation. To our left, lush, green plants grew in perfusion, what looked like a hothouse of tropical plants gone wild. Multiple varieties of palm, huge ferns, plus vines dangling from trees and snaking along the ground. Cedar, mahogany, and other trees I couldn't identify. And flowers in every color of the rainbow.

"Tell more about this food you hope to find," I said. My rumbling belly chastised me for pushing aside the half-eaten plate of bacon yesterday. I'd almost kill for a buffet right now. Even Jax's anemic, cheese-less omelet would be awesome. "Do you think we'll find bananas? They must grow everywhere here." Silly me for not thinking about them first. I could picture myself peeling back the skin, my teeth sinking into the sweet, soft flesh. How wonderful it would taste. My stomach howled, pissed off at me for teasing.

"The cultivated bananas you buy in the supermarket are the only edible variety." He held a branch out of the way so I could pass by, then caught up, waving away a cluster of mosquitos that had descended the moment we left the sunlight. "Which…isn't completely true. You can eat most any banana, but the ones that grow in the wild are full of seeds and have very little pulp. I imagine you'd need to collect a lot of them to get more than a few bites. Too much work for so little nutritional value."

"All this talk about food has stirred up my appetite."

"I don't know what we'll find on this island, but the odds are good we'll locate something." He glanced up, frowning. "We'll get our shelter built then I'll look around. We need to be under the space blankets and a mesh of palm branch walls tonight to keep us from getting wet." He grinned. "And we'll build off the ground so we're sure we don't have too many critters in our new home." Tipping his head back again, he squinted.

I also looked up, but didn't see much besides leaves, tree branches, and more leaves. "What are you looking for?"

"A good place to set up shop." He pointed to a cluster of trees ahead. "And I think this will do. It's far enough into the jungle we've got cover, yet not far to travel if we hear potential rescue."

"During tours with the military, I've slept on the ground, slept in the back of a pickup truck, and even slept once on a fairly flat roof," I said. "But I've yet to sleep in a treehouse."

"This one won't be far off the ground." He pulled his knife. "It's going to take some time to build a decent structure and there would be no way we could get up high. But we can make something that'll get us away from whatever creeps around on the jungle floor."

Definitely didn't want to go there. "You've built something like this before?"

"Rougher, but yeah." He peered around then stepped forward and sliced through the base of a long palm frond. "I'll gather a bunch of these and shave off the thorns while keeping an eye on the ocean for rescue. Can you collect some downed tree branches? We'll tie them together to make the floor of our shelter. If you lay them out on the ground over there—" He gestured to a flat, relative vegetation-free area. "You'll be able to tell when you've got enough. I'm thinking of a room about the size of a twin bed."

"Twin?"

"California king would be nice but we can snuggle."

"Works for me." Stepping forward, I wrapped my arms around his waist and kissed him. "Twin-sized is more than enough for us. Did you happen to grab those condoms before we ran from the room?"

He tickled my spine, making me laugh. "I have a bunch in my pack. You think we'll need them?"

I stroked his jaw. "I know we'll need them." Turning, I sashayed toward the jungle, knowing he was watching. "You staring at my ass, Chief?"

"All the time, Chief. All the time."

My laughter rang out again, but I stifled it fast. Yes, we were probably safe here for a short time, maybe long enough to find a way off this island, but the Maestro's crew could drive up to the shore or fly overhead within the hour. We needed to remain as quiet as possible.

If they came here, would the Maestro be with them? We didn't know who he was, but Gabe and I had been in Mexico to make contact with someone who hinted they had clues about the identity of the head of the cartel.

My vision wavered…

The person moved forward, leaving the car headlights behind them. The voice… The way the person moved… The clothing…

A man.

If only I could see his face, but it was in shadow…

As fast as it came, the memory spun from my mind. My skin clammy, I took in a deep breath but I couldn't stem the panic rising inside me. It wasn't long after this that we were on the road, racing away from…

I growled as the thought slipped away.

If only I could remember. Whatever I saw that night could be why someone was determined to kill me. He must believe I'll remember and tell. If I was the elusive head of a drug cartel, I'd be desperate to keep my identity secret, too.

Had he been desperate enough to make sure Gabe

died as well? The thought dumped through me, slowing my pace as if my veins had been filled with cement.

"You said…" Not turning, I gulped back tears, struggling to swallow back the pain. "You said Gabe died from his injuries. Someone didn't come after him after they life-flighted him out, did they?"

"You mean like they've been trying to kill you? No. He had bad injuries. He wasn't expected to survive."

Gabe. His loss flooded me with sadness all over again. I was going to miss my friend.

A month ago, in Cancun, someone shoved our vehicle off the road, which made me suspect Gabe and I had learned the true identity of the Maestro. Gabe had died before he could reveal what he knew, but the information remained locked deep inside me.

There had to be a way to force it to the surface. Remembering what happened that night might be our only chance of survival.

I wiped my eyes and struggled for control. Focusing on Gabe wouldn't get this shelter built, now would it? And Gabe would want me to fight to survive. To remember. And to make whoever killed him pay.

So I got to it. I bent down, untangled a long branch from the underbrush, and dragged it back to our camp area.

"You okay?" Jax asked, looking up from the palm branch he held out while he sliced off the thorns. He tossed it onto a small pile he'd started and picked up another.

"Yeah, I'm fine." I wasn't, but we needed to focus on living.

Survival shows on TV made it look easy. Surviving long enough to get off the island might be the biggest challenge Jax and I would face in our lives.

There were plenty of decent-sized branches lying around, courtesy of hurricanes and strong winds. Deadfall was common in a forest and the jungle was essentially a tropical version of the woods back home. With bonus, poisonous spiders and other creepy crawlies I'd rather not think about.

I dragged more branches over and dropped them near where Jax continued to clean palm fronds.

"I assume I'll lash these together with the nylon twine you used to trip the guy on our cruise ship balcony?" I said. "It worked well, by the way. I didn't have a chance to tell you until now. But when he fell, it gave me time to get ready to bash him with a bath bomb."

"I knew you'd appreciate those bombs."

"Sad I didn't get to use all of them. Some smelled pretty."

"I'll buy you a thousand more bombs when we get off this island and somewhere safe."

"Will you sink into the tub with me when it smells like strawberries?"

"I'll sink into a tub with you even if it smells like roses."

I smirked his way. "I'm going to hold you to that promise."

Mosquitos buzzed around us, a cloud of humming pests, and I swore and waved my arms in the air. Like that would do any good. They dive bombed my head the second I stopped waving.

"Try this," Jax said, handing me a small packet containing an insect repellant wipe.

"You sure I can't marry Dwayne?" I said, sighing and moaning as I swiped the stinky bug stuff across my exposed skin.

"Hey! I added these to the list."

"Okay, then, I'll marry you." The joke slipped out before I had a chance to think about how it would sound. My fingers rushed to my lips as if I could pull the words from the air and stuff them back inside my mouth. "Sorry, I—"

"Maybe you should," he said quietly, tugging another palm frond off the ground to de-thorn it.

"Is that a proposal, Mr. Ramsey?" While the words came out sassy, my voice shook because I half meant them.

His fingers stilled on the branch. "While it's early in our relationship, what if I *was* proposing?"

"Then…" I didn't hesitate because I had doubts. I'd been crazy about Jax for months now. I couldn't believe he felt the same. "Is this what you want?"

His gaze met mine, probing as if he hoped to learn all my secrets. I'd share them with him if he asked.

"What if it is?" he said softly.

"Then I'd say yes," I croaked out. *Way to lay your heart on the line, Haylee.*

He blinked. "Really?"

Dropping the two branches I'd dragged out from the

bushes, I strode up to him, not stopping until our chests bumped together. "Really, really."

His hands braced my forearms. "Fuck."

My laughter burst out. "Now? Thought you wanted to make that twin bed out of branches first?"

"Haylee."

I tilted my head. "Yeah, Jax?"

"I love you."

Tears sprang up in my eyes. What was it with this guy? Whenever I thought I'd figured him out, he surprised me all over again.

"Jax," I sighed.

He tugged me close and wrapped his arms around me. "No pressure. If you want, I can say I was just joking."

"You just kind of sort of proposed to me and now you're playing takesy backsies with your heart?"

"No taking it back. It's yours for as long as you want it."

So, my chest was going to explode. Holding my emotions inside had been killing me. "Jax. You're…" I grinned through my tears.

"I take it you're okay with that?"

Unable to say a damn thing, I nodded.

"Never thought my feelings would grow to this or that I'd be able to tell you how I felt. It's been building for a long time." He stared down at the palm branches lying on the ground. "I haven't said that to anyone since my mom passed."

Now I was really going to cry. All this time, he'd held himself back and protected his heart. He held it out to me, cupped in his hands, a fragile part of himself I never wanted to shatter.

"I love you, too, Jax. Never thought I'd have the chance to say it, either."

"So, did you fall for my natural charm once we were on the ship?"

"Fell for your natural charm ages ago."

"When you were sayin' my butt didn't have enough beef?"

My laughter spurted out. "I did say that, didn't I?" While working out one day. He was wearing snug shorts and one of those normally icky wife-beater tees that on him, looked awesome.

His lips quirked up. "Hurt my poor old feelings. I went home and cried in my pillow."

"Your butt is beefy enough." Sliding my arms around him, I grabbed it. "But to be sure, you might need to model it for me later."

"My turn for a tease?"

I couldn't imagine how much I'd enjoy watching Jax sway while pulling off his clothing.

"We're going to have a lot of date nights lined up for when we get home. Strawberry bath bomb and now a strip tease. I can't wait."

He tugged me closer. "We're gonna get off this island, Haylee." I loved that there wasn't a hint of doubt in his voice. "We're gonna have those dates and a thousand more." He tipped my chin up and kissed me, a slow, deep kiss that felt filled with promise and everything inside him. I drank it in, held it close, then sent it back to him tenfold. "I won't let anyone stop it from happening. We may be trapped like bugs in a jar, but it won't be for long."

"We're a team. We'll protect each other, fight for each other. We'll watch for rescue because the Maestro won't be the only one looking for us. Helicopters don't go down in the ocean without governments finding out. The Maestro won't be able to brush this accident underneath the carpet. And if not the coast guard, a fishermen will come by and see our signal. We'll get to Belize and disappear until Flint can get us home safely."

"And then we'll be together."

"We're together starting now and for always."

He kissed me, long and deep, his hands warm on my back, his body pressing against mine. I wanted him more than I had on the ship. Knowing he loved me made this purer. Sweeter. Sexier. I refused to let life bring us this close to perfection only to rip us apart.

"Let's get this shelter built. And then set things up so, when it rains, we collect as much water as possible. Then you can go fishing." He smiled. "While you clean the fish, I'll forage and set a few things up in the forest."

"What if I want you to clean the fish while I forage and set things up in the forest?"

"Then that's how it'll be."

"I actually don't mind cleaning fish."

"Anything but spiders."

"You got it."

We pulled apart, and I returned to hauling branches while he continued to de-thorn palms.

Once I'd collected enough, I lashed them together. Then Jax showed me what he was made of.

"How the hell did you do that?" I stared up at him, scratching my head. With barely any effort, and only a piece of rope, he'd shimmied up a tree and now stood on a broad branch about ten feet off the ground, staring down at me.

"I loved climbing trees when I was a kid."

"This is more than random tree climbing," I said in complete amazement. "This skill is going to come in handy when we want coconuts."

"Before Mom died, I competed in a few tree climbing events. Even won a few times."

Hands on my hips, I shook my head. "Such a thing exists?"

"It's cool. Fun." He tossed down one end of a rope. "Tie our platform onto this and I'll hoist it up."

"And do what with it?"

"Lash it down, add trusses to make a simple roof structure that I'll cover with space blankets. And then I'll use the palms for walls. This location is inside the jungle enough no one will know we're here unless they look up while walking past."

"So, um, I haven't competed in any tree climbing events," I said. "While I was decent on the climbing wall back in the military, I'm not sure that skill will come in handy in the jungle. How am I supposed to climb the tree?"

"We'll get you up here. No worries."

To say I was skeptical was an understatement, but I trusted Jax. If there was a way up, he'd show me.

In no time, he'd lifted the floor I'd made of branches lashed together, then added the roof and walls.

Watching him work—so at home in this environment while I floundered—was more fascinating than the time I'd binge-watched an entire tree house construction series. While Jax's treehouse wasn't as fancy, it would serve its purpose: protect us from the elements, get us up off the ground and away from both predators and creepy crawlies, and hide us from view.

After securing the space blanket roof and walls, he leaned out the front of the structure. "Want to come up and check it out? It's awesome. Cable should be installed by dinner, and I bet we can catch a football game on the big screen."

"Ha ha." I propped a hand on my hip. "I'm more interested in the kitchen. Is the propane hooked up to the cooktop yet? And I hope the hot tub's coming up to temp. I plan on lounging around in the water tonight."

He shimmied down the tree as easily as he'd ascended earlier. I still didn't get it. There were no handholds. Nothing for his feet to grab onto.

"Watch this," he said. He wrapped a braided piece of the nylon cord around the tree, leaving a long piece with preset loops dangling, then added another higher up on the tree.

He stepped into the lowest loop and used the next loop to climb higher, keeping the upper braided piece in hand. Once standing suspended on the upper loop, he moved the top section up and then inched up the bottom section.

"I can appreciate the concept," I said. "But I can't see how this will help us get into the treehouse quickly."

"Wait and see," he said.

Once he reached the top, he poked his head out of the opening again. "Your turn."

"But you have the pieces of cord up there with you."

"How about this, then?" A simply made rope ladder fell from the treehouse and dropped in front of me.

"Dwayne?" I said with a smirk.

"Me, sweetheart."

I latched onto the ladder. "I thought I was the queen of tease but you had me there for a minute."

"The way I showed you works when you don't have a ladder, but you're right, we need a quick way up to our house. I made this earlier."

"So much for resting from that head injury."

"We can rest when we're home."

It didn't take me long to reach the top. Jax inched backward on his knees, deeper into the treehouse, while I climbed inside with him.

"Cozy," I said, looking around.

My branch "raft" made up the floor, more branches had been set up in an A-frame design as roof trusses, covered with space blanket, and he'd tied palm fronds along the front and back. Simple yet effective. "This'll keep out the rain."

"And hide us from overhead drones."

"I'll make the bed while you make nachos."

He chuckled. "I wish we could have nachos."

"I wish we could have a bed. A nice big squishy one with soft sheets and fluffy blankets."

Taking my hands, he lay back on the rough surface and tugged me down on top of him. "You can lay on me all night, if you want."

"Your poor back." I could only imagine how "fun" it was going to be lying on sticks all night.

"We can put our clothing underneath us. That'll help a bit."

"Any plants or leaves we can use?"

"Probably not." He winced. "Bugs."

"Let's avoid bugs."

Because I could and I wanted to, I dropped down to lie fully on him. "This'll be okay."

"Easy for you to say. You're on top."

"You know what I mean."

He nodded. "Give me a kiss and then we can go fishing."

The kiss turned steamy but we both know we couldn't make it last, let alone do anything else. My question about condoms had been a joke. I doubted we'd dare lose ourselves in each other when we needed to focus on our surroundings.

After removing a few things from his pack and leaving them in our treehouse, he brought his pack down to the ground, where he suspended it from a piece of nylon twine he'd tied to our treehouse, I assumed to keep insects from getting inside.

I joined him with my wrist slingshot in hand, and we walked the short distance out to the beach.

"No one out there so far," I said, shielding my eyes with my hand while I watched for movement. Other than waves cresting the reef and smaller ones lapping against the shore, teal blue water stretched endlessly toward the horizon.

"A nice old fisherman coasting by in his boat would be too much to ask for, right?"

"Nothing about this adventure has been easy."

"Except me." He grinned. "Where you're concerned, I'm easy."

"Make that two of us."

"Have you ever fished with a slingshot?"

"I've gone deep sea fishing a few times, and I've been known to toss a line into a brook or two back home, but with this baby?" I held it up. "First time for everything."

"You're our best shot, so I'm going to leave that part of dinner to you."

"You go lounge in the shade. You need to rest." I frowned. "How's the head, by the way?" I hated that he had to work so hard in the heat when he should be doing nothing. But if we both didn't put full effort into our survival, our odds would drop substantially.

"While I'd love to kick up my feet and take a siesta, I've got other plans." He glanced over his shoulder, toward the jungle. "I'll be in the jungle for a while."

"I assume I need to watch for the usual stuff out there. Jellyfish, rays, sea urchins. I'll wear my sandals. Not the best protection but I need to keep my sneakers dry."

He strolled down to the shore, and I followed.

"Best way to see if there's a jellyfish threat is to look for them at the waterline. If they're hanging around, some wash up on the shore." He stooped down and pointed. "See this baby? Moon jellyfish. Mostly harmless."

"Mostly." I stared at the gelatinous creature lying dead just above the water line.

"Not all jellyfish sting. Although, the Portuguese man-of-war has been known to kill humans. They're rare, though. Doubt you'll see one here."

"And what variety of fish should I look for? I'm used to hauling in trout, mackerel, and bigger ocean varieties those few times I went deep sea fishing."

"A trunkfish looks kind of like a flounder only with leopard spots and bulging eyes. Another good one to catch would be a red hind, which is a regular sized fish. It's a pinkish color. Lots of fish near the reef. I think you'll find it easy to collect a few. Mackerel are common, too, though greasier. Snapper, of course."

"Sounds good. I imagine I'll find something. Hopefully soon."

His gaze drifted toward the sky. "Yup. Still looks like rain tonight."

"Do you have more than the one container to collect water?"

"I have four. I'll set them up tonight plus I can suspend a space blanket for a larger collection area. They're waterproof."

"Will anyone see it from shore?"

"I'll put it in an open area deep in the jungle, suspended up in the air if possible."

I stripped down to my underwear and draped my clothing across a branch, hoping that would keep the beasties away from it.

Jax's low whistle rang out. He stalked over to me,

stroked my hair off my shoulder, trailed his fingertips down my face to my chin. "You're gorgeous."

"Thought you had to go play Tarzan in the jungle?" My voice came out low and husky, like it did whenever he came near. Would I always feel this way?

I had a feeling I would.

"I do, but I can't resist touching you."

"You go do your thing." I nudged him toward the jungle and strapped on the wrist slingshot. "I'll go do mine."

He tapped my ass as I walked away.

"None of that foreplay, Jax," I teased over my shoulder.

Grinning, he headed into the jungle.

Stooping down, I collected a bunch of smooth rocks then splashed into the water, smiling when I heard Jax whistle again.

I slowed my pace, taking care where I put my feet, moving through the clear, blue water until it reached the bottom of my thighs. To think I'd pulled Jax past the largest part of the reef last night.

Was it just last night? It felt like days ago.

I spotted a lot of coral and more fish than I'd seen in my life. And jellyfish swishy-floating on the current, but I left them alone and they did the same. No need to get stung today.

When I got close to the reef, I placed my feet in a sandy area and waited. The sun poured down on me, making me sweat. If I caught a bunch of fish fast, I could put them up on the shore and swim. The water felt warm and salty-buoyant and I couldn't wait to submerge myself in it.

I also kept my eyes and ears wide open. If someone came by, I'd slink low in the water and watch to see if they were friend or foe. So far, I heard nothing.

Jax was right, this area teemed with fish. Ah! A red snapper. I carefully pulled back the pouch. Aiming at the fish, I released the stone.

Missed.

Some sharpshooter I was. But that was with a gun on a range. Shooting rocks with a slingshot through water was a completely different animal.

Fortunately, I hadn't scared the fish away. They seemed curious about me and ventured closer.

My next shot hit closer. Still missed the fish, but at this rate, I'd have food for us in a week or so.

I shot more stones, each making fish dart away only to have them replaced by others.

A grayish fish that looked like a flounder only a bit fatter, floated near, curious like all the others. I pulled back the stone in my pouch and sighted along the side of the slingshot.

Careful breath in. Hold my hand steady. Snap. I released the stone and it flew through the water and smacked into the fish's head.

Stunned, it floated sideways, its fins no longer propelling it through the water. I reached down and grabbed it.

I killed another then took the fish up to the shore.

After locating a decent-sized piece of beach glass, I

broke a new edge on it since the rest had been worn smooth by sand and time.

After descaling the fish, I washed them and used my improvised knife to gut them, rinsing them again in the water. I took the fish up the beach and after finding driftwood sticks, I speared the fish and stuffed the other end into the sand to keep them up off the ground.

Then I walked back to the water and submerged myself.

I floated on my back, savoring the warm water, the sunshine, the completely relaxing moment.

I'd turned over and was about to start paddling back to shore when I heard a boat motor grinding this way.

21

Jax

After locating and/or enlarging a few hiding spots, plus building a second platform—this one high in the canopy, hidden among the upper branches—I pulled the bag of goodies I'd asked Dwayne to pick up for me from my pack.

I couldn't be gone long from shore, but I did need to get a lay of the land and set up some simple traps we could use in a pinch. It never hurt to be prepared.

Best part about hiking around was I'd found food to supplement our dinner. We'd avoid eating the protein bars for as long as possible, saving them for times when we couldn't forage or we got desperate.

I returned to the beach to find Haylee crouched in the bushes, staring toward the sea.

"Boat," she said softly. "Gone now. I don't know if they'll come back again." Her breath shuddered from her lungs. "It was them."

Putting my arm around her shoulders, I squeezed in support. "How many?"

"Four men. The two who fired on the chopper, the one you threw off the deck, plus someone I didn't recognize from here. Tall." She shook her head. "Average build. He had a hat on so I couldn't pin down his features."

"Doesn't matter unless they come back and investigate the island. There are plenty of places we could be hiding in this area, which means they'll spend a lot of time investigating without finding anything. With luck, they won't be back."

"We'll see. Luck never seems to be on our side."

I studied the water for a long time, watching and listening. The fact that they hadn't returned was a good sign, but I'd keep my eyes and ears wide open.

Who needed to sleep?

She straightened and gave me a smile while lifting two sticks. "Look what I caught."

"Two trunkfish? Decent sized, too."

"I was feeling pretty cocky until the boat came along." Her shoulders slumped. "I'd gone swimming and was lounging in the water, pretending it was a giant bathtub. Now, I'm afraid again. I'd hoped…"

"Yeah, me, too. But we're alive. The odds are good a fishing boat will come by. And I found this." I held up my bag.

She leaned the sticks against a tree, keeping the fish from touching anything and, frowning, came closer. "Any chance there's bacon in there?"

I snorted. "I wish!"

Her lips pursed. "It's not healthy, per our conversation at breakfast."

"At the moment, even I'd eat a plate full of bacon." I opened the bag and pulled something out. "Plantain."

"Looks like a banana but not. They're starchy, right?"

"We'll sauté them with your fish."

She tilted her head. "How are we going to sauté them?" Her finger rose. "Wait. I know. Dwayne, my new hero, included a frying pan in the never-ending treasure trove pack I'm thankful I rescued from the chopper."

I did love how she teased. "I put the frying pan on the list."

Walking right up to me, she put her arms around my waist. "Then I owe *you* my thanks."

Just like that, my body overheated. I ditched the plantains and my bag and, arms around her, tugged her closer for a kiss. Definitely needed to find safe alone time with her soon.

We pulled apart, both knowing we couldn't take this further.

"Once the sun goes down and we're sure there won't be anyone passing by we can hitch a ride from, I've picked out a good spot for a fire."

Her nod shouted approval. "Lots of vegetation above to dissipate the smoke."

"Exactly."

We set up our rain collectors and stretched out the two remaining space blankets, tying them to bushes with pieces of twine.

Please, let it rain. My mouth was drier than a paper towel.

There was no way I'd complain about my thirst,

because sharing it would only make it worse. And while Haylee would be sympathetic, there wasn't a damn thing she could do about it. If she was like me, knowing the other person needed something would only make me try harder to fix the problem.

I climbed a palm tree and knocked down two coconuts. The sweet liquid inside helped quench our thirst, but it sure wasn't easy to extract. I'd bored holes then we tipped it up and it trickled into our mouths. It was a hell of a lot of work for only a cup of liquid.

We lounged on the beach underneath a cluster of palms, enjoying the gorgeous view surrounding us. It was hard to feel upset with a crystal clear, tropical ocean view and your feet buried in powdery white sand. All that was missing was a lounge chair, a good book, and a mug full of beer. And people who weren't trying to kill you.

The sun dropped below the horizon, taking some of the day's heat along with it. Sadly, no fishing or tourist boats passed our location.

Before it got too dark, we worked our way deeper into the jungle, heading roughly in the direction I'd come from earlier. I purposefully didn't go the same way, not wanting to stomp down too much vegetation that would suggest anyone was on the island if the guys came back and did a cursory search. Wouldn't want to leave an obvious trail that would lead them right to us, either.

I'd set things up earlier, wanting to make as cozy a place as possible for Haylee. When we reached the area where we could prepare our food, I propped my flashlight in the crook of a tree to give us a bit of light.

Couldn't risk using much, but there was no reason to stumble around in the dark.

Haylee was scared, with good reason. She'd been horribly hurt. Who could blame her for being afraid, especially after seeing the same guys who'd tried to kill her on the cruise ship passing close by, looking for us?

"Aww," she said when she saw what I'd done. She turned to me, and tears shimmered in her eyes. "You did this?"

"I'd do anything for you, Haylee. You know that, right?"

She leaned into me. "Yeah. I do. And I'd do the same. You know that, right?"

My heart felt squished against my ribs. "Yeah." My voice was husky. I couldn't contain my emotion, and I no longer wanted to try. I'd give her everything if she asked.

"I'm sorry I keep crying," she said as she swiped at her eyes.

"Why?"

"Because…I can't help it. It spills out of me, and I hate it because it means I'm weak."

"It's not a sign of weakness."

"It is," she huffed then pointed to her face. "Look. I'm at it again. They keep falling, no matter what I do! I'm messed up, Jax. The accident, Gabe dying, all this…" Her hand flicked to the general area but I knew she didn't mean the island or what I'd arranged to please her. She meant life and how it had dragged her down. "It broke me. I'll never be able to patch myself together again."

"You're not broken." I gathered her into my arms, wishing I could take on this burden for her. I'd do anything to make her feel more secure. "You're stronger than you've ever been."

"Not if I snap all the time. It's a flaw."

"It's a strength. I don't think I could've gone through what you have with the same grace. You amaze me all the time. Look at you." I waved to her body in general. "A little over a month ago, you were lying in a hospital bed, fresh post-op, and we were worried you'd never wake up. Now you're like an Amazonian from a legend."

"I guess you can say I'm Jane."

I frowned.

"You Tarzan, me Jane?"

My laughter snorted out. "I think you're the real Tarzan, sweetheart. You're the hero of this story."

She pressed her forehead against my chest and sighed. "Thanks."

I rested my chin on the top of her head. "Anytime."

Pulling away, she glanced around the tiny clearing. "I can't believe you did this for me."

I'd set up a tiny circle for our fire and dragged downed logs into the clearing to create a bench. And flowers. Women liked flowers, didn't they? I'd collected some for her, because I'd wanted to see her smile. I wanted to make her happy.

Earlier, I'd scraped a small pit into the ground that I'd rebury later. I leaned over the wood and dried leaves I'd placed in the depression, and lit it on fire. We soon had a tiny blaze crackling. That little bit of civilization brought warmth to my soul.

"It's the little things that make all the difference, isn't it?" Haylee said softly.

"Some people take things like a home or a secure place to rest your head for granted."

She put her arm around my back. "It's cheery. For as long as there have been people, a fire has meant safety. Protection from wild animals. A way to cook food. And a beacon in the darkness."

"Tonight, it'll bring us a bit of comfort. So we can face whatever comes tomorrow."

"Good idea. Focus on the moment, not on what ifs."

"Exactly. Have a seat. I'm playing chef tonight."

"Do you know how to cook?" Pure tease came through in her voice.

"I'll have you know that I once took a cooking class."

Her nose crinkled as she sat on the log. "Did you burn everything?"

"Only the water."

Rounding the fire, I offered her a plastic container, bowing low. "Wine, my dear?"

She took it like an old lady with a china teacup. "Thank you, kind sir."

"I found a tiny source of water in a cave partway up a cliff on the other side of the island, collected some, and purified it."

"Despite all my joking around, I know I have you to thank for all this, not Dwayne. You've been awesome." Blinking fast, she focused on the tiny flames licking around the branches. They crackled and popped. "I don't know what I would've done without you here with me."

"You would've survived. Fought them off if necessary. And taken back your life."

Her chin lifted. "You're right. That's what I meant. I… Sometimes, I feel as if I've lost everything."

"You haven't lost me." I knelt down in front of her and took her hands into my own. I'm here. I'll always be here for you."

"Jax." She stroked my face, now gone bristly. I hadn't thought to ask Dwayne to pack razors, and the ones I'd bought at the box store were still in the cruise ship bathroom. "I'm crazy about you."

"Feel the same, sweetheart."

Her belly growled, making us both laugh.

"How about I get that dinner going?" I said, straightening. "Someone I know caught us a couple of fish."

"And cleaned them, too."

"Perfectly cleaned. I'll get them going."

I pulled out the small frying pan and set it over the fire. After adding milk from a coconut plus a few small chunks of ginger root—I'd been lucky to find that—I cut up the fish and tossed it in with chunks of plantain. Simple, but the meal should taste wonderful, with a Thai flair. Even dirt would taste good when we'd eaten barely anything for twenty-four hours.

Once the food was cooked, I slid the pan off the fire and, sitting next to Haylee on the log, I dropped the pan onto the relatively flat surface between us.

"So, I don't have any plates or silverware," I said. "We can blame Dwayne for that."

The smile she rewarded me with almost made this worthwhile. "We'll eat with our fingers. It smells so good!"

We dug in and ate every bit within minutes.

"I thought two fish would be more than enough," she said forlornly, staring at the pan as if she'd like to lick it clean.

"We can catch more tomorrow. There's a reef full of them out there."

Her mood dimmed. "If they don't come back."

"We're gonna get out of this safe, Haylee. I promise."

Her fingers trailed down my cheek. "And I promise I'll do all I can to help make it happen. I know I can't keep up with you in the jungle. That's why you've been handling most of this on your own. But know I'm here to do whatever's needed."

"We make a great team." I grinned. "Believe me. I'll need help with some of this."

"Name it, and I'm there."

"I will. Hey, I almost forgot dessert!" Reaching into my bag, I pulled out an orange and dropped it into her waiting hands.

She cupped it to her chest and sighed. "It's beautiful. Where did you find it?"

"Went to the local grocery store and bought a bunch."

"Ha. But really."

"Found a scraggly tree, growing wild. We've got

enough fruit, fish, coconuts, and plantains to last for weeks, but I imagine we'll get sick of them."

"Not for a few days, at least. Hunger makes everything taste awesome, my grandmother always says."

I smiled, and I imagined it held a touch of sadness. "My mom always said the same thing."

"Good woman, your mom."

"The best."

She peeled the orange and split it into two halves, handing one to me. "I can't wait to try it. I've never had a freshly picked orange before. They don't grow in Maine."

It tasted heavenly, but I had a feeling even dry toast would taste awesome as long as I got to eat it with Haylee.

Sadly, our evening had to end when it had barely gotten started.

"I have to put the fire out," I said after we'd buried the orange peels beneath some damp leaves.

"I understand. We can't risk keeping it going for long."

I knelt down beside it and pushed sand I'd collected over the flames, snuffing them and our cheery evening out with a few strokes. It hurt, because the fire had made me feel better, too.

She stood and placed her hand on my shoulder. "We still have each other." This woman could read my mind and tug away the ache I'd been trying to hide.

"I'll clean the pan tomorrow morning with some sand and ocean water." I reached up into the tree and collected my flashlight. "You ready to get some sleep?"

She waved in the direction of the shelter. "Lead on. I can't wait to try out our bed of sticks."

Taking her hand, I guided her toward the sea. The crashing waves called to something deep inside me.

Yes, our situation was tenuous. We might not live beyond tonight. But like the ocean, my love for Haylee was endless. Timeless.

I'd cling to each moment as if it was my last.

22

Haylee

One thousand elbows were digging into my body.

Such was the rustic life. It was anyone's guess if we'd get much sleep tonight. Yes, I'd roughed it before, especially while serving in the military. I'd even gone camping a few times. But lying on lashed-together branches took rustic to the limit and beyond, even if we did cover it with a space blanket.

Waves rippled on the shore nearby and around us, the jungle had come to life. A symphony of insects chirped, and the air rippled with the croaks of frogs. Bird calls were punctuated by cries of small creatures. The wind stirred, rustling leaves overhead. And a storm approached, heralded by claps of thunder that gradually grew closer together and louder. Taps of rain danced on the leaves, soon giving way to a steady drizzle. Hopefully we'd wake to find we'd collected gallons of water. I'd just about kill for a tall, icy glass of tea. With or without lemon.

I couldn't stop thinking about how Jax had held me

earlier, how he'd comforted me near the campfire. He'd cooked for me, something no guy had ever done before. With each gesture he made, I fell more in love with him.

Some might call me silly, but I was worried about what tomorrow would bring. And the day after that. Everyone faced their mortality at one time or another, but few had to deal with someone trying to kill them on a regular basis. For all I knew, I might only have a few hours left to live.

Why waste these precious moments?

"I want you, Jax," I whispered.

"You've got me."

His voice came out gruff, as if he'd been asleep, but I'd known by the way he'd been shifting around—and from his respirations—he was awake.

"I want sex with you, I mean," I said. "Like, now." No one would ever accuse me of not speaking my mind.

He rolled over to face me. "Haylee." My name came out like a sigh.

We'd turned off the flashlight long before reaching the edge of the jungle. Even a tiny light could be seen for miles, especially if it was the only light on what was supposed to be a deserted island. The starless night had swallowed everything and being inside our windowless hut didn't help the lighting situation. If I wanted to see his expression, I'd need to use braille.

"We shouldn't," he finally said.

Shouldn't held more possibilities than *can't*.

"I imagine you think we need to be hypervigilant all night," I said. I mean, I understood why. The Maestro and his henchmen could be pulling up to the shore this minute. They'd hop off the boat and troop into the jungle with huge flashlights and endless weapons. We needed to be alert and ready to run.

"We can't risk being distracted," he said.

Turning his way, I rose up onto my elbow. "I get it. We also need sleep."

When I traced my finger down his jawline to his neck and then slid it along the skin above the neck of his tee, he muffled a groan.

"Yeah," he croaked.

"I also imagine you're wondering who would have to be on the bottom."

His snort of laughter rang out. At least I could make him smile.

"The thing is, this could be our last night together." This was practical, not maudlin. "I… I'm sorry." My voice cracked and my eyes watered. Again. But Jax was right, crying wasn't a sign of weakness. It meant I was strong enough to not only feel emotion but show it.

I loved him. And I wanted to be with him. I didn't want to think about what tomorrow could bring. I only wanted to live for this moment. To know that even for one tiny fraction of a second, we were safe with each other.

"You know I'll do anything for you," he said, his voice low and deep.

"I won't twist your arm, because you're right. We need to be cautious. On alert."

"I imagine…" He chuckled, using my go-to word. "I *imagine* we'd be safe for a little while. Dawn won't come for hours and someone would be foolish to try to take a boat across a reef in the dark. If they plan to approach the island, they'll wait until morning."

"I promise I won't scream."

"What if I like making you scream?"

Sitting up, I yanked off my t-shirt then shimmied out of my shorts.

"Haylee," he said, rising up onto his knees.

"I don't mind taking the bottom."

He tugged off his clothing. "I feel kinda bad."

"Why?"

"I promised you a strip tease."

There was no holding back my grin. "I'll take a rain check."

"You can have a couple hundred of them if you want."

"Deal."

"If you can bear lying down for a short while, I have a few things I'd like to do to your body."

Hell, yeah. I'd lie on hot coals for that.

A ruffling sound suggested he was spreading out his tee and shorts. It was followed by a pat-pat. "Right here, sweetheart. Let me show you how much you mean to me."

I dropped down onto my back, and he rose over me. His mouth met mine with a kiss that seared his name onto my soul. I sighed with pleasure, and he captured the sound and returned the feeling tenfold. His tongue met mine. Groaning, his palm—rough yet tender—stroked my side, my hip, and down my thigh.

I parted my legs to welcome his touch, and his

fingertips teased near where I wanted him most, before sliding up to my belly.

Leaving me gasping, his lips trailed down my neck to my chest while his hand stroked closer and closer again, but never quite touching where I needed.

"Jax," I panted. "Stop teasing."

"But you love to tease. And you do it so well." His tongue stroked across my nipple, and I released a high-pitched shriek. Insects that had been humming outside our shelter stilled before resuming their nighttime symphony.

"Like that, sweetheart."

"This is torture," I said with a moan.

"Can't be torture when I promise you complete satisfaction." Humor rang out in his voice. He took my nipple into his mouth and sucked while his other hand rolled the other nipple.

I bucked and thrust up my hips. "Cocky, aren't you?"

He lifted his head. "You like that about me."

"I do." Did I ever.

"And you like my alpha tendencies." His fingers slid down my belly to my thigh then down between my legs.

Close but not touching.

"Jax!"

"You want this, Haylee?" His palm cupped me then his finger stroked up my folds, stopping at the top to rub.

Another small shriek burst from my mouth.

"Thought you promised not to scream?" he said, full-on mocking.

He was so going to get it.

When his thumb slid inside me, I thrust up to meet him, driving him solidly inside.

"Yes, yes," I panted. "More."

"Like this?" He slid two fingers inside me all while rubbing at the top. Sucking my nipple inside his mouth, he pumped his fingers into me, going faster as I rose up to meet him.

I was gonna…

"Jax!"

"Yeah, sweetheart?"

"Now!"

"You want me?"

"Jax," I moaned.

His fingers slid out of me, leaving me wanting, and he dropped down onto the floor beside me. "Climb on. I'll be on the bottom."

Not so fast. While I was eager to sink down on top of him, two could play the teasing game. And, like he said, I did it so well. I just hadn't tried this form of teasing on him yet.

I did want to make tonight memorable.

Climbing over him, I spread my legs wide, straddling his belly, then kissed him.

His hands rose to cup my breasts and he pinched the nipples. It was all I could do not to impale myself on him. But, no. I wanted to tease him, right?

Hell, I was the one being teased.

Leaving his lips, I kissed down his chest, backing myself down his body until I could take him into my mouth.

He bucked upward and fisted my hair, holding me in place, not yanking me away. "Fuck. Haylee. Fuck."

"You like?" I asked before sucking him inside again. I ran my tongue from the tip to the base then back again, taking as much of him as I could.

Writhing on the floor, he groaned while pumping up to meet my mouth. "Fuck. Fuck. Fuck."

I released him with a pop but massaged with my hand while rising over him again. "Either I've stolen all your words except one or you're giving me a directive."

After sliding on a condom, he lifted my hips up and placed me over his cock. "Fuck me, Haylee."

"Oh, I intend to." I drove myself down onto him.

We both moaned.

"Yes, like that," he said, helping when I lifted up and dropped back down again. "Faster, sweetheart. Fuck me."

I'd never thought I could be turned on by a guy shouting for me to fuck him, but when Jax groaned it out, it was beyond erotic. I loved how he lost control, that I could drive him to the edge. But I needed him slamming into me, something my injured leg couldn't handle.

"If there was a wall, I'd wrap myself around you," I said. "But I don't think your pretty palm fronds could handle our action." Rising up and off him, I lowered myself to the floor. "Would you mind…"

"Hell. I'm sorry. Wasn't thinking. Shoulda realized I was causing you pain."

"The only pain I'm in right now is because you're not inside me."

"Fuck," he growled. "I can take care of that. You just enjoy."

Centering himself, he drove inside me.

My right leg, I splayed out to the side, where it could rest. But I lifted my other and wrapped it around his waist while he pumped into me, driving us closer and closer to the point I was going to shriek again.

He kissed me then moved his mouth to my breast, all while he drove into me over and over.

I clenched my fingers on his shoulders. "Jax."

He grunted and moved faster.

"Yes!"

Shuddering, his muscles bunching into tight knots as he strained, he groaned. "You with me?"

Too focused on the moment, I couldn't say a thing. But I moaned encouragement, my head thrashing on the floor.

We crashed together, flying all the way up to the stars. As the waves shook me, I trembled and muffled my shriek in his shoulder.

He collapsed but propped himself up on his elbows to keep from crushing me. His rough breathing fanned my neck and he kissed my collarbone, my shoulder, my cheeks.

"Damn," I said.

"Fuck," he added.

We both laughed.

23

Jax

Fishing was first on the agenda for the morning. The fact that the guys from the ship had come close to the island the day before made me eager to stockpile food for a potentially grim future. Maybe I was looking at this as a beer mug half empty instead of half full, but I didn't think that was the case.

My skin itched, which meant something was coming.

While Haylee fished, I foraged inland again. I lucked out and found a couple cacao bushes with mature pods. The white, milky innards could be eaten raw and tasted like honey. If we had the time and the inclination, the seeds could've been roasted and made into bitter chocolate, but there was no opportunity for that. I also located more ripe plantains that were best when cooked but could be eaten raw in a pinch, plus some scraggly oranges. I divided the food and cached it and the protein bars in various locations, where they could be accessed quickly. As for the water, I drank some and covered the rest, hiding it as well.

The fish, we'd smoke and dry tonight. Assuming we made it until tonight.

There I went again… Mug half empty. Maybe I looked at life that way because, while things had been great at times—thinking of Mom and Haylee here—my life had also been rough. When you measured your existence from one meal or a safe night's sleep to the next, it put everything else into perspective. You learned to appreciate the moment you were in and not worry so much about what the future held.

As I hurried back to the beach with a container of water for Haylee, the itching in the center of my spine grew stronger. Whenever it itched, I knew bad things were about to happen. Like that time when I'd been in Iraq and it twitched, only to have our mission go sour when we barely avoided becoming fodder due to an IED.

It had itched the night my mom died. And when I'd moved out onto the streets to make it on my own.

Because I couldn't scratch the tickle, I focused on making sure we were prepared for whatever might come next.

When I returned to the ocean, I found Haylee crouched in the bushes near our shelter. That itching feeling magnified tenfold.

I dropped down beside her and handed her the water. While she drank, I put my arm around her shoulders. The fish she'd caught had been suspended on sticks again and were propped against a tree.

"Looks like we're going to be stuck with sushi," she

whispered after draining the water and handing me the empty container to return to my pack.

Only blue sky and teal water stretched in front of me for as far as my eyes could see, but…

"They went by again," she added.

"Didn't stop?" Obvious but maybe they were just around the bend.

"They slowed but kept going." She turned to face me, concern heavy on her face. She'd pulled her hair up and secured it with the scrunched thing, and she was the most beautiful sight I'd ever seen. If only I could kiss her, love her all over again.

"I think they're on to us," she said.

"A hunch?"

She shook her head. Her cheeks and shoulders had pinkened from the sun, and sand dusted her calves and her arms. Water had seeped through her shirt, which showed me she'd thrown on her clothing and run directly from the ocean to hide. "They know."

"How can they?"

"It wasn't last night," she said defensively.

"No way."

"Right from the start, the Maestro has been one step ahead of us." She slumped onto her knees. "If only I could remember what happened. I think the key is locked in my mind."

"Nothing so far?"

"Just snippets. Someone in an alley…" She frowned. "It was dark. They got out of their car. It was a man. He stood in the light, but I couldn't make out his face. He didn't seem familiar at all, so I don't think he's on the inside."

"You had a head injury. Give it time."

She growled. "That's just it. We may not have any more time." Stilling, her head turned to the right. The rumble of a motor approaching made her rise back up onto her haunches. "They can't be passing by again, right?" Determination filled her voice. "It's a fisherman this time. We'll flag them down, swim out to meet them, and then we'll be…"

No fisherman I'd ever known used a powerboat for fishing.

But those hunting people might.

No, it could be tourists. My brain ran away with the idea. They rented a boat. They were planning to come to shore for a picnic. We'd greet them and hitch a ride to Belize.

Reaching around, I dug at my spine.

Haylee trembled as the whine of the motor grew louder.

"It's okay," I said as softly as possible. "We're well hidden here. Whoever it is can't see us."

"You're right. They don't know we're on the island."

A metallic red speedboat came into view.

"Is that the one you saw earlier?" I asked.

"Yeah. They'll keep going this time, too."

I wished I had her confidence. And I sure as hell wished this was a boat full of tourists, but I recognized one of the guys from the cruise ship.

My mouth flashed dry. This could be it. They were bringing it to us.

The boat slowed and we remained frozen, which made us less visible, even by an infrared device that could identify heat. If we ran, they'd pick up our heat signals. Right now, we had enough vegetation between us and them.

"They're stopping," she hissed, fidgeting like a doe in front of a lion, her muscles bunching to flee.

Four men on the boat.

One tossed an anchor over the side.

Were we about to finally meet the Maestro? He'd be crazy to risk revealing himself when he'd taken such care to remain hidden. Although…if he knew those seeing him wouldn't live long enough to tell, he might take a chance.

Two of the guys stooped down as if looking for something in the boat. One of the others pulled a bull-horn and lifted it to his lips. "Hay-lee!" The way he said it made him sound like a bully on a playground. "Come on out. We'll go easy with you."

Laughter sliced across the water.

My heart thudded once. Twice. My skin crawled.

A man wearing a broad hat leaned close to the one with the bullhorn, and he must've spoken because the guy nodded.

"You can't run, but on my word, can you walk fast?" I said softly to Haylee.

"You've got a plan. Share it soon, Jax." Her hands fluttered against her thighs. After what happened in Mexico, who could blame her for being scared. She was still wounded, vulnerable.

"Many plans." I gathered her into my arms. "If they

bring this to us, it's gonna end here. We're done playing this game by their rules."

Her voice came out muffled against my shoulder. "It's going to end for them, I hope."

"Someone tried to kill you in Cancun," I said in a low voice. "Succeeded with Gabe. They came after you in the rehab place. Then on the ship, which ended with them taking potshots at the chopper. We barely escaped with our skin."

"You're not reassuring me much here, Jax."

"Just sayin'. If they think they can take me on—take us on—and win, they're about to find out they've challenged the wrong team."

"Let's face it, I'm the walking wounded. I'm essentially useless."

"You're smart. Strong. And I love you. Nothin's gonna stop you from showing them they should've turned and run."

"Wait." Her head bobbed up, and her eyes met mine.

A quick glance at the ocean showed the man with the hat still talking while the other two did something inside the small cabin. The guy with the hat dropped down onto a bench surrounding the back of the boat and stared toward the shore. He put his feet up and cupped his hands behind his neck as if he was getting ready to enjoy a show.

"Jax," she whispered with tears forming in her eyes. "Love you, too."

It didn't matter how many times she told me; each would feel like the first. My chest expanded three times, and my heart felt like it was about to burst. "No matter what, we're coming out of this alive. We're going back to Maine, where we'll have a life together."

She smiled through her tears. "You moving in with me or am I moving in with you?"

I grinned back. "What size bed do you have?"

"It's a..." Her gaze was drawn to the boat, and her breathing jerked. "Down."

We flattened ourselves on the ground as bullets peppered along the shore, driving up toward the jungle where they ripped through the vegetation at about waist height. Leaves tore and sticks were severed. Bits of vegetation rained down on us.

Haylee remained quiet and motionless beneath me.

As quickly as the AK-47 had started firing, it stilled, leaving only the echo of the barrage rippling through the air.

"Haylee," the guy barked. "Jackson! If you two are still alive, we'll find you."

"Not on your life," I growled in a low voice. We remained on the ground in case they started firing again.

"If you don't come out, Haylee, we'll hunt you down. Boss here says Jax is toast, but you..."

Silence fell. It was easier to scare someone by leaving the worst to their imagination.

Anger burned through me like wildfire. The hell with me. They wouldn't touch her.

"Let's go," I hissed.

"Maybe I should..." The horror on her face when she rolled over made my heart stop. "If I go to them, you can run. Hide."

"You're not sacrificing yourself for me."

"I'm okay with it as long as you live."

"You ready to run?" Remaining crouched low, I offered her my hand. "Trust me, sweetheart. It's nowhere near over yet."

Her spine stiffening, she nodded. "Knew you'd say that." She rose and we crept backward, deeper into the jungle, keeping our gazes locked on the men in the boat.

"Us or them?" Haylee asked. "Is that how it's going to be?"

"They're bringing it to us. No rules any longer."

"They broke them back in Cancun."

"If they want a war…We've got one for them."

She grinned, her expression vindictive. "Cool." Her growl slipped out. "Let's do this for us and for Gabe."

Hell, yeah.

The guy with the hat leaned over the side and dropped a large, waterproof bag into the sea. It bobbed before nudging against the boat.

While he watched, the other three men jumped over the side. One snagged the rope trailing off the waterproof bag.

Then they started swimming for shore.

Haylee

J ax grabbed my hand, and we raced deeper into the jungle.

"Stay low and right behind me," he said shallow so his voice wouldn't carry. "We'll flatten some grass, though we won't make it too obvious."

"But then they'll see our tracks," I hissed, darting a glance over my shoulder. My belly surged up into the back of my throat. They were halfway to shore. "They'll know where to find us."

"Exactly."

I remained behind Jax and, as we curved along the rough path he was blazing, I looked back one last time. The terrifying scene carved itself into my mind. The guys splashed toward shore, one dragging the bag that must contain weapons, high-tech tracking equipment, and enough supplies to let them hunt us without having to stop to find food.

They'd be on our trail within seconds, fully armed. While we'd be scrambling to find ways to fight them off with a slingshot and a jackknife. All while hunger and thirst ate through our confidence.

We could hold them off for a day or two, but after that? We'd have to be careful, or we wouldn't stand a chance. We were outgunned, outnumbered, and we'd quickly run out of resources.

But we were tough.

Numbness and despair tried to grab hold of me, but I shook it off and made my legs keep pumping. As long as we both lived, I wouldn't give up.

Whispered conversation while running—hobbling in my case—was out, but I trusted Jax. He said he'd made plans. While I doubted my ability to keep up due to my injury, he wouldn't let us down.

We raced through the jungle that grew thicker around us, Jax shoving plants out of the way so I could follow without tripping. We kept going until my lungs ached from hauling in air and my heart rate drummed in my ears. A month ago, I would've taken my turn forging our path but now, my deconditioned muscles couldn't keep up the pace. Flagging already, my legs were slowing us down. Spasms arced through my thigh that screamed with pain.

Emerging from the jungle onto a narrow strip of tall grass, I stared up at a cliff face about three stories high directly ahead of us. Vines snaked all over it, a tangled, leaf-encrusted web. My limbs prickled. No easy hand-holds I could see. The cliff stretched into the vegetation on either side of us with no apparent out. I'd yet to build any stamina and, at this rate, it wouldn't matter.

"Where next?" I gulped out, trying to catch my

breath. "Left or right?" I bolted to the right, but Jax snagged the back of my shirt, bringing me to a full halt.

"Hold on," he whispered.

"Where can we hide?" I tripped, and birds nesting on the cliffside squawked and took flight. Crap. I'd draw them to us!

I wrenched a stick from the deep grass and whirled to face the jungle. "Showdown here?" I said. "I'm game. We can lurk near the edge and bash their heads in when they rush out. Or…I don't know, try to steal a weapon? Then we'll even the odds."

"No way. Why make it that easy for them?"

"Easy?" My god, how could he act so casual about this? I spun to face him and shoved hair off my face. Damn scrunchie kept slipping down the strands. "They're following us." I could hear them coming already. Stealth wasn't their strong suit. But why bother creeping when they held the upper hand? They could mow us down with fire power the moment they found us. No need to sneak up on us to do that. They'd herd us across the island, all the way to the sea, then stain the water with our blood.

"I've cooked up a little surprise for them," he said. "Come on." Turning, he jogged over to the cliff and jumped, snagging a clump of vines hanging about eight feet up. As it dropped, it unraveled in his hands.

My eyes widened. "A vine ladder?" I said, suitably impressed. "You've been busy."

"Just took care of a few things yesterday and this morning." He waved. "After you, sweetheart. When you reach the top, you'll see I've left party favors."

If this wasn't so scary, I'd laugh.

I gave him a quick kiss as I passed him. "Thank you." Grabbing the ladder, I snagged a low rung with my sneaker then hauled myself up. My arm muscles complained but would do as I demanded.

"Doin' all I can to keep you safe, Haylee." His hands on my hips urged my higher, helping support me. Lending me his strength.

"Watch out for yourself, too, huh?" I whispered. "I want both of us coming through this alive." I pressed for a smile, though it was tough. "Don't forget the plans we made for when we get back to Maine."

"Will do." He was right behind. "You're doing great. We're almost to the top."

My arms ached, and my leg kept twitching. "I'm holding us back."

"I'm not writing you off yet."

I shouldn't do it either, but it was hard. Stress, healing, and lack of sleep was eating away at my ability to push myself harder.

Reaching the top, I scrambled to my feet. He joined me and gestured to a waist-high stone wall he'd built along the edge. About four feet wide and three feet high, it had shorter sides.

"Behind there, everything you could ever dream about awaits you." His deep, throaty words tickled up my spine.

Not the time, Haylee.

But his ongoing humor kept me trying. It cracked through my fear and scattered it on the wind.

"This, I've got to see," I said in a slice of a whisper.

While he yanked up the ladder, I darted around the wall. "Nothing here, Jax."

With a low chuckle, he held out his hand. "Slingshot?"

I pulled it from where I'd tied it to a loop on my shorts and handed it over, watching to see what he'd do. When he finished making some quick modifications, I couldn't hold back my huff of astonishment. "What did you do to my baby?"

"Enhanced her." We dropped low, hiding behind the wall. Escape lay at our backs and in front, solid protection with a narrow slot about the size of a computer keyboard in the center.

"You built this?" I took in the well-constructed wall made up of large, flat stones stacked on top of each other, a barrier thick enough to withstand an AK-47 onslaught. "It's awesome."

"We won't need it for long." He kept his voice low, barely discernable. Lifting the wrist rocket, he pointed. "As you can see, I made a few changes."

"Wow, so…" I ran my finger along the adjustments. "Bamboo?" He'd suspended a short tube across the top of my slingshot with… "And you used an exercise band to hold it in place. I had plans for working out with this one."

"There's still a bit left."

I scrunched up my face. "Only a bit?"

"Check it out." Leaning close, he pointed. "I bound a strip of cloth with a hole in it over one end of the bamboo tube. It'll keep your trajectory stable. Can't have it wobble."

Snorting, I wiggled my eyebrows. "Can't have what wobble?"

How could I find the heart to joke at a time like this? Our tenuous position should be dragging my confidence through the center of the Earth.

Moving around me, he laid a bunch of sticks on the ground to my right. "Arrows. I found the perfect wood for them. Straight and dry."

"And sharp." Lifting one, I tested the tip.

"Wish I'd had time to make more."

"Like…jeez, Jax. You only made ten?" The more time I spent with him, the more he amazed me. "Did you do that in your sleep last night?"

"Yesterday and this morning. That and a few other things."

"More surprises."

He grinned. "Plenty of surprises waiting."

"You knew they'd find us."

"Suspected." His lips twisted and he stared through the opening in the wall, toward the jungle we'd recently run through. "Seems to be their pattern so far."

"This is fantastic."

His jagged smile made me glad we were on the same side. "More than enough arrows for a sharpshooter."

"Just so you know, I haven't practiced much with a bow."

"But you're deadly with a slingshot."

"Only with a stone, and on fish." I stared down at the arrow lying in my hand. "You think I can shoot one of these with the rocket?" The possibilities were endless. A stone could cause damage but arrows…

"The big question is." A grim mask fell over his face. "Can you kill?"

"In general? Yeah. Only if needed on a mission or in defense, though." Unease scratched through me, telling me where this was going.

"What about them?" He nudged his head toward where they had to be moving through the woods, following the trail we'd left for them.

"They're unknowns," I said. "There's no way to gauge how they'll behave." Except, they'd made it clear they planned to kill Jax and do horrible things to me before ending my life, too.

"They're amateurs," he said with disgust. "Doubt they're military. If I was them, I would've snuck on shore during the night. Laid traps then waited us out. Or brought in a small army and, outstretched, combed the island until they found us."

"I have to assume the Maestro will hire the best." In my debriefings back home at Viper Force, Flint told me he suspected the Maestro worked for the U.S. Government, which made sense. Only someone on the inside would have access to the information needed to run the stateside branch of the drug cartel in such a sophisticated manner. Only Viper Force's rogue, covert operations had made any progress in identifying the organization, and we were talking inches of progress, not miles.

Jax dipped his head in acknowledgment of my words.

"You know me." My pulse stuttered in my throat. "I've trained in martial arts for years yet the guy in the room almost killed me. If you hadn't arrived and flung him over the balcony, I'm not sure I could've bested him. They've had training."

"No one in the military would've blasted the bushes with an AK-47 when they couldn't know we were there."

Valid point.

"I think we can best them."

"Four on two."

"We're tough."

I couldn't hold back my wry smile. "You're tough. Sometimes, I'm not so sure about me."

"You're getting stronger all the time. Look at you. It's barely been five weeks, and you're holding your own already. Give it time."

Time was ticking down too fast.

"Them razing the bushes was a scare tactic," I said. "To put us on edge. Make us bolt. If we're worried, not thinking, we could slip up." Then they'd rip us apart.

"Not happening."

I held the wrist rocket toward him. "Maybe you should handle this." We had one chance. Once they saw we were firing on them, they'd melt into the jungle like mist at dawn. They could afford to wait us out then stalk us until we got tired or relaxed our guard. The island was decent sized but small. There were limited places to hide. And there was no way out. "I'd hate to miss."

"You won't." He said it with complete certainty. "But again, can you kill? Okay to back out, tell me it's not for you. I'll give it my best, but I'm no sharpshooter."

"What if I can't?" I wasn't weakening. Resolve to survive oozed from my pores. But did Jax have an alternative option to this scenario?

"I'll try or we'll keep going." His head tilted toward the hill behind us. "I've still got a few tricks planned."

"This isn't a game," I said softly.

He nodded.

"They're here to kill us," I said.

"Won't stop until it's finished."

One outcome. We either eliminated them, or they'd return the favor.

Frustration gnashed its teeth inside me.

Jax watched me patiently, giving me time to decide.

No true options. We needed to start evening the odds. I lifted my chin and tightened my spine. "There's no place for leniency in war." Turning, I spread the arrows neatly out on the ground and tightened my grip on the wrist rocket. "Firing this way is simple, huh?"

"If anyone can do it, you can."

"How did you dream this up?" I meant the modification.

"Read an article about weapons like this about a year ago. There's a decent online market for them. Seemed like a simple tweak to a basic slingshot."

Taking one of the arrows, I fitted it through the hole in the cloth. "I assume without your modification, the arrow will flip as it passes through the air, like when someone throws a knife."

"It can lose momentum."

"And pretty much guarantee I won't hit the mark." Not with a deadly enough blow to do damage.

Hefting the rocket to shoulder height, I pinched the end of the arrow in the pouch and tested pulling it back. It slid neatly through the hole, and I could see how the cloth would keep the arrow true until it was flying through the air. I turned my wrist and sighted down the grooves on the side, my preferred way to fire.

"Shoot to kill," I said with growing satisfaction in my voice. For the first time in days, I felt like I was grabbing control of the situation. No more waiting for someone to come after me. I'd bring the fight to them.

"We'll pick them off one at a time, either eliminating them or disabling them badly enough they're useless, then go after the guy guarding the boat," Jax said in a low murmur.

"Question him. Gain some clues about the Maestro?"

"Yep. If we end this fast, we can get out of here."

We'd be safe for the first time in months. Once we reached shore, we could activate the power of Viper Force. They'd fly us securely out of Belize and hide us in an unknown location. If the guy on the boat talked, the information we obtained could be used to bring down the entire operation.

Then it would be over, and we could go on with our lives.

We crouched and studied the jungle below through the narrow strip of window.

"Pick one and make it clean," Jax whispered.

"The others will be spooked." I'd love to see them run. It would buy us time. "If they're savvy, they'll ID our location and shoot."

"We'll be gone by then."

"Not back down the way we came up."

"I've made it a policy to always have a back door."

"And then what?" I asked, warming to the plan. Jax had thought this through. How had he found time while collecting food, making arrows, and building the stone wall?

"My goal is to avoid a shootout if we can." Frowning, he squinted toward the jungle where I'd yet to see movement. "We need to take them out before they know what hit them."

Below us, something shifted in the bushes…

I held up a finger then pulled back the arrow and sighted in that direction. My heartrate accelerated like a snowball rolling down a hill, picking up momentum.

"I've never killed anyone before, Jax," I whispered in a shaky voice. Doubts poured through me, weakening my resolve.

"All or nothing. If you're not in, and you don't need to be, I'll do my best." He held out his hand.

Like everything else so far, he'd do it for me. It wouldn't matter if he couldn't stomach the thought any more than I could or even if he felt his aim wouldn't be as true.

It wouldn't be weak for me to back down, but I wanted to find my way to the surface again. Not with Jax pulling me up when I floundered beside him.

Anger grew inside me at the idea of handing this task over. It felt too much like giving in. No, letting them win. These men—or others with them—had murdered Gabe. They'd nearly killed me.

They wouldn't stop. Even throwing one of them off a ship hadn't slowed him down. They'd fished him out, and he'd come with them for today's chase. Unless we eliminated this threat, it would follow us—hunt us—until we'd been eliminated.

"I can do it," I said with heat. This one was for Gabe.

As fury bound itself to the resolve building inside me, my trembling ceased. My breathing calmed.

One of the men crept from the jungle, the stock of his weapon snug against his shoulder. Keeping low and moving like a shadow, he looked around as he approached the cliff. He also studied the ground. Stooping down onto his haunches, he fingered our tracks. His head jerked back as if he'd scented us on the wind, and his gaze narrowed on the imprints we'd left in the grass during our approach to the cliff. Tongue sliding out to touch his upper lip, he tipped his head back, following the mesh of vines to the top.

He'd ID us in seconds.

I sucked in a breath and released the air with my arrow.

It smacked into his left shoulder.

A hoarse cry erupting from him, he stumbled backward, his weapon jerking up. Bullets sprayed the sky.

My heart crashing against my ribcage, I snatched up another arrow, slid it into the hole, then drew it back quickly.

Sight. Inhale. Release.

I didn't miss the second time.

Jax

After firing her kill shot, Haylee collapsed onto her knees. The wrist rocket thudded onto the ground beside her, spent. Turning, she leaned her back against the wall and tilted her face. She stared blankly at the sky.

I quickly tucked the rocket and arrows into my bag then looped it onto my back.

Scooting down in front of her, I lifted her trembling hands and kissed them. "Hey."

"Jax."

The pain in that solitary word stole my breath. I gathered her in my arms and held her tight. I'd give my soul to bring the spark back into her eyes.

But we'd soon be out of time.

Below, someone bellowed, a wrenching cry of anger and pain. "Gonna fucking kill you, dude," one of them shouted. "And you, girl. You're gonna pay."

Bullets peppered the cliff, the jungle, the wall, and the air around us.

Assholes were shooting at stone and it could ricochet

back and hit them, but who could blame them for being pissed off?

Two shots with a slingshot. Haylee was something else.

We'd evened the odds unless we counted the dude lurking on the speedboat. I assumed he was guarding the boat but could he be the Maestro?

"We've gotta go," I said, tugging her to her feet, though we didn't stand upright; we remained hidden behind the wall.

"Yeah. Time to run." As if she thought I needed reassurance, she pressed for a smile that came nowhere close to making it.

"Okay?" I asked.

She nodded. "I am."

But her voice trembled.

Hunched forward, we bolted across the top of the hill, leaving the guys to curse and fling firepower at a defensive barrier we no longer needed. We hit the top of a cliff on the opposite side of the hill, though this one wasn't as steep as the other.

Someone must've lived here at one time. Either that or large animals had roamed the island in the past, because a worn switchback path led down the side and would dump us back into the jungle.

That wasn't my destination.

"Come on."

We hustled down the narrow path, taking it as fast as we could without tripping up or tumbling off the side.

Partway down, I pulled her to a stop on a narrow stone shelf. To our right, the world dropped off. While a fall like this wouldn't kill 'ya, it would do considerable damage.

"Where to?" she asked, glancing vaguely around.

In shock, she'd need time to come back to herself. I couldn't rush it, or I'd break the fragile start she'd only recently found.

A profusion of lush vines draped down the side of the cliff, almost eclipsing the path. I parted them and revealed the cave I'd discovered yesterday while scoping out the island. This place was a treasure trove of hideouts.

"In here," I said.

She slanted me a skeptical look that made my heart surge up into my throat, because it meant she was still with me.

With my hand around her waist, I urged her into the cool darkness. I carefully erased our tracks outside and then let the vines flop back into place. I smoothed them to make sure the entry was completely hidden and encouraged her to keep going, deeper into the tunnel that sloped gradually downward. It would take someone days to explore all the channels. I'd followed one that led to a dead end. Another curved gradually upward and led to a small, grass covered hole exiting onto the flat on the top of the hill. A third ended at a small pool created by a trickle of water down a steep wall.

I nudged my head toward a two-foot hole on the right—barely discernible unless you had decent light. Stooping down, I followed her inside.

"It's only luck that I found this cave, but I'm damn

grateful I did. From the ground, no one can tell it exists."

She said nothing, just dully did as I said. I didn't like this. She was sinking inside herself. Hiding from what went on around her. I'd seen buddies do this overseas. Some never fully came back.

I turned on my flashlight and directed the beam around, showing her the somewhat cozy room I'd found —if a cave could be called cozy. I'd done what I could to make it comfortable, because I knew we might need a place to hide away where we wouldn't be heard while speaking in hushed whispers.

My light picked up the nest of leaves I'd created as a place to sit, the covered bowls of water waiting to be enjoyed, and the broad leaf filled with food in Ziplock bags I'd scavenged.

"You really are Tarzan," she said with awe that dropped off to a whimper. "Jax." Her voice broke. She turned and crumpled into my arms.

I held her. Nothing else I could do but offer her my comfort. She needed to work through this on her own. It was never easy to take another life, even if doing so was the only way to ensure your own survival.

Her tears slowed, and she sniffed. She wiped her eyes on the corner of her tee and looked up at me, sighing.

"Why don't I feel avenged?" she said. Raking her hands down her face, she shuddered. "I thought after I killed him, I'd feel…" Her shoulders lifted and fell. "I don't know. Glad? I should be happy he's dead. I mean, he sure deserved it. He's part of the group that killed

Gabe. He wants to kill me. But instead of feeling relief, I want to curl up into a ball and wail."

"If you found it easy to take a life, I'd be worried."

"I've held people in my arms as they died. It's not the death that wrecks me, though I still ache for each of the friends I've lost. It's…" Staring up, she blinked fast. "It's knowing I snuffed out someone's potential. Yeah, he wanted to kill me, and I'm all about my own survival. For all I know, he's murdered tons of other people. But now he has no chance of redemption."

"Not everyone is redeemable."

"So that makes it okay?"

"It'll never be okay. Death is… When you take a life, it's as if you're playing God."

"It's not my right to play God. I don't like it."

"You won't do it again."

She snorted. "Sure I will. There are three of them left. You and me? We're getting off this island, and we're not taking them with us. They came here, to what anyone would consider paradise, and they brought us a war. I won't let them defeat us."

"I know you, Hay. You'd never take a life but to save your own."

"I'd do it to save yours. My dad's. My friends at Viper Force. But I sure as hell hope I don't have to do it again too soon."

"I'll take care of the others." Wring their necks while she slept if I had to. Each time she killed would leave another scar on her soul.

"You say that as if you're sweeping dust underneath a carpet. Hiding it away where no one will find it."

What could I say to that? I didn't want to kill a person any more than she did. But even more, I hated watching her suffer.

"You hungry?" I asked, because we needed to focus on our survival.

We pulled apart, and she stared toward the leaf holding the food. "I need to eat."

"About the next part of the plan."

"I'll kill another guy whenever you're ready." Her head lifted. "Where will we wait so I can do it this time?"

"No need to shoot anyone else." Not ever again if I could help it. "The big question is, how nasty are you willing to be?"

She dropped down onto the seat made up of leaves, and I handed her a piece of fruit I'd picked this morning. Staring up at me, she lowered it onto her lap. "How nasty do you think *they're* willing to be?"

Nastier than us.

"The next trick is gruesome." Almost too gruesome for me, and I'd seen a lot of horrible things while living on the street.

"Will it kill another guy?"

I shrugged. "Put him out of commission for a long time." Which would be good enough for our needs.

"Let's do it then." Resolve rose in her voice, telling me she was fighting her way back to the surface.

"Eat fast, then, because we don't have much time. To the left of the cliff we climbed, there's another path that leads around to the base of the one outside the cave entrance. Took me about a half an hour at a run. From there, we'll have to weave through a bunch of boulders overgrown with trees. Plus get past the next surprise."

"Okay." She lifted the fruit and frowned. "What is this?" she said, staring down at what I had to admit looked like an oval pod filled with white slime.

"You'll like it."

Lifting it, she took a sniff. "Smells good."

I dropped down beside her with another. "It's cacao."

"Sure doesn't look like chocolate to me."

"Cocoa beans are in there, but we won't eat them. Normally, they're roasted and ground. But the white fruit around the beans tastes great. Give it a try." I handed her a container of water, and she took a long drink. I finished it off.

We used our fingers to scoop up the fruit, spitting the beans onto the floor.

"It's yummy," she said.

"Almost as good as bacon."

"Ha." Her lips curled up, making me feel infinitely better.

I opened a protein bar and we split it.

After finishing, she stood. "Let's get this over with."

"Okay."

We left the cave within ten minutes of arriving.

My belly churned at the thought of what we'd need to do next.

Haylee

A solitary shot rang out, making me freeze near the cave entrance. My hands shook, and I flashed back to the arrow embedding itself in that guy's chest.

Gulping back the water and fruit rising up in my throat, I shuddered.

"Close," I said in a bare whisper. "Sounded like it came from the other side of the hill. What are they shooting at?" Wasn't us.

He shrugged but his eyes darkened.

"They give themselves away," I said. "Why?"

"Maybe they saw a snake or something."

"Yeah. Should we wait them out here?"

"We need to draw them to the base of the cliff."

"Bait. Lovely." I struggled to tease, but my heart wasn't fully in it. "Just so you know, I left my wilted maiden outfit at home."

His grin rewarded my effort. "So want to see you wearing that when this is over."

No outfit, but I'd come up with something.

"If they chase us…" A frown creased his forehead. He held up his finger and tilted his head, listening. After a moment, he nodded and his shoulders loosened. "Follow me," he said in so low a voice, I could barely hear him. He slid the vines aside at the opening and stepped out, onto the path.

As I followed, fear rippled through me. I should feel brave after eliminating one of them but instead, I was scared out of my mind. Inside the cave, we'd been relatively safe. Outside, we'd be exposed.

"Once we get to the bottom of the cliff, we'll wait for them," he said.

Biting my lip, I nodded, and we hurried down the narrow, switchback path. When it spilled out onto the ground, I paused and studied the vicinity, looking for traps and ways out. Boulders that must've fallen from the cliffside eons ago covered the ground. Trees and dense vegetation made up of vines and snarled, thorny bushes had grown among the rocks, creating a rough, nearly impassable area. Anxiety climbed up my spine on steel spikes, and my skin flashed cold. Other than the path entering from around the hill on my left, there didn't appear to be a way out.

Jax wouldn't lead us into a trap, but that didn't stop my belly from rising up into the back of my throat.

Off to my right, the trail snaked up to two larger boulders. More trees beyond the rocks blocked my view.

With Jax in the lead, we hustled to the boulders and, after turning sideways to fit through the narrow passage between them, we emerged on the other side. To say my worry dropped a fraction would be an understatement, though we weren't safe yet.

Ahead, the thick, snarled jungle continued with the path cutting its way through. A low, swampy area bordered each side. I could see the possibilities of this already. One way out. One way continuing across this part of the jungle. Nothing in between and nowhere to hide.

What kind of trap had Jax laid?

He dropped to his haunches and tugged me down beside him, pointing to where the trail continued between a cluster of gnarly trees. "See that stick lying across the trail?"

It looked random, as it should. "Yeah."

"After we lure them here, as we're running to get away, I need you to jump when you reach the stick and land at least a foot beyond it. Don't step in between or you'll spring my trap. It's…"

Gruesome, he'd said back at the cave, but how? Squinting, I tried to see what he'd rigged but sunlight didn't penetrate this deeply in the jungle, and nothing appeared out of the ordinary. Which was the point, I supposed. "I'll be careful."

He stood and swiped his palms across the top of his head. His chest rose and fell, faster than it should since we hadn't exerted ourselves yet. He wasn't happy about what was coming next.

"Ready?" he breathed out.

"Let's do it."

He passed me, starting back toward the boulders,

where we'd act as bait, and I followed.

"Where will we go after we jump over that part of the trail?"

"To the next hiding spot."

"I imagine they—or one of them—will follow."

"Whoever's left may be delayed."

I was grateful Jax and I were on the same side. From his grim demeanor, I wouldn't want to face whatever he'd planned next.

"We'll pick away at them until none of them are left," I said.

"Then go for the boat."

"Steal it."

He chipped a nod. "That's the plan."

"How?"

"Any way possible."

Another challenge, then. The danger was worth it if we escaped and could return to civilization. Especially if we permanently eliminated the threat.

"We wait here," he said, peering through the narrow opening, toward the cliff.

"You're sure they'll come around from around the side?"

"There's a low, swampy area beyond the hill, full of snakes and creepy crawlies. No other way around."

My skin flashed with goosebumps. "Let's avoid the creepy crawly area."

"Also my plan."

"You know they're coming partly because there's no other way to reach this section and…"

His lips curled down as if he'd eaten something sour.

The realization sunk through me like a boulder. Why hadn't I remembered? Outside of tree cover, they had the means to pinpoint our location at any time. "They can see where we are." I rolled my shoulders but couldn't shrug off the dark shadows gliding across my skin.

"They couldn't locate us while we were in the cave, when we were under the space blanket, or when we hid in the deep vegetation. They'd be stupid not to use Google Earth or infrared to keep us in sight, but yeah. They'll know exactly where we are and will be eager to finish this. Especially after you shot the other guy."

I'd driven their anger to a higher pitch. "What's keeping them from calling in others to help in the hunt?"

"Nothing except time and resources."

"Which appear limitless to the Maestro." It was hard to hold back the overwhelming feeling of doom that seemed determined to run me over. Would I ever feel safe again?

Moving in between the boulders, we stopped and waited.

My legs restless, I held back their twitch. Sure, the guys could be watching us via satellite, but there was often a delay in sending images. And with the boulders, we'd be hidden—mostly—from infrared.

I couldn't get rid of the sensation of a bead centering on my spine. Someone's finger tightening on the trigger…

I didn't hear them coming. They wouldn't make that mistake again.

But when the tiny hairs stood up on the back of my neck, Jax nodded and held up his fingers to visually count down.

Three…

Two…

One.

"Jax," I said in a hushed voice that I knew would carry enough to be overheard but not come across blatant. "I think they're…"

Footsteps stomped in our direction and one of the guys snarled like a wolf snapping at the heels of a wounded doe.

"Run," Jax growled, making it clear where we hid. Not that there was an easier way out of the boulder-strewn area, but we needed to make sure they fell for his trick.

We barreled down the path and when we reached the cluster of trees overshadowing the stick, he leaped. I jumped as well, making sure I didn't land until I'd reached at least two feet beyond the stick. My right leg protested the jarring movement, but I kept going, my feet smacking on the ground behind Jax.

They followed and, from the sounds reaching from behind, they were gaining on us. Jax's plan better work or bullets would mow us down before we could hide.

My pulse roaring in my throat, I kept running.

We reached a bend in the path, and the curve put tree cover between us and the men. The dread clamping down on my spine eased a fraction.

"Follow the trail," Jax said, slowing and turning to look in the other direction. "I'll catch up in a sec."

He'd make sure the trap was sprung then join me.

I kept going, rushing through the jungle. Vines looped overhead like long, thin snakes, some draping so low, I had to duck to avoid brushing against them with my head. Thorny bushes encroaching on either side of the path snatched at my clothing. Beyond them, the swamp stretched into the distance. Trees with dense, tangled mangrove roots peppered the muddy area, as well as palms and mounds made up of grass and scrub brush rising out of the brackish water. I was grateful for the path, as I wouldn't want to make my way through the swamp.

A shriek pierced the air, and I dropped to a shuddering halt.

I peered back the way I'd run from.

"Jax?" I whispered when I wanted to scream out his name.

He couldn't be hurt. They hadn't caught him. My stomach churned, eager to reject everything inside it.

More screams followed, guttural, agonizing bellows of horror and pain.

Jax burst into view. "Go!" He reached me and swept me up, taking me along with him.

"What happened?" Did I really want to know?

"A snare," he chugged out, winded from the run. "Snagged him. Hauled him up by the leg."

Which wouldn't cause that much pain. What wasn't Jax telling me?

We left the swampy area and kept running through the jungle beyond.

"One guy or two caught?" I asked.

"One. Only dragged him up a short distance," he puffed.

"Won't the other guy…cut him down? He'll be after us again." We needed to go faster. I couldn't believe a barrage of bullets wasn't roaring this way already.

"Above him…" Jax slanted me a quick, stark look before his attention returned to the path we followed. "Paper wasp nest. Foot bumped the nest."

The gruesome picture painted itself in my mind.

Gulping back my horror, I swallowed the bile rising up into the back of my throat.

Us versus them. I had to repeat that litany in my mind or I'd go insane.

This would definitely slow them down. The first guy would… Didn't want to think too hard about that.

The other guy would cut his friend down and come after us. It was likely the first would've lost his thrill for the chase. He'd be lucky to live, let alone function after being exposed to the wasps. If it was me, I'd cut him down then leave him behind while I went after my prey.

The final guy would hunt to kill both of us. No eliminating only Jax while holding me back for a plaything.

While Jax was slowing, probably exhausted from rushing back to make sure his trap was sprung, he urged me to go faster. We emerged from the jungle. The ocean stretched ahead of us, plus a beach on the opposite side of the island from the one we'd originally landed on.

We ran across the sand together and into the sea. Turning right, we continued through the water that rose up to my waist. After going about three hundred feet, we left the ocean and crossed over a rocky area. Our wet footsteps steamed and would evaporate in minutes, hopefully before the guy caught our trail.

A cluster of boulders partly-submerged in sand lay ahead, and we ran around them. When we reached the other side, he tracked to the right, back into the jungle.

I ran beside him, my leg screaming and my lungs on fire.

No path this time. We slammed through the jungle. By now, with fear tracking down my spine and knowing the other guy would be full of rage, I didn't care if a spider dropped down on me.

We had to get away. Hide. Eliminate the guy before he hurt us. Then take down the final barrier on the speedboat.

Coming to such a stop, Jax pointed to the ground. "Inside here."

A hole?

"Feet first," he said, urging me to stoop down on the ground. "I promise. It's okay. He won't find us." He grabbed dead palm fronds and a cluster of brush he must've left for this purpose and dragged it closer while I dropped onto my butt and lowered my feet into the dark opening beneath the ground.

"How far does it go down?" I asked, my teeth chattering.

"Far enough." His head darted to the right, toward the ocean. "Hurry. He's coming."

The guy would take care not to make a sound, but I swore Jax could hear a feather hit the ground from a mile away.

I scooted down into the hole and my feet met dirt

sloping into nothing. Inching in farther, I touched bottom when I was shoulder level to the surface. Scooting the rest of myself inside, I poked my sneakers forward, testing the ground that continued only a short distance more. My shoulders brushed the sides of the dirt tunnel, and I was damn grateful I wasn't claustrophobic.

When I was fully submerged, I wiggled as far inside as I could to make room for Jax.

He scurried down onto the ground behind me and a scratchy-dragging sound told me he hid the entrance with the brush.

I stretched out my hands and, on either side, met cool soil. The space felt about three feet across, leaving barely enough room for both of us to fit.

Settling down beside me, Jax turned on a penlight and revealed the small hole in the ground, the walls and ceiling made up of sandy dirt with roots snaking through it.

"You dug this?" I whispered.

"Part of it. Expanded it so we could fit, really. Most of it was already here. Had to…evict the former tenants."

Best not to ask.

Another bag sat near his feet, likely holding more food. Hopefully water, as I was parched.

It was a decent hiding spot since the soil above us would mask us from both Google Earth and infrared cameras.

I leaned back against the wall and sighed while my body sunk into the moment to rest.

Jax dragged the bag over, between his knees, and opened it up, handing me a peeled orange he'd wrapped in what felt like a leaf. He also split a protein bar with me and I gulped both down, my hollow belly welcoming the food. I washed everything down with a few sips of stale water from a container he'd left in the corner, well-wrapped in a leaf to keep out bugs.

"One guy left," I said. Assuming the second guy was out of the picture. How could he be anything else after dangling near a stirred-up wasp's nest? My flesh crawled as I imagined how horrifying that must've been. Jax was right; his trap was gruesome.

They'd brought this to us, though. Had they expected us to give up our lives without a fight? There was no clean way to fight back.

"Yup, one guy."

"Much better odds unless the one on the boat joins the fray."

"We'll handle him, too, if we have to. "

"At least then we'll have access to the boat." When they'd arrived, I'd nearly given up hope. Three on two wasn't horrible odds but they were fully armed with enough technology to take out a small army. But Jax was an army all by himself. Alone, I wouldn't have survived but he'd upped the game tenfold. "Maybe we should—"

"We've got a problem," Jax said softly. Creases etched themselves across his forehead, and he winced as he shifted the bag back and stretched out his feet.

He tilted his right leg inward, crossing it over the other, revealing the outside of his thigh.

I followed his gaze to…

A knife stuck out from his thigh and blood dribbled around the hilt, down his leg, and onto the floor beneath it.

Jax

"Crap," Haylee hissed, terror coming through in her voice. "Your leg!"

Leaning forward, she fluttered her hands over the knife and I could tell she wasn't sure if she should pull it out or leave it alone.

It stung like a bitch. Had the entire time I ran here with Haylee. Only the fact that it was deeply imbedded had kept it from falling out from the jarring movement.

When I left Haylee on the trail, I'd crept back to make sure at least one of the guys was no longer a problem. I'd watched while one guy, caught in my trap, flailed, dangling in the air from one of the trees. A blurry cloud of angry wasps seeking revenge surrounded him.

The other guy had dropped his weapon on the ground. He'd pulled a knife and, after covering his upper body with a jacket, was attacking the loop holding his buddy suspended from the tree, swearing and waving the other arm as if that would drive off the wasps.

Rope severed, the man dropped to the ground, where he lay moaning.

I must've moved or the other guy sensed me watching through the trees, because he lifted his head and his furious gaze met mine. As I pivoted to run, he straightened from where he'd stooped down to check his friend.

Something thudded against my thigh, and I assumed I'd smacked it on a downed tree or branch. Knowing the guy would be after me, I hadn't taken time to look.

It was only when pain seared through me with every jolting step that I realized what happened.

I thought I'd got away, but…

"He saw you," she said, mouthing the words to stay quiet. I'd begun to believe we'd never have the chance to speak to each other again in a normal tone. "Oh, Jax." My name sighed out of her.

"Yeah," I said, equally low. "With his gun on the ground, I thought I'd get away before he could act but I didn't count on something like this."

At least it wasn't a bullet. Shit, who was I fooling? This could be worse than a bullet.

"We've got to pull it out," she said through clenched teeth. "We can't leave it there. You're…" Her shoulders curled forward. "Oh, Jax."

"I know I left a blood trail." Splashing through the ocean would buy us time while he sought us in both directions, but we couldn't remain here for long. I'd lead him right to us.

"We need to get it out and wrap the wound, stop the

bleeding." She looked around frantically. "Do you have a medical kit?"

Fat chance of that. "Nope."

Her jawline tightened. "You still have your jackknife with you, right?" She held out her hand. I pulled my blade from my pocket and dropped it onto her palm. "I'll cut strips from the hem of my shirt. Once we remove the knife, we'll bind it tight and run." She gulped. "If you can run. Does it feel like it severed anything vital?"

"Just muscle, from what I can tell." I'd run on it already and my leg had responded, which was a good sign. If the knife had hit an artery, I'd be bleeding more than I was.

Grimacing, I grabbed the knife handle. It was gonna kill me to yank it out.

"Do you have any other secure spots we can go to next? After we…" Her voice quivered, but I could tell she was scared out of her mind. We all took basic first aid in the military but we weren't often called upon to use it. "Our first shelter is out. If nothing else, we can return to the cave. At least we have food and water there, enough for only a meal maybe but it's better than nothing. I can forage, find water, protect us. And then, later, I can—"

"Haylee," I said, cutting her off with a hand on her arm.

"Yup?" she said, her face creased with pain.

"Get ready because I'm going to pull it out."

She swallowed, but her spine tightened. "All right. Let's do it. You, um… And I'll…" Yanking off her shirt, she dropped it onto her lap then gouged away at the hem. She ripped a strip off then started sawing at the shirt to create another.

"One'll work fine." I cupped her cheek and drew her face up. "It's gonna be okay."

I wished my belief in that statement was as strong as it sounded.

Her eyes swam with tears, and she blinked fast to drive them away. I'd caused this woman to cry too many times. Sadly this might not be the last.

"Don't worry about me. I'm here for you, Jax."

"I know you are, sweetheart." This woman. I wanted to rip my heart from my chest and hand it over to her.

But first, we had to get this knife out of my leg. Then get off the island. Because it was eating me alive that I couldn't end this and keep her safe.

After propping my flashlight on the bag, pointing it toward my leg, I tightened my grip on the hilt. Counting wasn't going to make this any easier.

Clenching my jaw, I jerked the knife out. Couldn't hold back my gasp because… Fuck, didn't that hurt.

Fresh blood seeped from the slit, like it must have dribbled down my leg as I ran.

Haylee pressed her shirt against the wound, holding pressure while watching my face. "Stay with me, Jax."

Words I'd said to her a thousand times while she lay on that hospital bed. Had she heard me back then?

The world spun. Never thought I'd be someone who'd pass out but damn, it was all I could do not to tip my head back and bellow. Tiny stars twirled in my periphery, telling me I was too close to the edge. I couldn't afford to go unconscious. The guy would find us and make sure I never woke up.

I sucked in air and released it. Again. But a third time still didn't cut it.

Clenching my eyes shut, I tried to block out the stars.

Haylee held pressure until she must've been confident the bleeding had slowed. While I braced my head on the wall, she ripped off another chunk of her shirt and, folding it, held it against the wound.

"Can you…" She nudged her chin to the folded scrap. "If you hold it there, I'll wrap it in place."

"It's gonna leak through in seconds once I start running."

"Not much we can do about that, but we can keep dirt off it. Dirt…" Her voice broke. "We need to soak it in salt water to help prevent infection. You need antibiotics."

"We'll get someone to look at it once we're off the island." There I went again, sounding confident we'd make it out of here alive.

"We're getting off the island," she echoed with complete certainty.

"Damn right we are." God, I hoped so. But I was going to slow us down.

She finished tying the knot.

"You ready to get out of here?" I said in a cheery voice, like everything was okay. While my body ached and I wanted to give her a chance to rest and regroup, we had to go. "The guy will be on our trail." If it was me, I'd already be here. "I do have one more location where we can hide." After that, we'd either hit the cave or be on a full run, but I wouldn't bring that up until I had to.

Hopefully, we'd leave the island with me at the helm of the speedboat. Then hiding would no longer be an issue.

Turning over onto my knees, I peered up through the brush but it was too dense to see through, even when I poked my head up among the vegetation.

We'd have to chance it. The longer we stayed here, the greater the odds he'd find us.

I sat down beside her and leaned close so only she would hear. "We don't have to go far, and once we're there, we can take a break. Rest up a bit."

"Good," she mouthed. "You need to give that leg a chance to scab over."

We wouldn't have time for that, but we could hide out until nightfall.

Then I'd go hunting, because there was only one left.

"Ready?" I said.

At her tight nod, I eased the brush to the side as soundlessly as possible then crept up out of the hole with Haylee right behind me.

We turned and continued deeper into the forest and this time, it was me slowing us down.

Haylee kept her arm around my waist. "Lean on me," she said below a whisper. "I can take it."

"I don't want you taking it," I muttered. "You're hurt, too. Worse than me."

"Oh, Jax," she said softly.

"Oh, Jax, what?" I said, equally quiet.

"I'm strong. You know that by now." Staring forward, she blinked fast. "Please."

Why did I deny her this opportunity to help me?

Maybe because I'd relied only on myself for years.

"It won't scar you for life to let me do this," she said.

Fuck. What was I doing to her? To us? I didn't need to hold myself back from this woman. Didn't want to, either.

"I'm sorry." Some of the stiffness went out of my shoulders. She was right. And my leg *was* killing me.

When I let her help me, she gifted me with the best smile.

"No problem," she whispered. "I get it."

She knew me better than I knew myself.

We worked our way through the jungle, moving in the general direction of my next hiding spot. Since we'd washed up on shore, I'd done my best to study the island, though there was still a ton of real estate I hadn't covered. As I searched for food and located good places to stash stuff, I'd kept my scope limited. Best to memorize a small section of the grid that we could cross at a run than take on more than I could handle. Then we'd be in danger of getting lost; the quickest way to get caught. Or killed.

We looped back toward the hill by another narrow trail weaving through the mangroves, approaching it from the other side of the boulders. We'd avoid the area with the wasp nest and the guy who'd tangled with it.

We hit a fork in the path and turned left.

"Almost there," I said. This direction would take us toward a part of the island we hadn't run through today.

"You're doing great," she said in such a low voice, I barely heard her. "How much farther?"

"A thousand feet or so." My breathing hitched, and my leg felt like it had been hit by a cannonball. I flicked my hand toward a denser part of the forest ahead. "Through there. On the opposite side of this grove there's a—"

Someone dropped down on top of us, driving us both to the ground.

28

Haylee

Tumbling forward, I met the ground with my palms.

With a growl, I flung myself to my side and came up in a crouch.

My thigh screamed. Damn thing would need solid workouts to get me up to speed once we got out of this.

Assuming we got out of this.

Jax and the man were on their feet, grappling together. Sweat and sticks and leaves flew through the air as they punched, kicked, and blocked each other's movements.

Blood had soaked through Jax's bandage.

The other guy looked like he'd been in a fight already. Rescuing the one who'd met up with the wasps hadn't done this man any favors. Pink splotches covered his face, neck, and arms, where the wasps had stung.

Grunts and snarls echoed in the tiny open area among the trees.

I hobbled around them, waiting for a chance to

jump in and take the guy to the jungle floor, but their motion was nearly a blur.

With a left jab, the man sent Jax backward a step. Not losing speed, he hit the guy with a crescent kick in the head, making him grunt. Jax followed the kick with a lift of his knee, hitting the man in the gut. The guy huffed and, when he bent forward, the front of Jax's elbow connected with the man's jaw.

My hands clenched, I punched forward, nailing the guy in the left kidney. He bent forward from the impact and spun, kicking out.

I stumbled backward, nearly losing my balance, but righted myself in time to land a few punches before he dove away from me. He rolled and sprang to his feet then raced toward Jax, grabbing his wrist and twisting. Jax's body followed the pull, turning to the side, but he stomped on the man's foot, making him arch backward and release Jax's arm.

Fist bursting forward, the guy tried to hit Jax in the neck, but Jax reeled away. He caught his footing while the guy's arm swung out again. Jax ducked and drove forward, punches swinging, slamming the other man in the chest.

Groaning, the man spun to the side. Squaring his feet, he pulled a knife. With a roar, he ran at Jax, who met him partway, blocking the descending knife with his forearm. Jax latched onto the man's wrist and deflected the knife to the side. Jax's leg swung out, sweeping the man's feet out from under him. He stumbled forward but righted himself and swung around, the knife swinging wide. Jax arched his spine backward to avoid being sliced wide open.

With the man's back to me, I saw my chance. I leaped forward and brought my clenched fists down on the back of his head, but he butted his head out, jarring the front of my skull.

My foot caught on a root and I slammed onto the ground, the wind knocked from me.

The thunder of my heartbeat echoed in my ears as the man dropped down on top of me, the knife swinging toward my throat.

But shock filled his face, and his arm stilled. His eyes rolled up in his head, and he collapsed on top of me.

Jax stood over us, his face florid, scrapes covering most of his exposed skin. He held what looked like a tree stump in his hands.

"Got 'im," he gasped out. The log dropped to the side, and he leaned over to haul the guy off me.

The guy flopped onto his back and lay still.

Jax wavered on his feet. Dropping to his knees, he sat and stretched out his wounded leg in front of him. "Fuck."

"Not now, sweetheart," I said. I grinned as I got to my feet. "Definitely later, though. Hold that thought."

I flipped the guy over onto his belly and nailed him in the back with my knee, and then pinned his wrists behind him. "You got a rope?" I wheezed. "We can tie him up."

Jax crawled over to the bag he'd been carrying and pulled a clump of the nylon twine from the side pocket. Stretching out his arm, he handed it to me.

I bound the guy tight at his ankles and feet and trussed him up so he'd never get free.

After, I dropped down beside Jax and leaned into his side. Or he leaned into mine. Without our arms around each other, it was hard to tell who held who up.

"Three down, though we'll have to look for the one who met up with the wasps," he said.

"One on the boat left to go."

"We'll get him next."

"We can take a breather first, right? Because I'm completely—"

The walkie-talkie strapped to the guy's side crackled.

"Pete?" someone said, coming through tinny-chirpy. "Come in, Pete."

Jax looked at me, and I looked at him. We both shrugged.

"Pete's not going to answer that," he finally said.

My snort of laughter rang out. Hard to believe I could find humor in this situation, but there it was.

"Someone needs to answer or he'll suspect Pete's out for the count," I said. "Maybe you should give it a try. I doubt he'll think I'm Pete."

"We want to board the boat without him knowing we're coming." Jax sighed as if heavily put upon. Leaning forward, he pulled the radio from the guy's belt. He pressed the button on the side. "Yeah?"

"Status?"

"Both dead," Jax said.

"Great. Return to the boat."

"It'll be a couple hours."

"Okay."

Jax's face tightened, and he dropped the radio in his bag before settling back beside me. We leaned against a big tree and let the tension leak from our bones.

"On the way, we can scout out the other guy," he said.

"Wasp man." I shouldn't joke about something so terrible, but the guy had been determined to kill me. Why should I feel sympathy for someone like that? "Bet he didn't think he'd kick a bee's nest when he came after us."

"If he's got any oomph left in him, I'll tie him up."

"I assume we'll leave them where he is."

"I'm not dragging him around the island."

"Me either," I chuffed out.

I removed another strip of material from my shirt, leaving me with not much more than a loose bra, and redressed Jax's wound, which still seeped. At this rate, it was never going to stop bleeding. But bleeding sure beat the alternative.

I struggled to my feet and offered Jax a hand to get up.

He took it without hesitation.

While I retrieved the knife from the bushes, Jax searched the guy but didn't find a phone or weapon, or anything we could use to increase our odds of survival.

We took our time walking along the path toward the boulders at the base of the cliff. While we were eager to swim out to the boat, we needed a break to rebuild our strength. As much as I wanted to get this over with one way or the other, it would be best to wait until dusk, which appeared about an hour away based on how the sun slanted through the jungle.

How had the day passed so fast? Oh, yeah, we'd been running for our lives.

As we got closer to the cliffs, we moved with more stealth.

We found the third man leaning against a boulder not far from the wasp nest, his florid face and arms grossly swollen from stings. He didn't open his eyes as we approached, nor when we backed away to a safe distance to talk after seeing if he still lived.

"Should we tie him?" I whispered, unable to stop staring.

"No need. We'll either be boating toward Belize within the hour or we'll be dead. This guy can make it or not on his own."

Jax approached the guy again and slipped the radio from his belt then walked around him, probably looking for weapons.

"Does he have a handgun?" I said in a low voice when he returned to my side.

"Not that I could tell. The AK-47 isn't anywhere nearby either."

No bag that I could see. They must've stashed the weapon in a secure location.

Bummer. I would've liked a better weapon than a knife when I boarded the boat.

"Let's get going, then," I said. "We can make our way to the shelter, eat and rest until sundown, then swim out to the boat."

He waved toward that direction. "On to the next challenge."

Hopefully the last.

We reached the shore forty-five minutes later, and I climbed up into the treehouse to retrieve our supplies. I joined Jax at the base of the tree, and we slunk through the jungle, stopping where we could see without being seen to scope out the boat situation.

The man who'd remained onboard stood near the cabin, staring down toward the hull. As we watched, he stooped over. With a beer in his hand, he crossed the open deck and settled in a seat. He kicked up his legs, then popped open the beer.

The fizz reached toward the shore.

My belly rumbled. Not for beer but for water, which we didn't have. We'd drained every last drop Jax had stored after the rainfall last night.

Last night? It felt like three weeks ago.

Since this was our last few minutes on the island, we each ate two protein bars and split an orange.

We settled on the ground and I checked out Jax's wound, which had seeped through again. Fortunately, we'd left clothing in the shelter, and I was able to dress in another shirt and use a clean one to rewrap his leg.

"We'll give it half an hour or so?" I asked softly, knowing sound carried on the water. "It won't be long enough for your leg to completely stop bleeding, but we need the rest."

He squinted toward the horizon, though the sun would set behind us. Already, long shadows stabbed across the shore, reaching ghostly fingers toward the water. "Forty-five minutes might be better."

I nodded and leaned into him. He dropped his head onto mine and wrapped his arm around the back of my waist.

If only I could sleep for even ten minutes, but I didn't dare. We needed to remain hyper alert to any threat. While we could see the remaining guy on the boat and the other two couldn't reach us, it never paid to relax your guard.

Time ticked down slowly as we worked out a plan. It was pretty basic. Get onto the boat without being seen then eliminate another bad guy. Question him about the Maestro if we didn't endanger ourselves.

When the sun winked out of existence and the forest came alive with insect chatter, we turned to face each other.

"This is it," I said, trying to sound brave. I'd always dived right into action, never thinking twice about the danger I might put myself in. But that was when it was just me.

Not us.

He cupped my face and kissed me, so soft and tender, my eyes stung from tears I refused to shed.

"No one else I'd rather tackle this with than you, sweetheart."

"Oh, Jax." I wrapped my arms around his shoulders and burrowed against his chest. He smelled good, despite no shower, a fight, plus running and crawling through sand and dirt. But then, I was partial.

"Love how you say that, oh, Jax."

"Love you," I mumbled against his neck. My heart ached for what we might no longer have. In a short time, it would be over. While I'd do my best to make sure we both survived, there were no guarantees.

If only we had more time…

"We're going to get out of this," he said.

"We are."

But it was clear we both knew how grave the odds were. One versus two, but we were beat, wounded, and worn out.

He kissed me again then pressed his forehead against mine. "You ready?"

I'd never be ready to lose Jax, but waiting wouldn't make things better. Each second increased the risk.

"Let's go steal a boat," I said.

"We *are* Navy."

"Seabees."

"Can do."

He closed his eyes briefly and sucked in a deep breath. Rising to his feet, he extended a hand to me.

We crept out of the jungle and slunk across the beach to the water.

29

Haylee

T he man wasn't on the boat.

Jax leaned over the deck, staring down at me while I remained in the water. "He's not down below," he said by my ear. "Not up here either."

"Key?" I asked.

How had we missed the guy on the shore?

"Not in the ignition," Jax whispered.

Crap.

"Can you hotwire it?"

"Maybe. I'll try."

"I'll go around to the back and board."

He nodded and turned.

I floated to the stern that had been built low to the water. Being careful not to scrape my leg on the propellers, I was boosting myself up onto the boat when someone came up behind me.

"Going so soon?" he said.

A final memory flashed through me, and I knew.

Striding forward, the man left the vehicle and walked up to me and Gabe. The gun in his hand winked in the headlights. He pointed it at Gabe. Then at me.

"I want the name of the contact," he'd said. "Tell me and I'll end it fast. Take your time and…"

I knew that voice. I'd love him my entire life.

And now, he wanted to kill me.

"Dad?" I'd stuttered out.

"Dad," I said now, turning with my heart a solid lump in my throat.

He smacked me on the head with a handgun.

I fell into the water, stunned.

My father grabbed a fistful of my hair and hauled me backward, dragging me behind him as he swam toward the reef.

He climbed up onto the coral and hauled me up to stand between him and the boat. He pressed the gun to my head and clicked off the safety.

"It's over," Dad yelled. "Come on out, Jax."

Jax rose up from the shadows of the boat and stalked to the stern, where he stood boldly in the moonlight. "Let her go."

"Sorry, but that's not an option."

"All this time…" I said. "You're the Maestro."

He said nothing, but I didn't need confirmation. I remembered. Gabe and I had located a new contact who'd said he had information. He'd asked us to meet him in the alley, saying he didn't dare name the Maestro except in person.

My father had come in the man's stead.

In the alley, Gabe had jumped Dad. They'd wrestled for the gun but it had skidded beneath the car.

Gabe and I ran. We jumped into our vehicle, then sped through town with Dad right behind.

"You drove us off the road," I said while Jax watched in horror.

"I couldn't let the information get out."

"But you're my father," I bleated. Pain crashed through me, making me weak. "All this time, you've been trying to kill me!"

"Would've done it at the hospital if Jax and the government agent hadn't been hovering around all the time."

"Why?" The word leaked from me with the last of my wind. My knees crumpled as shock took over. He'd killed Gabe. He was going to kill me.

"Your mother—"

"Stepmother," I growled. Anger shoved aside my pain and lent me the strength I needed to remain on my feet.

I felt Dad's shrug, though the gun never wavered. One move, and he'd put a bullet in my skull. It was clear he was not only capable of doing it, but willing.

It hurt. You'd think after learning he'd been trying to kill me for months, I'd hate him. Why couldn't I hate him?

"Stepmother, then," he said. "She likes nice things. The house. Jewelry. Trips overseas. Those things cost money."

I'd never asked him to choose, but he had, maybe from the moment he met her. Her needs were more important than my life, and that crushed me.

"So you're bringing drugs into the states?" Jax said.

My dad chuckled. "It's quite a lucrative business."

"And you fed Flint jobs so you could keep an eye on how they were handled."

"Yes," Dad said. "I needed to watch my investment."

"You never intended for us to locate a new contact," I said.

"Gabe should've gone to Cancun alone," my father said. "If you'd stayed home, you would've been safe."

"Really." The fact that he was willing to kill me didn't support that statement.

Jax's eyes met mine, and he darted his gaze to the water at my left.

Some jellyfish are bioluminescent. They emit light to attract prey. A huge cluster of them floated a foot or so from where I stood with my father.

I blinked twice to show I'd gotten the message, and Jax's gaze went to the stanchion-mounted light on the back of the boat.

Again, I blinked twice.

Diving toward it, Jax turned on the light and swung the 1,000-lumen spotlight in our direction, blinding us.

Dad groaned, and his free hand rose up to cover his eyes.

Released, I whirled around and punched him in the neck. As he sputtered and choked, I wrenched the gun from his hand. Then I pushed him into the water. The jellyfish bobbed around him, disturbed by his impact.

He rose up to the surface then froze. A shriek erupted from his mouth, and he flailed toward us.

Jax turned the spotlight in his direction.

Gritting my teeth, I leveled the gun, pointing it at

my father's head. "Stop right there. If you hold still, they won't sting you any further."

"Something's biting me," he yelled.

"No worries," Jax said. "Last I heard, there aren't poisonous jellyfish around here. But do you want to test it out with a few more stings?"

Paddling in place, my father growled.

"Give us the keys to the boat," I said.

Jax left the boat and joined me on the coral.

My father smirked. "I'm not sure I remember where I put them."

I tightened my grip on the gun. "Give. Them. To. Me."

"You won't shoot," he sneered. "You can't hurt your own father."

I pulled the trigger, and his right shoulder bloomed with color. It seeped into the water, creating a red fog around him.

He screamed and floundered, his head going under. He bobbed back up to the surface, pain etched on his face. "You shot me."

"I'll do it again if you don't give us the key to the boat." I tipped my head toward the open ocean behind us. "Heard there are a lot of sharks in these waters. Sad that you're bleeding because it'll call them right to you."

Jax slipped into the water and swam over to my father. "Give us the key, and we'll give you the same chance you gave us on the island."

At least until the cops arrived.

"You'll pay for this," my father said, reaching into

his pocket. He dropped the keys into Jax's hand, and Jax swam back to the boat and climbed onboard.

"I think I've already paid the price," I said softly as I watched the man I used to call my father swim toward shore.

I eased into the water and floated over to the boat, where I climbed up to stand beside Jax.

We watched as the Maestro reached the shore and dragged himself up out of the water.

He didn't stop. He walked into the jungle, disappearing among the vegetation.

He didn't look back.

Epilogue
JAX

Three Months Later

Most would consider it a sad thing if they had to spend Christmas Eve at the office. Not me, because my buddies and Haylee would be there, too, and they were my life.

I'd asked Haylee to meet me at the shop, saying I had an errand to run, which I did. I did not, however, tell her what the errand was, despite her considerable…persuasion.

That woman was going to kill me, but I'd die with a grin on my face.

After Haylee's dad melted into the jungle, I'd gotten the boat running and pointed it toward the open sea. Haylee had joined me at the wheel and leaned into my side. She'd hiccupped and then turned into my chest and sobbed.

Gnashing my teeth and wishing I could slam my fist into her father's face, I'd held her with tears of sympathy in my eyes. There was no way I could comprehend the pain she was feeling, knowing her father had wanted to kill her.

Once we reached the shore, we got in touch with Flint, and he sent a cleanup crew to the island. Haylee's father was found hiding in our cave and arrested. He was extradited to the U.S., where he was charged. His assets confiscated, he'd been unable to make bail. Until he could stand trial, he'd remain in jail.

I hoped they locked him up for a thousand years.

He'd passed a message through his lawyer to Haylee, asking her to visit. Said he had something so tell her.

She'd gone. I'd offered to be with her, but she'd said this was something she had to do by herself.

The haunted expression on her face when she returned had ripped me apart. I'd held her while she cried and shared his words.

He was sorry. He'd done everything he could to keep her out of it, but at the final moment, he'd had no choice.

Hell, no. He'd had plenty of chances to end this before it went too far, but he'd chosen himself instead of his daughter. I'd never forgive him for that, even if Haylee could find a sense of peace for her father within her own heart.

While she still had bad days, she was getting counseling. She said there was no way she wanted to handle this on her own. Not that she'd ever be alone; she'd always have me. But I understood. It wouldn't be easy to get over this loss.

Driving down the last stretch of the road toward Viper Force, I took in the new fence and gate.

The guard, seeing me approach, left the heated security shack and waited for me to bring the vehicle to a stop.

Katrina smiled. "Welcome, Jax! The rest of the crew's inside already."

"Are you joining us?" Cold air dumped in through the open window, making my hands shake.

No, my hands shook because of that errand. Why had I told myself this was a good idea?

"Flint says I can lock up and head home once you're here," Katrina said. "My family and I are going to mass, then we've got a midnight feast planned."

"Then have a good one," I said as I shifted my truck back into gear.

"Oh, I plan to!" she said, grinning again. "Happy Holiday!"

"You, too." I drove through the open gate and parked next to the other vehicles out front.

Lights shone through the windows, and Mia had strung twinkle lights around them to add to the festive atmosphere.

I tapped the bee cutout above the door and to the left of the discrete sign stating, *Viper Force R&D*, with a gold fouled anchor mounted beneath it.

Enveloped in warmth from the moment I stepped inside, I stopped and took in the scene.

Becca, Flint and Mia's aunt, stood on a ladder,

placing the angel on the top of the tree Flint had set up in the corner.

Ginny sat with Cooper on the sofa next to the tree, cups of eggnog in hand, both watching Becca. I could tell Cooper itched to jump up and take care of the angel himself. Not because Becca couldn't do it but because he, like me, worried she'd fall while climbing down the ladder in her four inch heels.

Mia and Eli entered the room from the kitchen and strolled over to me. "Cookies in the break room," Mia said with a smile. "Your favorite."

"All cookies are my favorites," I said.

"These are the best cookies you'll eat in your life," she said with a twinkle in her eyes. "You know why?"

I shrugged, feelin' like this was a trick question.

"Haylee made them," she said with a grin.

Haylee appeared in the doorway. "Oh, hey, Jax. You're too late. I ate all the cookies." She smirked, and I was happy to see a bit of her old spark in her eyes. "They had strawberry filling."

I strode right up to her and brushed the crumbs off her chin, then braced my palm on the doorframe near her head. "You're sweeter than any cookie, sweetheart."

"Just keep that in mind," she said, ducking underneath my arm. She trailed her fingertip along my jaw as she passed and, like every other time she touched me, I lit on fire. "If you're extra nice, I'll bake you some cookies later." She winked, but before she could saunter away, I tucked my arm around her and pulled her close for a searing kiss filled with endless promise.

"Jax," she whispered after, her voice trembling.

Hell, I trembled, too. Always did when I touched her.

Her fingers played with a button on my shirt. "I'm so going to jump your bones the second we get home."

"We'll jump each other's bones."

"Holding you to that."

I released her and she walked over to the tree, where the others had already gathered.

Becca had survived her descent from the ladder and had leaned it against the wall. She strode around the desk and flicked a switch, turning up the music. Dancing along with *I'll be home for Christmas*, she rejoined everyone at the tree.

Flint entered the lobby from the hall leading to the offices and the back warehouse where we tested equipment. He went over to a table set up along one wall and scooped up a cup full of eggnog. After he joined Becca, his deep voice picked up the song as they swayed together to the music.

Ginny pointed to mistletoe hanging overhead and she and Cooper kissed. Engaged, they'd soon be married.

Mia leaned into Eli's side and his arm tickled up and down her spine.

I stood and watched, feeling separate but not completely alone for the first time in my life.

My chest squeezed tight as raw emotion overwhelmed me.

I hadn't had a family in years, not since my mom died.

But I did now.

These people, my friends from Viper Force and the woman I loved, were my home.

Haylee turned and smiled. She held out her hand and I strode forward, took her fingers, and then leaned in to kiss her.

My errand could wait. Later, after she'd paid me back for eating all those cookies, I'd ask her a very important question.

Once she'd said yes, I'd kiss her sweet lips, thank the stars for my good fortune, then slide the ring on her finger.

~THE END~

About the Author

Marlie writes books with heart, humor, and a guaranteed happily-ever-after. When she's not writing romance, you can find her in Maine, where she works as a nurse. She lives with her own personal hero, her retired Navy Chief husband. They have three children, too many cats, and a cute Yorkie pup.

Other Books by Marlie May

Crescent Cove Contemporary Romances

SOME LIKE IT SCOT

SIMPLY IRRESISTIBLE

TWIST OF FATE

(A time travel romance set in ancient Pompeii)

Viper Force

FEARLESS

RUTHLESS

RECKLESS

CALL IT LOVE

After Lark Harpswell's boyfriend leaves her with an empty fridge and a maxed-out credit card, she's done with men. If she needs romance, she'll live vicariously through her favorite historical Highlander novels. So when gorgeous Dag Ross asks her out, she turns him down.

During the day, Dag lounges in bed or works as a part-time handyman for a friend. At night, under a secret pen name, he writes wildly popular romance novels featuring a brawny sword-wielding Scotsman. Though he's convinced true love doesn't exist outside fiction, Lark blindsides him. When he sees her with one of his novels and she hints she'd date a hero like his Duncan MacLeod, he can't resist the challenge.

Dag dressed in a kilt and spouting Scottish phrases is hotter than Lark imagined, and keeping him at arm's distance isn't easy. She's determined not to get screwed over again, though, especially by a man who's erected walls around his heart.

Call it Love features laugh-out-loud moments, plenty of swoony romance, on-the-page heat, no cheating, no cliffhangers, and a guaranteed happily ever after. Each book is standalone and can be read in any order. Look for Call it Fate, Roan's story.

Turn the page for chapter 1…

Chapter 1
LARK

Most women would rather go out on a Friday night than stay home with a hot man dressed in a kilt.

A fictional kilted man, that is.

Not me. Which was a problem. Admitting I preferred reading over a hot date suggested I was well on my way to cat lady status. It also implied I'd hit the bottom of the dating scene barrel and needed an intervention.

Which was true.

I'd offered to take my sister, Paisley, out for her birthday tonight, which showed I was making an effort. Putting myself out there.

We crossed the road and stepped up onto the sidewalk. Only a few blocks left to go before a night of possibilities stretched ahead of us. For Paisley that is, because she was on the prowl. I was in this for the socialization. And the beer.

Paisley smiled over her shoulder. "Keep up, slowpoke."

Groaning, I pretended to hobble. "My legs are tired."

"What did you do today? Three? Four miles?"

"Ten."

"Jeez, Lark. Maybe you could take a few days off? You're wearing yourself out."

Since I competed in half marathons to benefit the Sweetwater Cancer Foundation, I couldn't slow down now. Unhappy with my last finishing time, I'd stepped up my training in preparation for an event in the upcoming Highland Games. Good finishing times guaranteed generous sponsors. As well as tired Larks.

A gust of wind snatched up leaves and skipped them along the pavement like thin stones tossed across a pond.

Paisley hugged her jacket close. "Brr. Tell me again why we decided to walk and not to take a cab?"

"Because extra money translates into more beer."

"Oh, yeah. I like the way you think."

It was so cold, my cheeks ached, but that was spring in Maine for you. June had recently shoved out its timid cousin, May. But while people in warmer climates might be wearing shorts, this part of the world had barely moved beyond mitten season.

We passed a man coming from the opposite direction who smiled and tapped the brim of his baseball cap. "Evening, ladies."

"Evening." Paisley barely held in a giggle.

My lips twitched. While Paisley paused and stared after him, I continued toward the Crescent Cove Brew

House—the only place downtown guaranteed to serve alcohol after eight.

Paisley rushed to catch up, her heels tap-tap-tapping on the pavement. She leaned near and whispered, "Where are you going? It was a *man*."

I rolled my eyes. "I have it on good authority they're not threatened with extinction."

"Cute ones are."

He *had* been cute, but cute was off limits. For that matter, *not* cute men were also off limits.

Paisley pouted. "You're taking all the fun out of my special day."

"By not flirting with strangers on the sidewalk?" Even though Paisley had been milking her birthday celebration since yesterday, she was right to call me out for being a grump. I linked my arm through hers and laid my head on her shoulder. "I'm sorry."

With Paisley taking summer classes and me working all kinds of hours at the diner, sister time was rarer than…well, hot, kilted men. And that thought brought out my full grin. "What do you say? Should we hunt him down?" Stalking men could take our Friday night to a whole new level.

Her lips twisted. "He wasn't that cute. Let's take our hunting elsewhere." Paisley hauled her hat down over her ears, making her blonde curls stick out on each side like corkscrews. Her pink nose wrinkled, but her eyes gleamed with happiness.

Inside the Brew House, I unzipped my jacket and soaked in the warmth. Music swirled around me, and my hips caught the rhythm and swayed along.

Taking stools beside a window looking out on the street, we ordered two pints of beer. Clear glasses topped with a healthy dose of foam were soon placed in front of us. The bartender also slid a bowl of pretzels down the bar, in case the urge to balance hops with salt overcame us.

Paisley took a long drink of her beer. She clunked the glass back on the counter and smacked her lips. "Ahh. Nectar of the gods."

I sipped my cranberry wheat, savoring the tart pinch in the back of my throat. "It is good, isn't it?" I rocked my drink back and forth on the smooth wooden bar top surface, making the amber liquid slosh.

Paisley danced in her seat in time with the music. "Thank you for my present." She hugged me. "We haven't done anything like this together in ages."

I couldn't remember when we'd last gone out. Between working at the diner and getting everything ready for the first Highland Games Committee meeting, I'd barely found a moment to think. Playtime always got shoved aside for later, and later never came. Sometimes, just keeping up with life overwhelmed me.

"How's the job hunt coming along?" Paisley asked.

"I've got an interview next week for a managerial position at the indie bookstore near the mall." In the town next to ours. If I was lucky, I'd soon get to use my business degree. Standing at college graduation a few weeks ago, it hadn't mattered that at twenty-seven, I was one of the "older" students. Sure, it had taken me nine years to finish, but I'd gone part-time. Checking off that goal was all that mattered. But it was time to find full-time work in my new field.

"How can they not hire my wonderful sister?" Paisley toasted me with her beer. "Don't forget to mention what you do for the Foundation."

"It's on my resume already." I'd been asked to help with the upcoming Highland Games, an event the Sweetwater Cancer Foundation was hosting to raise money. My half marathons guaranteed a good donation to the Foundation, but the Games would give the organization the financial boost it truly needed. I'd never find a way to fully repay them for what they'd done while Paisley was sick with leukemia a few years ago. Thankfully, she was in remission now.

Paisley slid off her stool and nudged her head toward the hall with the bathrooms. "I'll be right back."

Facing forward, I tapped my fingernails on the bar. A pretzel spiked my appetite, so I ate another, washing it down with beer. I glanced around, but still no Paisley. There must be a long line for the bathroom.

I opened my purse and pulled out my book. A soft smile lifted my lips as I traced my fingertip along the cover model's muscular chest. *Revenge of the Highlander* was one of my favorites in this series.

Opening to my bookmark, I started where I'd left off earlier.

Duncan dispatched the last kidnapper with a thrust of his claymore. While the outlaw gasped his final breath, the brawny Scottish warrior turned to where Lenore was tied to the back wall of the cave. He stalked toward her, the folds of his blue and green kilt shifting across his muscular thighs.

Halting, he stroked her face, and a growl rumbled in his chest. "Och, lass, what have they done to ye?"

"Tis nothing," she said. "I feared for your life. Those men—"

He kissed her forehead. "Dinnae fash yerself. All is well now."

Pulling his dirk, he made quick work of her ties. As he gathered her into his embrace, his scent, heavy with the thrill of battle, swirled around her.

His lips descended. His tongue slaked across hers, stirring her fire. She—

"Jeez, Lark." Paisley settled on her stool. She waved at the worn paperback. "I can't believe you're reading when we're supposed to be out celebrating."

"You were gone a long time." Heat filled my face as I tucked my book away in my purse. I'd only planned a quick peek, but like every other time, I'd been sucked into the life of Duncan Magnus Ferguson MacLeod. His broad shoulders. His chivalrous ways. His heady kisses.

No real man could compare.

"S'okay." Paisley glanced sideways and shifted around to speak by my ear. "Hottie alert at nine o'clock. Did you see the guys at the other end of the bar?"

I leaned forward. A man with wavy brown hair sat beside a blond guy. Both looked a few years older than me. As if sensing my attention, the darker-haired one raised his eyes to meet mine. My neck tingled, and I wrenched my gaze from his.

"Pretty sweet, huh?" Paisley asked.

I fanned my face. Was he ever. Chiseled jaw line. Muscular build. Drop-dead gorgeous. Unfortunately, like every other cute guy out there, Mr. Tall Dark and Everything was probably aware of his blinding appeal.

"We should go over and introduce ourselves," Paisley said.

"Not tonight." I snatched a pretzel from the bowl and chased the saltiness with beer. The Brew House sure knew how to keep their customers drinking.

"Why not?"

"Because I've come to a momentous decision recently."

Paisley lifted her eyebrows.

"I'm swearing off dating."

She snorted. "For good?"

"For now."

"Because of Ted."

"He burned me so badly, I'm contemplating signing up for firefighter training."

"Decent career. And firefighters?" Paisley wiggled her eyebrows. "They're smokin' hot."

"I'm not hooking up with a fireman." Although, there was something appealing about muscle-bound men striding around with their bare chests hanging out. Posing with puppies for calendars. Sliding down those poles…I shook my head, sending my long brown hair onto my back. No more men for me.

"I know you've had a dry spell since Ted…left, but the best thing to do is get back on the camel."

I snickered. "One problem. The saying includes a horse, not a camel."

Paisley shrugged. "If we were in Egypt, we'd be saying camel."

"If we were in Egypt, we'd be drinking in an oasis." I waved my glass at the room in general. "But I'm not seeing palm trees or blue pools of water."

"Or sheiks. Don't forget the sheiks."

"With you here, I doubt I could." Why was I picturing the cute guy at the end of the bar dressed in sheik's robes? With a sexy beard.

Astride his horse, he pursued me across the desert sand. His mocking laughter rang out. Ye will be mine, lass, he said.

No, wait. That was Scottish, something Duncan would say. And a sheik would say…well, I wasn't sure what a sheik would say. Something Arabic, I supposed.

My imagination must be ruling my brain tonight. Or stupid Cupid had decided to tease me the second I'd announced I was taking a dating hiatus.

"I don't plan to marry them," Paisley said. "I only want to get to know them better. One of them, anyway." Her face scrunched. "I'm not into threesomes."

Neither was I. For months, I'd only been into onesomes. Maybe I *was* going through a dry spell. Unable to help myself, I peered in their direction again. Mr. Tall & Brooding's gaze pinned me to my seat. Delicious shivers raced through my bones, but I needed to ignore the feeling. "Already told you. Not interested."

"What's not to like? They have all their teeth, they're decently dressed, and from what I can tell from here, they're not drunk. Yet."

"I'm not setting myself up to get hurt again. Whenever I trust someone, he turns into a jerk." Well, except

for Duncan. Who was unavailable because he was ficti-
tious. But that was being picky. My Highlander made
the perfect dating material. To go out with him, I only
had to open one of his books, flip through the pages,
and drool during the steamy parts. And when I got tired
of him, I could put him back on the bookshelf until our
next interaction.

"You just haven't found the right one yet," Paisley
said.

I stabbed a pretzel circle and shook my finger at my
sister. "I tell you, there are no *right* ones out there." My
ex-boyfriend, Ted, had lounged around my house all day
and spent the rest of his time eating a path through my
fridge. I'd kicked him out, but not before
he'd *borrowed* my credit card and racked up enough debt
to drown Paisley's camel. "I'm not going out with
anyone until I'm convinced he's decent," I said. "I can
take care of us, but I draw the line at letting some guy
leech off me again. Hey. Maybe I should use my new
degree and treat dating like a business. Before I go out
with someone, I'll check his references."

"References. Really?"

The idea wasn't that far-fetched. My potential dates
could fill out applications. I'd interview their former girl-
friends and maybe their moms. Well, moms might be
taking it too far, but—

"Why not ask them to get DNA testing while you're
at it?"

I tilted my head. "Do you think they've identified the
jerk gene yet?" I chuckled, but I wasn't exactly joking.
"You're implying this is complicated, but I don't actually

need much in a man." With my fingers, I ticked off what I considered decent dating material. "He needs to be trustworthy, single, employed, use his own credit card, not mine, and…"

"And what?" Paisley asked.

"Bonus points if he's a hero."

"Like Spiderman?" Paisley grimaced. "Not into spiders."

"All those webs." I shuddered. "I was thinking about the heroes in my books."

"Oh, like the Highlander one you were just reading? Nothing like a man in a kilt."

"Men like that don't exist." A lifetime of longing weighed down my sigh.

"I still think you should've kicked Ted's loser ass to the curb long ago. And made him pay. It's not like *you* owed the money. He's the one who used your card for those sites."

What a way to convince a woman she wasn't fun enough between the sheets. I'd tried not to translate his porn addiction into a lack of appeal on my part. Told myself that turning down an invitation to join me under the covers to jerk off instead was his problem, not mine. But it hadn't been easy. It still hurt.

"It's been three months," Paisley said.

"It'll take longer than that to put it behind me." I forced a grin. "But let's not talk about me anymore. It's your birthday, which means we need to indulge your every desire."

"Since this night is about fulfilling all my wishes, we should start by sampling each brew on tap." Paisley lifted the menu. "They have some new ones. Apricot jalapeño, chocolate stout, a peach IPA—"

"Hello. Apricot jalapeño?" I squinted over Paisley's shoulder. *Sweet, fruity flavors that lull you into a mid-summer night's dream, only to shove you out of bed with a fiery kick in the morning.* This place used *the best* descriptions for beer. "How about we order a couple sampler flights?"

"Can we get some curly fries, too?" Paisley asked. "I'm famished."

"Deal." The Brew House's fries were better than sex. Any sex I'd ever experienced.

Out of the corner of my eye, I saw the men stand.

Mr. Smoldering, Dark, and Too-Cute spoke to his friend before moving around the end of the bar. He was tall, like six-two or three, and he moved like a panther on the prowl.

Oh, my.

When his gaze locked onto mine, my heart flipped.

Pick up Call it Love!